breakdown

■ ■ ■

Ellie Grace

Breakdown
Copyright © 2014 by Ellie Grace

Cover Design by Sarah Hansen of Okay Creations
http://www.okaycreations.com/

Interior Formatting & Design by Angela McLaurin, Fictional Formats
https://www.facebook.com/FictionalFormats

ISBN: 978-0-9914060-7-4

For all the readers who gave this rookie author a chance.

part one

. . .

chapter one

Amy

My entire life, I've been part of a set. An eternal duo. A pair. One half of a whole. I can't remember a time when I wasn't lumped together with my twin brother, Dex. From the moment we began sharing a womb, we became a team. Right from the beginning it's been us against the world.

There are a lot of really great things about being a twin. You always have someone to play with or talk to. Someone who consistently has your back and is there to look out for you, no matter what. And most importantly, you have a best friend for life.

Of course, there are also a few things that aren't so great.

When you're a twin, you share everything: your identity, birthdays, friends, and in some cases—like mine—you even share clothes occasionally. It didn't matter to my parents that Dex was a boy and I was a girl. Since Dex was always bigger than me, I was frequently getting stuck with his hand-me-downs. Needless to say, after all those years of dressing up in my brother's clothes, I became quite the tomboy. It didn't help that I spent most of my time hanging out with him and his other boy friends. I didn't own any Barbies, play with dolls, or host imaginary tea parties. Instead, I played sports, rode bikes, and basically rolled around in the dirt. I was one of the boys.

It wasn't until I got into junior high that anything really changed. Dex and all our friends started getting interested in girls, and apparently they finally realized that I was one. All of a sudden they started acting weird around me and stopped inviting me to hang out with them. They ignored me at school, treating me like I had the plague or something. I still had Dex, but even that wasn't the same. All the girls thought I was weird because I dressed and acted like a boy, and none of the boys wanted to be my friend because I *wasn't* a boy. It was a pretty lonely time.

Finally, when I got into high school, I made my first real girlfriend. Savannah had just moved to Charleston from Maine, and she immediately took me under her wing and helped me learn how to be a girl. I ditched the baggy tee shirts, track pants and sneakers and learned how to style my hair in ways other than a messy ponytail. I'm still not a girly-girl by any means; I rarely wear dresses or make-up, but at least people finally know that I *am* a girl.

With Savannah by my side I've managed to actually enjoy high school. I have a close group of girlfriends, I get good grades, and I've already been accepted to my top-choice college for next year. There's only one aspect of my life that I'm failing miserably at.

Boys.

I'm halfway through my senior year of high school and I haven't been kissed or even been out on a date. For the most part, I think I'm fairly decent-looking. I guess I'm a little plain, and definitely not drop-dead gorgeous like some of the girls I go to school with, but I'm not ugly either. So why am I seventeen years old and totally inexperienced?

Dex Porter.

My overbearing, overprotective twin brother has made sure that I am completely unattainable to all males within the vicinity of Charleston, South Carolina. Any time a guy has shown even the slightest interest in me, Dex steps in and scares him away. People have always been intimidated by my brother, but now that he's spent the last year training to join the Marines, becoming a solid brick of muscle, it's only gotten worse. No guy wants to risk going up against him, and there's nothing I can say to change it. I've long since accepted the fact that I'm going to be the most inexperienced freshman on the entire college campus.

It never used to bother me all that much, because there weren't any guys in our high school who really interested me. There's only person I've ever truly wanted to date, kiss, or do anything with, and he is totally, one-hundred-percent off-limits. Not only does he go to our school, but he's also my brother's best friend.

Nate Miller.

Dex and Nate didn't become friends until high school, so he's the only one of my brother's friends who doesn't know me as the little tomboy twin who wore her brother's clothes and ran around with the boys. All the idiots who I was friends with back then still look at me like I'm one of the guys, but not Nate. When Nate first glanced my way, he just saw *me*. The first time I met him, when Dex invited him over to the house, Nate smiled at me, and my stomach did somersaults. I'd never reacted that way to anyone before. I couldn't peel my eyes away from his gorgeous green eyes, perfectly messy dark hair, and the way his perfect lips curled up in an adorable, boyish grin. Everything about him was different from all the other boys I knew, and no matter how hopeless it was, my crush only grew from there.

Even now, as I watch him saunter across the high school library, I feel those same butterflies that I felt the first time I saw him. My eyes always manage to find him in a crowd, as though I'm attuned to his presence, and the moment I see him tingles begin creeping up my spine.

He joins a group of guys who are seated at a table on the other side of the room, and I peek out from behind my book, hoping to hide the fact that I'm staring at him. His dark hair is disheveled, as though he's been running his hands through it, and he's wearing a faded old pair of jeans with a tee shirt and Converse sneakers. In all the time that I've known him, he's never been the type to care about his appearance or what he's wearing, and yet he always looks gorgeous. Even when he's walking around with engine oil stains on his clothes from working with his dad in the garage, he couldn't care less. He's perfectly and effortlessly beautiful.

"Earth to Amy," Savannah says, smacking the wooden tabletop to get my attention. "Are you listening to a word I'm saying?"

"What?" I snap my attention from Nate to where my best friend is sitting across from me. "Sorry, I was distracted."

"Clearly," she says with a knowing smirk. She leans across the table and lowers her voice so no one but me can hear her. "I was trying to tell you that Scott Henderson has been staring at you for the last ten minutes." Her eyes swing to the left, and I follow her gaze to where he's lounging on one of the couches nearby. He smiles when my eyes meet his, and I immediately jerk them away.

"What do you think that's about?" I whisper to Savannah, too scared to risk another glance in his direction.

"Who knows?" She shrugs. "I heard that he and Becca just broke up. Maybe he's got his sights set on you now."

I roll my eyes. "Yeah, right. He's in my English class. I'm sure he just wants me to help him with the paper we have due next week."

Scott is good-looking in a hipster sort of way. He's not hugely popular, but he has his own crowd of friends that he hangs out with and seems to be the kind of guy who gets along with everyone. He's also been dating a gorgeous blonde cheerleader named Becca for most of the year. Even if Savannah's right and they broke up, there's no way that he's interested in me.

"Well, you're about to find out because he's heading this way," Savannah mutters under her breath.

I sneak a glimpse at him, and, sure enough, he's walking right toward us. My whole body stiffens, and I pretend to be immersed in the pages of the book in front of me as he approaches.

"Hey, ladies," Scott says with a smile as he pulls out the chair next to mine and sits down. "I'm sorry to intrude, but I was wondering if you might let me make a copy of the assignment for English. I managed to lose mine sometime between third and fourth period."

"Sure, no problem," I stammer, digging through my bag to find my English notebook. "I have it in here somewhere, just give me a minute."

As I'm rifling through the pages in my folder, Scott suddenly reaches out to stop me, placing a hand over my arm. "Okay, I have a confession to make. I don't actually need a copy of the assignment."

I look up at him, confused. "You don't?"

He shakes his head. "No, I just needed an excuse to come over here and ask you something, but I didn't want to seem creepy. Now I feel bad that I've got you digging through all your stuff, so I figured I should cut to the chase before you dump out your whole bag for no reason."

I let out a nervous laugh, dropping my bag back down to the

floor. "Um, okay. So what did you need to ask me?"

"Is there any chance you'd go out with me tomorrow night?"

"Me?" I ask dumbly, unable to comprehend what's happening. "Are you sure?"

Scott laughs. "Yes, I'm sure. I know it seems out of the blue, but I've been sitting behind you in English class all semester, and I can't seem to take my eyes off you."

"Awww," Savannah swoons from across the table, where she's clearly listening in on our entire conversation.

I can't help but glance over at Nate, who's still chatting with his friends, oblivious to my presence and what's going on. As much as I want him to be the one asking me out on a date, I know deep down that it's never going to happen. Scott, on the other hand...

"It's crazy to me that all the guys in this school let your brother scare them away from you," Scott continues, noticing my hesitation. "But I think that's ridiculous. I'm not about to let idle threats keep me away from a beautiful girl."

He might actually be the one who's crazy, since even I know that there's nothing idle about my brother's threats. However, I decide to let it go because I may have found the one person who's too brave... or too stupid... to be scared of my brother. Scott may be my only chance to gain some dating experience before starting college next year. Besides, he's cute, funny and charming. Maybe I could feel for him what I feel for Nate if I give him a chance.

"Okay," I answer softly. "Tomorrow night sounds great."

Nate

Dex isn't going to be happy about this.

I'm flipping through the pages of *Car and Driver* magazine when I catch sight of Scott Henderson cozying up to Amy in the library. I can tell right away that he's trying to put the moves on her because, well, I've pulled that same stunt enough times to recognize it. He's got a phony, calculated grin on his face that I'm sure he thinks is charming, but I can see it for what it really is. A strategy.

Unfortunately, Amy seems to be falling for the act, because she's giggling along with him and eating right out of the palm of his hand. I'm more irritated than I should be, but something about the whole encounter just isn't sitting well with me. Amy is too sweet and innocent to be getting mixed up with a guy like this, and even though she's not my sister, I have the sudden urge to put a stop to it.

Dex takes the role of protective brother very seriously, especially when it comes to Amy's dating life. I know he loves her and wants to keep her safe, but the poor girl is about to go to college, and her brother is still scaring off any guy who comes close. I've always thought that Dex was being unfair, but now that I'm watching this asshole blatantly attempt to get in her pants, I can understand why he does it.

Amy's unlike any other girl I know. She's not pretentious, shallow or vapid. She doesn't care about her image, or fitting into a certain mold, and she doesn't cover herself with fancy clothes and makeup merely because it's expected of her. I don't even think she *wears* any makeup; not that she needs it. She's genuine, kind, intelligent, and not afraid to be herself. I really like that about her, because who she is, is really awesome. I haven't known her as long as the rest of the guys, but I've spent enough time at the Porter's house over the last four years to get fairly close with her. She hangs out with us a lot, and the crazy thing about it, is that it's not weird at all. Normally hanging out with girls our age for extended periods of time is exhausting and annoying, but Amy is actually fun to be around. She can watch sports without asking questions about what's going on, she's witty, she's not afraid to laugh—like really *laugh*—and most importantly she's just... real. She's special, just the way she is, and I'd hate to see some idiot swoop in and ruin her. There's something about her that makes you want to protect her. She's kind and trusting, always seeing the best in those around her, and there are people out there who would take advantage of that.

So, now I'm in quite the predicament. Do I tell Dex, who will undoubtedly put a stop to the whole thing, and risk upsetting Amy at the same time? Or do I let it play out and risk seeing her get hurt?

I'm leaning towards telling Dex, but when I see the cute, cautiously happy smile on Amy's face when Scott walks away, I know that I can't ruin this for her. As much as I hate the asshole who put that look on her face, I'd hate myself even more for being the one to take it away.

■　　■　　■

I have a free period at the end of the day, so I leave school early and head over to my dad's auto shop where I work as a mechanic. I've had a job here for as long as I can remember, working alongside my dad and learning everything there is to know about cars. I inherited my dad's passion for cars early on, just as he inherited it from his dad before that. My mom always says that the men in our family have motor oil running through our veins instead of blood. In a few years when my old man retires, I'll take over the business and work here full-time. While some might think of it as a burden to carry on the family business, I couldn't be happier.

School has never been easy for me. From day one, I was constantly struggling to catch up with my classmates, and no matter how hard I worked to learn the material, I was always falling behind. I eventually got held back a year in middle school, but even then it was an uphill battle that made me feel stupid and inadequate compared to everyone else.

When there's an engine in front of me, I understand what to do. I know all there is to know about every single part and component, and what needs to be done to it. I never struggle to find the answers or solve the problem. When it comes to cars, I'm smart. I know what I'm doing, and I'm good at it. It's the one thing in life that has always come easy for me.

So despite the fact that I managed to fight my way through school, I have no plans for higher education after I get my diploma. College simply isn't for me, and I'll happily spend my future underneath the hood of a car with permanent grease stains on my fingers.

When I enter the garage, my dad is elbow-deep in the engine of an old Volkswagen Beetle.

"Hey, Pop," I call out to him as I walk inside. "Got anything for me to work on today?"

"Don't I always?" he says with a grin, peering up from the engine. "There's a Jeep parked out front that needs to have the all the brake pads replaced. If you can tackle that job, then we can head out early today. Your mama's making her famous pot roast tonight, and you know she'll kill us if we're late."

"Oh, I know it," I say as I grab my coveralls from the hook and put them on over my clothes.

My mom has dinner on the table every night at six-thirty on the dot, and I don't think my dad has ever once been late for it. He also stops every Wednesday, without fail, to buy her flowers from the stand across the street from the shop. It's been the same routine for as long as I can remember, and yet my dad looks at each meal like it's the best he's ever had, and my mom gasps with surprise every Wednesday when he hands her the flowers he bought for her. They've been together for more than thirty years, but for them, every day is their honeymoon. It took them a long time to get pregnant with me, so they're a bit older than most of my friends' parents are, but I know that I'm damn lucky to have two parents who love each other, and me, as much as they do. I'll consider myself the luckiest man on earth if I ever have something half as special as what they have. Unlike all my friends, who go through girls like they go through socks, I'm looking for that one person who will be my lifelong best friend. I see real, true love every day when I look at my parents, and that's what I want, too. I want the real thing.

My parents found each other when they were fifteen years old. I don't want to miss out on true love simply because I'm too blind or immature see it. When I find her, I intend to hold on to her. I don't care if that makes me a pussy, or whatever else my friends call me.

That's just the way I am.

chapter two

Amy

"Where's he taking you?" Savannah asks me as we sit down at a table in the cafeteria.

It's Friday afternoon, and tonight is my date with Scott. I've been a bundle of nerves all day, and just thinking about it has my stomach in knots. I can't decide if what I'm feeling is excitement or dread. I've gone back and forth about canceling the date at least a dozen times since he asked me. I'm terrified that I might do or say something wrong and end up humiliating myself, but the idea of going off to college as a naïve, inexperienced freshmen is enough to prevent me from backing out.

"He mentioned dinner and bowling," I tell her, biting my lip. "Apparently a few of his friends are going to meet up with us after dinner."

"That sounds like fun," she says with a cheerful smile. "Why don't you seem excited about it?"

I shrug. "I guess I'm just nervous."

She looks at me with narrowed eyes. "Are you sure this doesn't have anything to do with a certain best friend of your brother's?"

Savannah knows all about my hopeless crush on Nate. She's the only person I've ever told, because I can trust her with anything.

"This isn't about him," I say, glancing around to make sure that there's no one in earshot of our conversation. "I mean, maybe it is a little bit, but I can't keep waiting around, hoping for him to notice me. Nothing's ever going to happen with Nate. He doesn't see me as anything more than his best friend's sister, or another one of the guys. If I keep holding out for him, I'll end up a lonely, pitiful thirty-year old virgin!"

"That's never going to happen," she laughs. "And maybe you're right about Nate, but maybe you're not. You'll never know unless you actually tell him how you feel."

"No way," I say, shaking my head. "Have you forgotten about my brother? Dex would never let me get involved with one of his friends, and Nate is way too loyal to do anything that would jeopardize their friendship. Trust me, the best thing for me to do is to try and get a little bit of dating experience under my belt, and then I can go off to college and finally move on. I'm sure I'll forget all about Nate once I'm no longer seeing him every day at school, or watching him play basketball shirtless in my backyard."

I can't help but let out a small sigh when I think about Nate's bare, sweaty torso in all its perfection. He's tall and lean, with the faint ridges of a six-pack on his stomach. He doesn't spend as much time at gym as Dex and their friend Teddy do, but he takes good care of his body, and to me he's absolutely flawless. I've spent far too many nights lying in bed, fantasizing about tracing my tongue over every curve and contour of his firm chest and tasting his tan, salty skin.

My thoughts are interrupted when my brother drops into the seat next to mine, slamming his overloaded lunch tray onto the table. Teddy and Nate follow behind, sitting down in the empty chairs next to him.

"What's up, sis?" Dex says as he begins digging into his food.

"Do you think you got enough to eat?" I tease him, glancing sideways at the enormous amount of food stacked up on his lunch tray.

"I'm a growing boy," he says with a grin in between mouthfuls.

Nate chuckles from his seat on the other side of the table. "Yeah, but you're growing *out* instead of *up*. That poor tee shirt you've got on is working overtime. Looks like you're about to bust right out of that sucker."

"Ptfff, I'm pure muscle," Dex responds, gesturing to his upper body. "I'd be happy to take my shirt off and show you."

"Keep your damn clothes on!" Nate insists with a groan. "I see enough of that shit at the gym." He smiles, his green eyes flickering in amusement as they meet mine from across the table. "Is he this bad at home, too?"

"Yup, unfortunately," I laugh, attempting to hide my body's reaction to him. "I consider it a good day when Dex actually decides to put on pants."

They all laugh, and Dex shrugs unapologetically. The guys are always messing with each other, so I'm used to the playful banter between them. That's the way they are. Dex occasionally turns it on me, but I've learned to dish it out pretty well over the years, so I never let it bother me.

"So Ames, are you going to watch the big fight with us tonight?" Teddy asks. He's been using that nickname for me since we were kids. Of all the boys I used to run around with as a kid, Teddy is the only one that I'm still friends with today. He's also the only one, besides

Dex, who never ditched me for being a "girl." In a lot of ways, he's like a second brother to me.

"Uh, no… I actually have plans tonight." I stare down at my tray, silently praying that Dex doesn't ask me about it. I've managed to make it this far without him hearing about my date with Scott, and I don't want him to find out now. I can see him out of the corner of my eyes, looking at me curiously, but thankfully he doesn't say anything.

"Aw, too bad," Teddy says. "You're missing out!"

"Uh, hello?" Savannah interjects, glancing around the table. "Aren't you even going to *pretend* to invite me to your little fight or whatever?"

"Trust me, Savannah, you don't want to come," Teddy tells her. "It's not something that a girl would be interested in."

"*I'm* a girl," I grumble.

"You know what I mean," Teddy says, waving his hand dismissively. "It's not something that an *actual* girl would be interested in."

Gritting my teeth together in frustration, I stand up from the table and dump the remaining contents of my tray in the garbage before heading to my next class.

■   ■   ■

Savannah meets me at my house after school and proceeds to spend the next three hours working her girlie magic to get me dolled up for my date. Under most circumstances I would never allow the whole "makeover thing", but after what happened at lunch today, I feel like I have something to prove. I know that Teddy's comments weren't meant to offend me, but I'm sick and tired of being lumped in with the guys. For once, I want people to look at me and see something different, see someone beautiful. I want to experience that moment of awestruck silence when a guy looks at me, and he can't take his eyes off me. I want someone to be so captivated by me that the last thing on his mind is the big fight or the score of the game.

Of course, I had no idea what I was in for when I enlisted Savannah's help getting ready. She's been buffing, polishing and curling for what seems like hours, and I'm beginning to regret my decision. That is, until I catch a glimpse of my appearance in my bedroom mirror.

"Wow." I'm barely able to recognize the person looking back at me. I look older, more sophisticated, and maybe even beautiful. I actually look like a woman.

"I know, right?" Savannah smiles proudly, admiring her hard work. "It's amazing what a little bit of makeup and a curling iron can do. Since you're already blessed with those high cheekbones and long, thick eyelashes, all you really needed was a little blush and some mascara to emphasize your natural features. Then we just added some waves to all that gorgeous brown hair of yours, and *voilà!* You're a total sex goddess!"

I laugh self-consciously, my cheeks immediately flushing pink. I've never been sexy, and all the makeup in the world couldn't change that. All of a sudden, the whole makeover seems like a huge mistake. There's no way I can pull this off. I don't know how to be the person who goes along with this new look.

"Stop overthinking it," Savannah scolds, as if reading my mind. "You look amazing, and you're going to have a great time tonight."

I frown, biting my lip nervously as I look in the mirror. "I'm not sure I can do this."

"Don't be silly, of course you can do this." She grips my shoulders, spinning me around to face her. "A little bit of makeup and some curls doesn't change anything. Underneath it, you're still the same gorgeous, smart, funny person that you've always been. Just be yourself. You'll be fine!"

I let out a breath. "Okay, you're right. I can do this."

"That's the spirit," she smiles. "Now we just need to find you something amazing to wear. I went ahead and brought a few things of mine for you to choose from, since we both know there's nothing in your closet that will do you justice tonight."

Nate

"Oh, hell no," Dex shouts angrily from the bottom of the staircase. "You have got to be kidding me. No fucking way."

Turning, I follow his gaze to where Amy is coming down the stairs, and my tongue immediately gets stuck in my throat.

She's all dressed up, wearing a tight black dress that hugs her curves and lands well above her knees. Her long brown hair is no longer in her signature ponytail, but falls in waves around her shoulders and down her back. As she gets closer her eyes lock on mine, causing a blush to spread across her cheeks, but I still can't tear my eyes away. I've never once seen Amy wear makeup, but tonight her hazel eyes are sexy and smoldering, and her full lips are glossy and tinted pink. My eyes drop lower, skimming down her body until they land on a pair of black high heels. God, her legs look like they're ten miles long, and I'm suddenly picturing them wrapped around my waist, with those black heels digging into my back.

Fuck.

Amy's always been beautiful—even with the messy ponytail and jeans—and I'll admit to being attracted to her when I first met her. However, when Dex and I started hanging out more, she automatically became off-limits. I never let myself look at her that way again. She's always just been... Amy. My best friend's sister and a cool girl who I actually consider to be one of my friends. But now, shit... I don't know if I'll ever be able to *stop* looking at her. She looks like my every fantasy come to life, and I will never get her image out of my head.

"Go back upstairs and change your clothes," Dex demands, pointing up the stairway that she just climbed down. "Now."

Amy shifts her eyes away from me as anger invades her features. "No," she says forcefully, gritting her teeth and glaring up at Dex as he towers over her. "I happen to like the way that I look. Stop acting like such an asshole."

I happen to like the way she looks, too.

"Where the hell do you think you're going, dressed like that?" Dex asks roughly, glancing back and forth between Amy and Savannah, who is cowering at the bottom of the stairs.

Amy bites her lip, and for the first time she appears nervous. "Actually, I have a date."

Dex looks even angrier. "With who?"

"Scott Henderson," she says, shrugging her shoulders.

"No fucking way," Dex growls, his jaw clenched tight. "You are not going out with that douchebag, Amy. Call him and cancel it."

For the first time, I completely agree with him, but I don't know if my sudden change of heart has to do with backing up my friend, or my growing hard-on for his sister.

Mrs. Porter comes around the corner from the kitchen and glares at her son. "Dex, behave yourself and stop harassing your sister," she says sternly. "She's nearly eighteen years old, and if she wants to date, then she's going to date. It's about time that she finally found someone who isn't afraid of you."

Dex has his hands fisted at his sides but doesn't say anything.

"Amy, you look beautiful," Mrs. Porter says with a smile, just as the doorbell rings. "Have a great time and grab a jacket in case in gets cold, okay, sweetie?"

"Okay, Mom." She grabs a jean jacket from the coat closet before swinging the front door open.

Scott stands on the front porch, his cocky smile faltering for a moment as he looks in and sees the crowd of people surrounding the front door like a security detail. Dex is grilling him so hard that I have to give him props for not running off like a scared little girl.

"Uh, hey, Amy," he says, shifting his feet uncomfortably. "Are you ready to go?"

She pauses, making me think for a moment that she might say no and cancel the date after all, but then she nods. "Yeah, I'm ready."

Her eyes meet mine once more before she turns to leave, and it hits me deep in the pit of my stomach. I don't like this. At all.

My thoughts are interrupted when Teddy lets out a low whistle. "Well damn, your sister's pretty hot, Dex. I guess little Ames is all grown up."

Dex glares at Teddy with murder in his eyes. "Don't even think about touching my sister. I don't care if you're my best friend, I will beat the fucking shit out of you."

Teddy laughs, slapping a hand on Dex's shoulder. "Relax, dude, I'm just messing with you. None of us are stupid enough to go after your sister."

■ ■ ■

"I'm starving," Teddy announces at the end of the fight. "Where's the pizza? If I don't get some food in me soon, I can't be held accountable for my actions."

The boxing match just ended, and we're sprawled out in Dex's living room. It's been a few hours since Amy left for her date. I'd be lying if I said I haven't been keeping one eye on the clock waiting for her to get back. I guess that means she's having a good time, and I'm trying to remind myself that it's a good thing. The best thing that could happen would be for Amy to end up in a relationship. That way I could push these weird feelings aside and stop fantasizing about those full pink lips, wondering how they taste.

It's just Amy. The same Amy who is my best friend's twin sister and is downright untouchable.

The doorbell rings, announcing the arrival of the pizza we ordered, and Teddy jumps up to get it. When he comes back in with the boxes, I reach into my back pocket to grab some cash and realize I don't have my wallet on me.

"Shit, I left my cash in the car," I tell them. "I'll be right back. Try not to eat both pizzas before I get back."

"Can't make any promises," Dex teases, shoving nearly an entire slice in his mouth.

It's a clear, beautiful night. I take a moment to look up at the stars in the sky, the tiny, bright flecks of light spattered across a black canvas. It's not often that you get such a good view, but the storm that passed through earlier in the day left a perfect night in its wake.

After grabbing my wallet from the car, I'm making my way back around to the front of the house when I hear something coming from the backyard. It sounds like a low whimper, or something whining, and I take a detour around back to check it out.

It only takes me a few seconds to find the source of the sound. I can see Amy sitting on the bench in the backyard, obscured by the darkness with her head in her hands, crying softly.

"Amy?" I say, approaching her slowly. "Are you okay?"

"Just go away," she says without raising her head to look at me.

"Did he… did he hurt you?" I ask quietly. I'm trying to remain calm, but the thought of him doing something to hurt her has anger pumping through my veins. If that asshole touched her, he doesn't stand a chance.

Amy shakes her head. "No, he didn't do anything to me."

My entire body relaxes as I move to sit next to her on the bench, careful not to spook her. "What happened?"

She finally looks up, her gorgeous hazel eyes full of tears. The heartbroken expression on her face makes my chest ache, and I need to know what happened to put that look there.

"I'm such an idiot," she says, twisting her hands together in her lap. "Scott was never interested in me. He was just using me to make his ex-girlfriend jealous. She was there at the bowling alley, and as soon as she saw him walk in with me, she came over to confront him. Within ten minutes, they were back together, groping each other in the corner, and he completely forgot about me. I had to pay one of his friends twenty bucks to drive me home."

She starts sobbing again, and it's probably the worst sound I've ever heard. I drape my arm over the back of the bench, resting my hand on her back in an attempt to comfort her.

"How long have you been out here?" I ask, wondering where she's been all this time if the date ended as early as she said it did.

"A couple hours, I guess." She slumps her shoulders, wiping stray tears from her cheeks. "I couldn't stand the idea of coming home and having to explain what happened. Not to mention proving Dex right. God, it's so embarrassing."

I shake my head angrily. "Scott's the one who should be embarrassed, Amy. Only a total coward does something like that. I mean, come on, what a fucking pussy."

A faint smile appears on her lips. "I don't know why I'm so upset about this. I honestly didn't even like him that much. I was just fed up with being the only girl my age who hasn't been on a date or had a boyfriend. I haven't even had a real kiss yet!"

Her confession takes me by surprise. I know that Dex is protective, but how the hell is it possible that someone like Amy has managed to avoid being kissed? Ever? The whole thing blows my mind. I guess high school guys really are just as stupid as everyone thinks we are.

"I'm afraid of going off to college next year with *zero* experience," Amy admits. "There must be something seriously wrong with me. Am I not pretty enough? Or am I just not kissable? What is it?"

"There's nothing wrong with you," I tell her, scooting closer and tilting her chin up so she meets my gaze. "There's something wrong with *him*. He's a fucking idiot for passing up a chance with you. That girl he's with is nothing compared to you. You're gorgeous, smart, funny, caring… any guy would be lucky to have you."

The sad, vulnerable look in her eyes has the truth pouring out of my lips before I can stop it. The only thing that matters to me right now is making her feel better.

"You're just saying that."

"No, I'm not," I say truthfully. My fingers begin tracing small circles over her back and shoulders, and somehow my other hand finds its way to her warm, bare knee. A faint shiver runs through her, and she shifts her body slightly, closing the remaining distance between us, allowing me to feel her warmth against me.

"Amy, when you came down the stairs tonight, you completely took my breath away. I'd never seen anyone so beautiful in my whole life."

I hear her sharp intake of breath, and suddenly her small hand is resting on my side, timidly grasping at the material of my tee shirt. She bites nervously on her bottom lip, and all I can think about is sucking that lip into my mouth and tasting it. My body suddenly develops a mind of its own, and my palm drifts further up her smooth thigh, until my fingers are teasing the hem of her short dress.

"Nate," she gasps, tightening her grip on my shirt and pulling me closer. Her eyes are locked on mine, inviting me in and pleading for me to kiss her. I'm too weak to try and fight it.

My fingers trail up her back and over her shoulders to the nape of her neck. I brush my thumb over her damp cheek, wiping away any traces of her tears. Gently I pull her toward me, sloping my body closer until I feel her soft lips against mine. The kiss is hesitant at first, and then she lets out a soft moan as she begins moving her mouth over mine.

Every fiber of my body wants her, and I'm aching with the need for more. I want to kiss and touch every inch of her body and feel her wrapped around me as I bury myself inside her. I'm fighting to restrain myself, held back only by the knowledge that this is her first kiss.

Her hand sneaks under the hem of my shirt, tentatively skimming my bare skin with her fingertips and igniting a fire inside of me. Unable to control myself, I slide my hand further underneath the hem of her dress, creeping closer and closer to her warmth. I run my tongue along the seam of her lips, begging entrance into her mouth, and she immediately opens for me. My tongue barely sweeps against hers when I hear Dex.

"Nate, where the fuck are you?" he calls out from the front of the house. "If you're not in here in thirty seconds, we're eating your goddamn pizza!"

His words are like a bucket of freezing cold water, soaking us and drowning the moment. I jerk away from her and jump up from the bench, instantly brought back to reality.

"Fuck, Amy… I'm so sorry," I tell her, dragging my hands over my face as I attempt to regain control.

Her chest is rising and falling as she catches her breath. "Nate, no, it's okay. I—I want this."

I shake my head furiously back and forth. "No, this was a mistake. I shouldn't have done this. It's my fault. I'm so sorry."

Turning on my heels, I walk away as fast as I can, ignoring the painful look of disappointment in her eyes as she watches me go.

part two

. . .

two years later

chapter three

Amy

My eyes keep darting to the clock as my English professor wraps up his lecture at the front of the classroom. It's Friday afternoon, and this is my final class before a long weekend. I'm anxious to get back to my dorm room and start packing.

I'm making the two hour trip home from the University of South Carolina to spend the weekend with my family, who I haven't seen in a few months. Dex and Teddy have a rare break from their Marine training and decided to take a quick trip home to Charleston, so they've been there for the last few days. Now that they're in the final stages of training, they're based in Quantico, Virginia, and they seldom have any time off. It's been ages since I've seen my brother, and I miss him like crazy. I wanted to skip classes to get home earlier, but Dex insisted that I finish out the week. By the time I finally get home, I'll be lucky to get a day with him before he has to leave again, but I'll take what I can get. Pretty soon his training will be complete, and he'll be halfway across the world fighting a war.

Just thinking about that is enough to send me into a panic.

When my class is dismissed, I exit the building and find Duncan waiting for me outside. Since he has class in the same building at this time, he always waits for me so we can walk back to the dorms together.

"Hey, baby," he says, wrapping his arm around my waist and dropping a kiss on my cheek. "Want to stop at the dining hall to grab some lunch?"

"I wish I could, but I should probably start packing." I offer him an apologetic smile. "I need to get on the road soon if I want to make it home at a reasonable hour."

I feel bad for not spending time with him before I leave, but I'm anxious to get home. If Dex wasn't such an overbearing brother and had let me skip classes like I wanted, I would already be there.

"I wish you were staying here this weekend," Duncan says, grabbing my hand as we start the short walk across campus. "I'm going to miss you."

I met Duncan at the beginning of my sophomore year, and we've been dating for about three months now. My freshman year had been just as pathetically uneventful as I expected it to be, and aside from a few brief and forgettable encounters with the opposite sex, I ended that year with the same amount of dating experience that I'd had when it started. Instead, I spent the year focusing on school and taking a few extra classes to fill the time. On the bright side, my meager social life has put me way ahead of the game when it comes to earning the credits I need for a degree in education.

This year, everything turned around for me. I came back in the fall with a new attitude, determined to make my sophomore year a memorable one. I got a new roommate who was eager to welcome me into her clique of friends and introduce me to the social side of college that I'd been missing out on. At the very first frat party they took me to, I met Duncan. Never in a million years did I think that someone like him would ever be interested in me. He's smart, good-looking, rich, and not only a member of the most popular fraternity, but also the football team. When he started pursuing me, I thought he was just messing with me—I'd had a bad experience with that, after all—but much to my disbelief, he actually wanted me. *Me*.

After that, everything happened pretty quickly. All the years of experience I'd been missing was rolled up into a few months—dates, kissing, sex—it all just… happened. Not that I'm complaining, it just wasn't quite what I'd expected it to be.

I thought that all of my "firsts" would feel like that first kiss I shared with Nate. The build-up and anticipation, the nervous stomach flutters, and the frenzied, desperate desire. While I feel some of that with Duncan, I don't feel it to the same degree as I did with Nate.

Of course, Duncan actually decided to stick around. Unlike Nate, who went out of his way to pretend like the whole thing never even happened. After the kiss, the only time I ever really saw him was when my brother and his friends were around; so after a while, things went back to normal. I put the whole thing behind me and decided to move on. As much as it had killed me to hear him say that the kiss was a mistake, he was right. The only reason he'd kissed me in the first place was because he liked the way I looked that night. He was attracted to the makeup and the tight dress, and I went along with it because I wanted to believe it was me who he wanted.

Lesson learned.

Duncan and I are almost at the entrance to my dorm when he suddenly turns to me. "Since you can't stay this weekend, why don't I just go home with you?"

"You want to come home with me?" I repeat, dumbfounded. "Like, to meet my family?"

"Why not?" He smiles. "I'm probably going to meet them at some point anyway. And this way I won't have to stay here all alone, missing you."

This idea sounds like a recipe for disaster. Especially considering the fact that my brother is going to be there. Not to mention that it feels... soon.

"I thought you had football practice this weekend?" I throw out, hoping to steer him away from the idea without hurting his feelings.

"Coach decided to cancel it." He reaches for my hips and pulls me up against him. "Come on, it'll be fun."

He brushes his lips against mine, and I let myself melt into him. Maybe I'm being stupid about this. My parents have been asking to meet him, and I'm sure they'll force Dex to be on his best behavior.

"Okay," I concede with a nervous smile. "Let's do this."

As soon as I'm finished at the shop for the day, I head down to the Seaside Bar & Grill to meet Dex and Teddy for a bite to eat.

While I've spent the last two years here in town with a full-time job at the shop with my dad, Dex and Teddy have been working their asses off to get through their extensive Marine training. I haven't seen much of them since they started. Even when they were close by at Parris Island for basic training, they never had any free time. Now that they're up in Quantico, Virginia for advanced specialty training, it's a miracle that they have a few days off to make the trip home for a visit. No matter how busy they are, or how intense their training is, we always do our best to keep in touch. As much as it sucks to be the one here by myself, I'm glad that they have each other, and I couldn't be more proud of them for what they're doing.

When I walk into the restaurant, I notice the two of them immediately, mainly because they stick out from the rest of the crowd like sore thumbs. They're both huge, solid blocks of muscle from all their training and conditioning, and they have identical military buzz cuts. Not to mention, they're surrounded by women. I can't help but chuckle when I see all the girls tripping over themselves to try and gain their attention. What is it about men in the military that makes women so crazy?

They both stand up when they see me, and we meet each other with the standard masculine half-hug, half-handshake that men use to greet each other. Not that these two need to worry about appearing feminine. I'm fairly certain that they would look macho even if they were painting their nails and shaving their legs.

"I still can't believe that you guys came all the way down here for, what, three days?" I shake my head as we sit down at the table.

Dex shrugs, as though seven hours of travel is no big deal. "God knows when we'll have time off like this again, so we couldn't pass it up. It's nice to be home, even if it's only for a little while. I haven't seen my family in months, either. If they knew I had time off and I didn't find time to see them, they'd probably kick my ass."

"They must have been psyched to see you," I say. Both Dex and Teddy are really close to their families, and I know all the time apart is hard for them.

Dex laughs. "Yeah, they went a little nuts when I told them. Amy even tried to get away with skipping classes so she could come down earlier, but I wouldn't let her. She should be here some time tonight."

My ears perk at the mention of Amy. I've mastered the art of hiding my reaction to hearing things about her, but I can't keep myself from noticing.

"How is Amy doing? I ask, trying to sound casual.

"She's doing well, I think." Dex frowns slightly, narrowing his eyebrows together. "Apparently she has some boyfriend up at school, which she's failed to mention. My mom finally told me about him today, right before she informed me that he's coming down with Amy for the weekend to visit."

Teddy chuckles in amusement. "Oh boy, I can't fucking wait to see this!"

I can't fake a laugh because I feel like someone just punched me in the gut. It's stupid, because I knew Amy was going to end up with someone eventually. For years I wondered how she managed to stay single for so long, but now that I hear she's seeing someone, I don't want to believe it.

I clear my throat, choking back my irritation. "So, what do you know about this guy?"

"Not a damn thing," Dex complains. "My mom hasn't met him yet, and Amy hasn't said much about him. All I know is that he's some fucking frat boy named Duncan who plays on the football team. Sounds like a total douchebag to me."

"I'm sure he's not that bad," Teddy reasons. "Amy's a good girl with a decent head on her shoulders. Although it will definitely be way more entertaining to watch you torture the poor kid."

Duncan? I have to agree with Dex on this one. He sounds like a total douchebag.

I'm not a complete hypocrite. I know that I have no right to pass judgment on anyone who Amy dates. I gave up the right to act jealous or possessive the second I walked away from her two years ago. When I left her alone on that stupid bench and ignored the heartbroken look on her face as she watched me go.

"I want this."

Her words from that night have echoed in my mind at least a million times since they fell from her sweet lips. I never knew that Amy had feelings for me or thought of me as anything other than her brother's best friend. But that night I'd seen it. I saw the longing... the desire... on her face when she looked at me. I felt it in the way she touched me, in each caress of her lips, and in the way she responded to my hands on her body.

I knew she felt something because I did, too.

Which is exactly why I had to walk away. I had to distance myself from her so I could douse the fire that had ignited between us, before it erupted into something that I couldn't control. It was the only choice.

What happened between us was a mistake. Or at least, it *should* feel like a mistake. The truth is, it felt... right. Even though I know it's wrong, I don't want to take that moment back. The taste of her lips, the sounds that she made, the warmth of her palm on my skin... it's all burned into my memory. It's there in my mind for me to replay over and over again.

Unfortunately, it doesn't matter how good or how perfect it felt. One of the main rules of friendship is that your best friends' family members are always off-limits. It's a boundary that I refuse to cross, because it would ruin my friendship with Dex. Regardless of how close we are, I know that he would never be okay with it.

"Don't even think about touching my sister. I don't care if you're my best friend, I will beat the fucking shit out of you."

I don't have any siblings, but Dex and Teddy are the closest thing

I have to brothers. They aren't just my friends, they're my family. I won't do anything to jeopardize that. It's more important now than ever, as they're preparing to ship off to war and put their lives on the line. I owe it to them to be a good friend, to be someone who they can trust and rely on, no matter what.

chapter four

Amy

The sun is just beginning to set as Duncan turns his car onto the quiet road leading to my parents' house. I'm so anxious to get there I can't seem to sit still. I've been impatiently tapping my foot ever since we crossed the bridge leading to my hometown of Folly Beach.

"Would you knock that off?" Duncan says, gesturing to my bobbing knee. "You're making me nervous."

"Sorry," I mumble half-heartedly.

The moment we pull into the driveway, I see Dex standing outside waiting. Before the car is fully stopped, I'm jumping out of the passenger seat and running toward him. A smile appears on his face seconds before I crash into him, throwing my arms around his neck.

"I missed you so much!" I shriek as his strong arms squeeze me tight and lift me up into the air.

Chuckling, he lowers me to the ground. "I missed you too, little sister."

I smack his arm playfully. "I'm not your little sister, you idiot. In case you forgot, we were born at the same time."

"But I'm bigger," he argues. "And older."

"Only by three minutes!"

A wide grin spreads across his cheeks. "Still counts."

I don't bother bickering with him about it. I'm so happy to see him that I don't care. Besides, it's impossible to be mad at Dex when his typically stern face is lit up with a smile like this. I really missed him.

His smile slips when he looks over my shoulder, and I spin around to see Duncan cautiously walking toward us. "Be nice," I hiss under my breath so only Dex can hear.

Duncan sticks his hand out to introduce himself. "Hey man, I'm Duncan. It's nice to meet you."

Dex just stares, scrutinizing him from head to toe without saying a word. Finally, he reaches out to shake his extended hand. "Dex. Nice to finally meet the boyfriend I've heard nothing about."

I roll my eyes. "Geez, Dex, I wonder why I don't tell you anything." I shift my gaze to Duncan, who's standing there uncomfortably. "Just ignore my brother. My parents dropped him on his head a lot when he was a baby."

Dex laughs. "Relax, Amy, I'm just kidding around." He wraps his arm around Duncan's neck in what appears to be a friendly headlock but is definitely tighter than necessary. As he drags him inside, he says, "Come on, let's go introduce you to the rest of the family."

The parental introductions go a lot smoother, with both of them seeming to approve of Duncan. There's no doubt that he's charming, and he certainly knows how to make a good impression. Dex is not as easy to win over, but he eventually stops shooting daggers out of his eyes and actually starts warming up to Duncan a little bit.

After we finish eating dinner, Duncan kindly offers to help my mom clear the table and I pull my brother aside. "Thank you for not killing him," I say. "I should have told you about him sooner, and I know it was a surprise to have him come here with me."

"He must be pretty important to you for you to bring him down here to meet the family," Dex points out. His words are casual but I know that he's digging for information and assessing my feelings.

"I suppose," I shrug. "I haven't spent much time analyzing my feelings yet. Obviously I like him, but this whole dating thing is still new to me. We've been together for a few months, though, so bringing him here seemed like the right thing to do."

He's quiet as he weighs my answer. There are questions in his eyes, but there's also guilt.

"I guess it's my own fault that all of this is so new to you," he says finally, shifting his weight uncomfortably. "I know that I haven't always been fair to you when it comes to dating and all that shit."

"Well yes, you are a tad bit on the protective side," I say, teasing.

Dex looks at me seriously. "I hope you know that I only do it because I care about you. It's not because I'm trying to keep all guys away... I'm just trying to keep the *wrong* guys away. I want you to have someone who deserves you and will fight for you. If a guy chooses to stay away from you simply because I tell him to, then he's not worth your time."

I study him curiously. Not once have I considered that Dex's intentions were anything beyond keeping all guys away from me in general.

"Someday you'll meet a guy who really sees you," he continues. "He'll see you for who you are, beneath everything else. It won't matter what I say, or threaten, to try and keep him away from you, because you'll be worth it to him. He won't be scared of me, and he'll fight for you, because nothing I could ever do to him would be worse than not having you."

With that, Dex drops a quick kiss to my forehead and leaves me there to absorb everything he told me. All those years of resenting my overbearing and overprotective brother fly out the window in an instant.

Turns out, I have the best, most caring brother in the entire universe.

■   ■   ■

By the next morning, I sense that Duncan is getting restless being stuck in the house with my family. As much as I want to spend my time with Dex before he leaves, Duncan *did* come all the way down here with me, and it doesn't seem fair to neglect him. Since he's never visited the Charleston area before, I decide to show him around a little bit and take him to a few of my favorite spots.

The small seaside town of Folly Beach where I grew up is only a few minutes outside of downtown Charleston. It has amazing beaches and a quiet, laidback atmosphere that I've missed since being away at school. Nothing quite compares to being here, and I'm eager to share it with Duncan.

One of the places that I want to show him is the swimming hole at the back of my parents' property. As we drive down the old, rural dirt road to get there, I find myself cringing every time the undercarriage of Duncan's BMW sedan scrapes against one of the deep potholes. He's driving slowly and carefully to avoid them, but since his car is so low to the ground it's nearly impossible. With his jaw clenched tightly and his hands fisted around the steering wheel, his anger grows with each scrape of his car on the dirt. Duncan is *really* into his car. I mean, totally obsessed. I'm about to suggest we turn around and skip the swimming hole altogether when I hear a sharp hiss of air right before the car veers unevenly in the road.

"Fuck!" Duncan yells, hitting the brakes and slamming his hand against the steering wheel. He climbs out of the car to assess the damage and I follow behind.

Sure enough, one of the front tires is blown out and completely destroyed. Duncan looks like he's about to lose it.

"Great," he complains. "Fucking perfect!"

"It'll be okay," I reassure him. "Do you have a spare? We can change the tire, and then bring it in to get the tire replaced."

"Uh no, actually we can't," he says, eyeing me with contempt. "First of all, I'm not qualified to change the tire on this kind of car, and second of all, I'm not going to risk further damage by driving on this godforsaken road for one more second."

Translation: Duncan has no idea how to change a tire.

"You could've warned me that we were going to be driving on a bunch of desolate, rinky-dink roads in the middle of Hickville, USA," Duncan grumbles under his breath.

"In case you forgot, I suggested that we take my mom's SUV out today, but you said no," I snap back, no longer able to hide my irritation. Duncan has a tendency to turn into a real prick when he gets angry. Lashing out at those around him seems to be his way of handling tense situations. I've learned that fighting back only makes it worse, so I bite my tongue and take a deep breath. One of us has to remain calm, and it sure as hell isn't going to be him.

"I'll call Dex and see if he can come help us out," I say calmly, reaching into my pocket for my cell phone. "He used to work for a mechanic, so he'll know what to do."

Dex answers on the third ring, sounding out of breath. I realize he's probably at the gym with Teddy and I feel bad for interrupting, but I know he doesn't mind. Dex has always been there to bail me out and take care of me, and this time is no different. After I explain our situation, he tells me to give him thirty minutes and he'll be here to get us out.

Not even fifteen minutes later I hear the loud rumble of an engine echoing through the trees. A few moments later I see the huge flat-bed tow truck coming down the road towards us, and I breathe a sigh of relief. When it comes to a stop I walk over with an appreciative smile, but it falters and I stop mid-stride when I see someone other than Dex climbing out of the tow truck.

My stomach automatically twists into knots. "What are you doing here?" I ask in a shaky voice.

"Is that how you treat people who come out to rescue you?" Nate says with a smirk.

"I'm sorry," I respond quickly, shaking my head. "I didn't mean to sound so rude. I was just expecting Dex, that's all."

"He called me to ask if he could borrow the tow to come out here and get you. I was at the shop anyway, so I offered to come instead."

I feel bad for how I reacted to seeing him, especially when he came all the way out here to do me a favor. "Thank you, Nate. I really appreciate it."

"Any time." His lips turn up in a warm smile that lights up his whole face, making me go weak in the knees. For a brief moment we stand there looking at each other, neither one of us saying a word.

Everything else drifts into the background until Nate's eyes suddenly shift from mine, his smile dissolving as he finally notices Duncan standing behind me. I'd nearly forgotten that he was here, and heat spreads across my cheeks as I turn around to face him.

Clearing my throat, I force a smile as I introduce them. "Duncan, this is Dex's best friend, Nate." I bite my lip nervously before turning to Nate. "Nate, this is my boyfriend, Duncan."

Nate presses his lips together, glancing one last time in my direction before stepping forward and extending his hand. "Hey, man, nice to meet you."

Duncan examines him skeptically and then reluctantly shakes his hand. "Yeah, you too."

It's almost funny to watch them size each other up. Nate towers at least six inches taller, but it doesn't stop Duncan from scowling at him. I don't understand why he's treating Nate as though he's some kind of threat. I know better than anyone that he doesn't see me that way, and it irritates me that Duncan is behaving like a predatory jerk when Nate is only trying to help us.

"So, Nate, do you think you'll be able to get us out of here?" I ask, hoping to relieve some of the tension.

"Shouldn't be a problem." He moves around to the front of the car to assess the damage. "Do you have a spare that we can throw on there, or do we need to tow it?"

"I don't want to use the spare," Duncan insists.

Nate looks at me with raised eyebrows, and I merely shrug in response. "Okay, then," he says. "Let's get it up on the flat-bed, and we'll bring it into the shop for a new tire."

Once the car is securely loaded on the back, I climb up into the cab of the tow truck and settle into the middle seat, making sure to leave enough room for Duncan and Nate on each side of me. Nate jumps into the driver's seat, and I suck in a sharp breath when I feel his body align next to mine in the cramped space of the cab.

While we wait for Duncan to retrieve his cell phone from the car, Nate looks at me with a teasing grin and nudges me with his shoulder. "So, your boy doesn't know how to change a tire?"

"I was thinking the exact same thing!" I say with a hushed giggle as Duncan climbs into the truck next to me.

Nate

There seems to be some major tension between Amy and her boyfriend. The drive over to the shop is filled with awkward, uncomfortable silence as the three of us remain squished into the small space of the cab. I'm having a hard time concentrating with the way that Amy's tight little body is pressed against me. Her shorts do little to cover the smooth, creamy skin of her thigh, and I'm fighting the urge to reach out and drag my fingers over it. If I move my hand another two inches to the right I could touch her, feel her warmth. I grip my own leg instead, keeping it firmly in place as I remind myself that she's not mine. She belongs to the arrogant little fuck sitting on the other side of her. The one who doesn't even know how to change a goddamn tire.

When we finally arrive at the shop, I jump out of the cab as fast as I possibly can and busy myself with unloading the car and getting it into the garage. As soon as I start working on the car, I'm able to forget about everything else and focus on what's right in front of me.

Duncan is hovering over me, watching closely and scrutinizing my every move as I position the jack underneath the car and start to raise it up.

"Are you sure you know what you're doing?" he asks, crossing his arms over his chest as he tilts his chin toward the car.

"Seriously?" I say, cocking my head. "It's just a tire change."

"Yeah, but this isn't just any car. It's a BMW M3. It cost more than you make in a year."

"Duncan!" Amy gasps, her mouth falling open. "What is wrong with you?"

"It's okay," I tell her calmly, not the least bit worried or affected by his opinion of me. I've worked on cars that make his overpriced, piece-of-shit BMW look like junkyard garbage, but I don't bother telling him that. Let him think what he wants about me. At the end of the day, I couldn't care less about him. The only thing that bothers me is the fact that Amy is stuck with this prick.

"Sorry," Duncan says with a shrug, sounding anything but apologetic. "Just be careful with my baby, okay?"

His baby?

Amy rolls her eyes at him behind his back, and I turn away to hide my grin. This guy is something else.

I love cars. My life is all about cars. But there will only ever be one "baby" in my life, and you can bet your ass it won't have four wheels. It'll be the woman who ends up by my side. A car is just a car. It's nothing more than bunch of metal on four wheels. Sure, it's fun to drive around in, and some of them are pretty damn nice, but no car can compare to the love of a good woman. That's the kind of thing you fucking cherish.

It doesn't take long to get the new tire on, and thankfully Duncan keeps his mouth shut. I want to catch up with Amy and hear about how school is going, but it feels weird to do that with her boyfriend around. It shouldn't, since we're just friends, but it does.

"Thanks for everything, Nate," Amy says when I'm all finished. "I'm sure this isn't how you planned on spending your Saturday afternoon."

"You know I'll always be there to help you out." Her big, brown eyes focus on mine, and my heart stalls in my chest. She's so fucking beautiful.

"I know," she says with a coy smile, slowly backing away. "Um, I guess I'll see you later then."

"Wait." I stop her, not ready to say goodbye yet. "Will I see you tonight?"

She furrows her eyebrows curiously. "What's happening tonight?"

"We're having a bonfire at the clearing, since Dex and Teddy are leaving tomorrow. Nothing major, just some beer and music with a few people. You should come." I glance at Duncan, who's waiting in the car. "Unless you guys have other plans."

"No, I'll be there." Her mouth curves up into a smile, and she chews nervously on her lower lip. "Uh, I mean, we'll be there."

■ ■ ■

I bring the bottle to my lips and tilt it back, enjoying the cold taste of the beer as it spills down my throat. My eyes are fixed on the bright orange flames of the bonfire as they flicker and dance around the wooden logs, brightening the field around us and reaching high into the dark night sky. The heat caresses my face, and everything around me blurs as I focus on the sparkling embers and the drowsy rhythm of a country song that pours from the speakers nearby.

I'm instantly thrown back in time to all the nights in high school that were spent here in this exact place, doing just this. In a lot of ways, it *is* the same. The same group of friends, the same fake I.D. used to buy beer, and the same need for a brief escape from reality. This place carries a sense of freedom. Being out here, deep in the woods and hidden from the rest of the world, it's easy to forget everything else and just… be.

I glance up and see Dex and Teddy, laughing and drinking, and I have to wonder if being here still gives them that same reprieve. Their lives are so different now, so... real. Soon they'll be halfway across the world, risking their lives to fight for our freedom. I can't even imagine being in their shoes.

My life hasn't changed too much since high school. I guess you could say I chose the safe route, but the truth is, I'm happy with it. Sure, it's a little boring and lonely sometimes, seeing as how most of my friends left town after graduating high school, but for the most part, I enjoy my life here.

Swallowing the last sip of my beer, I stand up to toss the bottle in a trash bin. As I'm walking over to the trunk of my car to grab a fresh one from the cooler, I notice the black BMW pulling into the clearing. Duncan's shiny black sports car looks completely out of place parked next to the huge, muddy trucks around it. I watch as the passenger door opens, and my breath hitches in my throat when I see Amy step out of it. Her dark hair hangs loose past her shoulders, and she's wearing a short blue sundress with thin straps, showing off her delicate shoulders and long, tan legs. The light material of the fabric flutters around her slender body, and although it's a warm night I can practically feel the slight shiver that runs through her. It makes me want to wrap myself around her and share my warmth.

Duncan climbs out of the driver's seat, mumbling something to her before walking off in the direction of the keg. Amy doesn't follow or wait for him but instead moves toward the bonfire where Dex and Teddy are sitting.

I grab an extra beer and walk over to meet her. She seems a bit uneasy at first, glancing around the small crowd, but as soon as she sees me, her face lights up.

"You made it," I say as I approach her. "I was starting to think you might blow me off."

"Of course not." She smiles. "I was glad to get out. I needed a change of scene."

I sit down on the big log next to the fire, gesturing for her to sit next to me. "Want a beer?"

"Sure, thanks." She takes a seat beside me, carefully arranging her dress to cover her legs.

I pop open the two beers and hand one to her, intentionally grazing my fingers across hers when she takes it from me. Even the slightest contact with Amy is full of electricity, and I know she can sense it, too. Her cheeks flush slightly as she lifts the bottle to her full lips and takes a long sip.

Damn, I'd love to feel those lips again.

"So, how have you been?" I inch my body closer to hers. "How's school?"

Her proximity is distracting. Her fruity, coconut smell invades my senses and draws me in. I know that I should put some distance between us, but I can't seem to make myself pull away.

"I've been pretty good." She shifts toward me, letting her thigh bump against mine. "School is… well, school. It's a lot of work, but I like my classes, so I don't mind it. How's everything with you?"

"Can't complain," I say with a shrug, trying to hide the fact that her touch makes my head spin. "Things have been hectic at the shop, so I'm keeping myself busy."

I take a long pull from my beer, and her eyes are fixated on my throat as I take a deep swallow. I'm so engrossed in her reaction that I don't notice Duncan until he's standing right above me.

"Got you a beer," he says flatly, holding a red plastic cup out to Amy.

She offers him an apologetic smile as she holds up the beer I gave her, and I can't help the pleased feeling that spreads through me. "I already got one, sorry. I wasn't sure how long you would be."

"Whatever." Duncan jerks the cup away, lifting it to his mouth and draining the entire contents at once. When he's finished, he carelessly tosses the cup aside, looking at us as he sneers, "More for me then."

chapter five

Amy

I can't help but cringe when I hear Duncan's angry tone, although I probably should've expected it. Things have been tense between us ever since we left Nate's shop this afternoon. I couldn't believe the way he'd acted toward Nate, all smug and pretentious, and frankly I was embarrassed by it. When I confronted him about it on the drive home, he didn't even have the decency to act remorseful or offer any kind of explanation. All he did was laugh, as though he's actually *proud* to be that way.

Things only went downhill from there.

Now, I'm wondering how much I *really* know about Duncan. We've been together for a few months now, and I thought he was a decent guy, but maybe I've been oblivious to what was right in front of me. Perhaps I so desperately wanted him to be right for me that I've been allowing myself to overlook his true character. I was hoping to get some space from him tonight so I could clear my head, but evidently that's not going to happen.

Duncan plunks down in a beach chair a few feet away from where I'm sitting, staring straight forward into the fire as he drinks from his remaining cup, not bothering to acknowledge me or even look at me.

Nate rests a gentle hand on my lower back, and when I turn to look at him, his eyes are full of concern. "Are you okay?"

"Yeah, I'm fine. Let's just say it's been a long day," I say with a short laugh, rolling my eyes in Duncan's direction.

"Okay, but all you have to do is say the word, and we'll kick him out on his ass." Nate winks, the action making my stomach do a somersault.

Dex and Teddy come over a few moments later, sitting down next to us and relieving the awkward silence. Pretty soon we're all laughing and chatting away, and eventually Duncan decides to join us. He seems to have lightened up, joking around with the guys, and exchanging banter with Dex and Teddy. I'd like to believe that the sudden lift in his mood is due to a change of heart, but I think it has more to do with all the beers he's consumed. He still barely acknowledges me—or Nate for that matter—but at this point I couldn't care less.

Teddy's in the middle of regaling us with one of his many hilarious stories from boot camp, when someone comes up and asks Nate for help getting his car to start.

Nate, being the generous guy that he is, immediately stands and follows him to the area of the clearing where the cars are parked. I watch him as he walks away, already feeling the loss of his presence next to me, and I only hope that whatever the issue is, it won't keep him away for long.

When I finally turn my attention back to the group, I find Duncan eyeing me. His jaw tightens, and I can only assume that he caught me gazing after Nate. I offer him a gentle smile, hoping to brush it off as an innocent gesture, even though we both know it wasn't. It doesn't work though, and Duncan quickly goes back to ignoring me.

I should probably be more concerned about what's going on with my relationship and try to come up with a plan to fix it, but the truth is, I'm not. As horrible as it sounds, I don't care what happens between Duncan and me after tonight. This weekend, I've observed a side of him that I don't like, and I know there's no way I'll be able to go back to my previous state of blissful ignorance.

Nate returns a few moments later and reclaims his seat next to me on the log.

"Did you get his car started?" Dex asks him.

Nate nods. "Yup, it was no big deal." He looks over at Duncan with a teasing grin. "Nothing complicated like changing a tire. Right, Duncan?" His tone is playful, but Duncan glares at him with a murderous look in his eyes.

I realize immediately that this isn't going to end well.

"Fuck this," Duncan spits out angrily, rising from his seat. "I don't need to sit here and listen to this shit." Scowling down at me, he motions his finger between Nate and me. "And I definitely don't need to sit here and watch my girlfriend flirt and make googly eyes at this fucking grease monkey. I'm out of here."

With that, he spins around and storms off toward his car. My cheeks flame, and I keep my eyes fastened on the ground, trying to hide my mortification and avoid the confused looks on Dex and Teddy's faces.

"Well, that was fucking weird," Teddy says with an amused laugh.

"Are you okay, Amy?" Dex asks. I can feel his eyes on me, and when I finally peek up at him, his expression is full of concern. "What the hell was that all about?"

"We've just been fighting a lot," I respond with a shrug. "It's okay though, really."

"You sure?" Dex doesn't seem entirely convinced, but thankfully he drops it. "Okay, well I'm going to go get another drink and make sure he's out of here. I'll be around if you need me."

"I'm right behind you, buddy." Teddy stands up with Dex and winks at me. "Don't worry, Ames. We got your back."

I can't help but smile as they walk away. Those two are like my own personal protectors, and I love them for looking out for me. They've always been a team, but it's become even more evident since they entered the Marines together. They're fiercely loyal to one another and always have each other's backs. They take the "No man left behind" aspect of the Soldier's Creed very seriously.

Nate has been quiet, and when I finally turn to face him, his eyes are full of regret when they meet mine. "Shit, Amy... I'm so sorry," he says, scrubbing his hands over his face. "I swear I was only joking around with him. I didn't think he would react like that. I should have kept my fucking mouth shut. If I'd known it was going to start a fight between you two, I never would've said anything."

"Don't worry about it." I wave my hand dismissively. "You have nothing to be sorry about, Nate. It's not your fault that he's uptight and can't take a joke. Besides, we were fighting long before you said anything."

"Are you sure?"

"Positive," I assure him. "I'm actually relieved that he's gone. Things have been really tense between us since we got here, and I needed some space."

He tilts his head, drawing his eyebrows together. "What happened when you got here?"

"I'm not exactly sure," I try to explain. "It's like I suddenly saw this whole other side of him that I hadn't seen before. I don't like it."

"Well, I wasn't going to say anything, but he is kind of…"

"An asshole?" I finish his thought.

Nate laughs. "I was going to be polite and use a word like 'pretentious,' but yeah, that works too. How's he managed to hide it from you all this time?"

"I guess it was different when we were at school. We were always hanging around with the same people and doing the same things. We were in our own bubble. But now that I've seen that side of him, I don't think I can go back to the way it was."

"Good," Nate says, taking me by surprise. He rests his hand on my knee and gently lifts my chin up with his finger, forcing me to meet his gaze. "You deserve better than him, Amy."

His gentle touch ignites my body with heat, quickening my pulse. I say breathlessly, "You think so?"

"Yeah, I do."

I feel his thumb begin tracing small circles on my thigh, and a dull ache settles between my legs, intensifying with each brush of his skin against mine. Every fiber in my body wants him, and any delusion I had of being "over him" goes up in smoke, drifting away into the night sky.

His eyes fall to my lips, studying them hungrily, and my mouth gently parts as if begging for him to seize it. We're both frozen in place, lingering in a battle of wills and waiting for the other to decide what happens next.

The sound of Teddy's voice breaks through the haze, and Nate squeezes his eyes shut as he pulls away from me.

"Hey." Teddy has a curious look on his face as he glances back and forth between Nate and me, but in a flash it's gone. "Dex and I got invited to join a couple of lovely ladies back at their place, so I think we're going to head out." Turning to Nate, he asks, "You want to come with us, or do you have something else going on? I'm sure they can dig up a friend for you if you're interested in a little fun." He waggles his eyebrows suggestively.

My gut twists uncomfortably at the idea of Nate joining in on the "fun" with those girls. I stare nervously at the ground while I wait for him to answer.

"Nah, you guys go ahead," Nate replies without hesitation. "I think I'm going to call it a night."

Relief floods through me, and I try to conceal the smile that appears on my lips.

"Suit yourself, man," Teddy says. "I'll catch up with you guys later."

Teddy hurries off to rejoin Dex and the girls, leaving me alone with Nate again. After a few beats of weighty silence, he turns to me with a cautious half-smile. "Can I give you a ride home?" His voice is deep and smooth, and heat simmers in his green eyes, causing a fresh wave of excitement to crash over me.

"Sure," I respond breathlessly.

He rises from his seat and holds his hand out to help me up. I stand on unsteady feet and follow him through the clearing. The bonfire has died down, darkening the field and making it difficult to see. Nate rests his hand on my lower back as he steers me toward his car, and there's something about that simple touch that feels familiar and possessive in a way that I crave.

The blue paint of his classic Ford Mustang sticks out in the dark, and I smile when I see it. When Nate first got the car, it was a rusty old hunk of junk. He bought it dirt-cheap from a salvage yard and spent all of high school restoring it, little by little. Clearly he's still working on it now, because when he opens the passenger door for me

I notice that the interior has been completely redone since I last saw it.

"Wow, the car looks great," I observe, sliding into the comfortable bench seat. The black leather that used to be tattered and torn is now sleek and pristine.

"Pretty nice, right?" Nate grins proudly as he climbs into the driver's seat and turns the ignition. "I could never afford to fix up the interior when I was still in school, since all my extra cash went under the hood to get the thing running. I was psyched when I was finally able to get it done."

After a few minutes of driving in silence, I scoot into the middle seat and reach toward the radio in the center console, hovering my fingers over the dial as I peek over at Nate. "Do you mind?"

"Go ahead. I'll be the chauffeur and you can be the DJ." He glances down to where I'm fiddling with the radio, and when his eyes shift back to the road, his expression is strained.

Confused, I look down and notice that my dress is hiked up around my thighs, exposing a large portion of my bare leg. I move to adjust it, but when I see the way Nate is gripping his fists around the steering wheel, I stop myself. I like knowing that I can affect him like this, and I want him to get a taste of the wild desperation that he makes me feel whenever he's around.

We're almost to my house, but I'm not ready for the night to end just yet. In a rare moment of boldness, I scoot even closer to him, letting my dress inch further up my thighs. I don't miss the subtle downward shift of his eyes when he sneaks a peek, and I bite my lip to conceal my pleased smile.

The car comes to a sudden stop, and he turns off the engine. It takes me a few seconds to realize that we're parked in the driveway of the vacant house across the street from my parents'. I turn toward

Nate, and his eyes are burning into mine. He's breathing heavily, and before I can ask him what we're doing, he lets out a deep groan and reaches toward me. Grabbing onto my thighs, he hauls me into his lap so I'm straddling him. I let out a sharp gasp as his mouth crashes into mine. He pulls me tightly against him, and when his tongue sweeps over my lips, they instantly part for him.

At the first caress of his tongue against mine, I wind my arms around his neck and sink further into him until his hardness is pressing perfectly against me. A moan escapes my throat, and my hips automatically rock against him.

"Shit, Amy…" Nate runs his hands up my thighs and underneath my dress, gripping me firmly as he flexes his hips up, grinding his length along my aching center.

"Oh God, that feels so good." Feeling him through nothing but the thin material of my panties is overwhelming, and dampness pools between my legs. I know that I'm soaked, but I'm too caught up in how amazing he feels to be embarrassed about how much I want him.

He kisses along curve of my neck, grazing his tongue over the sensitive spot behind my ear and driving me wild. I wind my fingers into his hair and grip him tightly, unable to control the sounds that pour out of my mouth.

Nate tugs at the thin straps on my shoulders until the top part of my dress falls down, exposing my lacy strapless bra. His fingers gently trail over the swell of my breasts, and he looks up at me when I suck in a nervous breath.

"You're fucking beautiful," he says softly, before placing tender kisses along my collarbone and over my cleavage.

"I want you so bad, Nate." My voice is needy and breathless, and my body simmers with anticipation. "Please touch me."

I feel his smile against my skin, and he tilts his head back to look at me. "Where do you want me to touch you?"

"Everywhere," I breathe.

He tugs down one side of my bra to expose my breast and covers it with his mouth. "Here?" he murmurs, gently licking and sucking my nipple until I cry out desperately.

"Yes," I pant.

He brings his hand down to my stomach, dragging it over my belly button until he reaches the edge of my panties. His fingers tease the elastic with his fingers as he looks at me and says, "Here?"

I'm unable to form words, but thankfully he doesn't wait for an answer before dipping his fingers underneath the material and rubbing my slick flesh.

"Christ," he groans, circling his fingers around the most sensitive part of me. "I love how wet you are for me."

I can already feel myself beginning to climb, utterly disarmed by his sure and steady movements. When he sinks a finger inside of me, I let my head fall back as his name tumbles out of my mouth on a sigh.

He continues to work me until the last shudder leaves my body, and in the next instant he has me on my back, pressing me into the smooth leather seat. Hovering over me, he melds his mouth to mine and thrusts his tongue between my lips. When he settles his hips between my legs, I can feel every hard, thick inch of him against me, and I'm overcome with the need to feel more of him. I reach for the bottom of his tee shirt and start lifting it up over his torso. Nate separates from me just long enough to pull it over his head and toss it to the side before realigning his body on mine.

His bare skin feels hot and perfect against me, and I run my hands up the taut muscles of his back as he rocks his hips into me. I'm already desperate for more, and when his rough palm covers my breast, I reach between us and hastily fumble with the button on his jeans until it pops open. The stiffness of his arousal presses against the zipper, and his breathing accelerates as I begin to lower it. Slipping my hand under the waistband of his boxers, I wrap my fingers around his silky smooth length, and he hisses gruffly into my ear.

"Amy, fuck…" His voice is thick with desire, and it completely turns me on. I begin moving my hand up and down, slowly at first, and Nate groans into my ear. "God, that feels so damn good. Just like that, don't stop."

He thrusts into my hand, and I stroke him faster, relishing the deep, sexy sounds that he makes as he gets closer to his release. As much as I want to get him there, I don't want it to happen until he's deep inside me.

I tilt my head up and ask, "Do you have a con—"

Headlights pour into the car, and we both freeze. They're gone almost immediately, but Nate still doesn't move.

"Shit," he mutters softly, pulling back and separating himself from me.

"What's wrong?" I look up at him without moving, and watch as he fastens his jeans and tugs his shirt over his head. "Who was that?"

He scrubs his hands over his face and lets out a heavy breath. "Duncan. He just pulled into your parents' driveway."

Just as he says the words I hear my phone ringing, and sure enough it's Duncan's name on the display. "I guess he didn't get the hint," I say, hitting the button to ignore the call.

"You should go talk to him," Nate says quietly without looking over at me. "We shouldn't have done this. It was a mistake."

My mouth falls open, and I stare at him blankly, too shocked and confused to form any words. When I finally do, they're barely above a whisper. "No, it wasn't."

"Put your clothes on, Amy," he pleads, his expression tight.

I've barely registered the fact that I'm still lying half-naked on the seat of his car. I should feel self-conscious about the fact that I'm on display, but the only emotion I have room for right now is anger. I tug my bra back into place and pull my dress up over my shoulders as I glance over at Nate, willing him to look at me. "Why are you doing this, Nate?"

"I never should have let it happen to begin with." He finally turns to me, but his eyes are cold and seem to look right through me. "I had too much to drink, and I wasn't thinking clearly. I let things… get out of hand. I'm so sorry." Gripping the steering wheel with both hands, he stares straight ahead as he says the next words. "You should work things out with Duncan."

"You don't mean that." My voice trembles, and pain hits my stomach, like a knife twisting in my gut. I shake my head as tears fill my eyes. "You know he's not who I want. He never was."

He visibly winces and drops his chin to his chest, staring at the floor. "It doesn't matter. This is for the best." When his eyes shift to mine they're full of pain and regret, but they're determined. "This is the way it has to be."

"Nate, tell me you don't actually think that Duncan is right for me."

"No… but I do know that I'm not right for you."

I don't say another word as I slip out of the car, because there's nothing left to say. Somehow I manage to make it through the front door of the house before the first tear escapes down my cheek. As I lean back against the wall and let my body crumble to the floor, the rest of them follow.

Nate

I don't think I've ever hated myself as much as I do at this moment. I hate myself for telling her to work things out with that douchebag, Duncan. I hate myself for lying to her about drinking too much. I hate myself for putting that awful look on her face when she climbed out of my car.

I especially hate myself for wanting her as much as I do.

If I thought it was hard walking away from her after sharing a brief kiss with her, it's nothing compared to how it is now that I've felt her... tasted her... heard her. I'm not sure that anything will ever compare to that. The way she came apart in my arms, the way she touched me, and the breathless way she uttered my name. Fuck... nothing has ever felt as good as that. Nothing has ever felt so... right.

But it wasn't right.

I don't know what got into me tonight. It would be a lot easier to blame alcohol for my inability to control myself, but I barely had anything to drink tonight. The only thing I was intoxicated by is Amy. When she's close to me, I seem to forget about all of the reasons why I should be keeping my distance from her. Shit, if I hadn't been nearly blinded by Duncan's headlights pouring through my car window, I would probably be buried deep inside of her right now.

Letting out a groan, I adjust my pants for the third time. Thoughts like that do nothing for the hard-on I've been sporting ever since I caught a glimpse of her bare thighs in my car. I need to push those thoughts from my head. Immediately.

My mind shifts to Dex, and that instantly does the trick. When I first saw those headlights, I thought it was him, and I was certain that we were busted. The whole scenario played out in my head over a few seconds. Dex would come barreling over to my car and start banging on the windows, screaming when he saw me lying on top of his half-naked sister, who had her hand wrapped around my dick. Then he would pull me out of the car, beat the living shit out of me, and tell me he never wants to see me again.

I can't let that happen.

The fear that passed through me at that moment was enough to halt me in my tracks and bring me back to my senses. It was like a warning bell; a silent alarm going off in my head to remind me of what I was risking and what I had to lose.

Because as much as I hate turning my back on Amy like I did, it would be even worse to lose my best friend. Dex and Teddy are far too important to me to risk destroying our friendship. And I know, without a doubt, that this would.

■   ■   ■

When I graduated from high school and decided to get my own place, I didn't move far. Only about fifty feet, actually. I suppose I do still *technically* live with my parents, since I moved into their garage apartment, but for the most part, it's my own place. Either way, I happen to enjoy living here. The rent is cheap, it's close to the shop, and I get to enjoy my mother's cooking whenever I want.

Like for Sunday breakfasts.

Throughout my entire childhood, my mom always prepared a huge breakfast on Sunday mornings. She always said that we needed a good meal to fuel ourselves up for the week, so she went all out. I'm talking the works: pancakes, eggs, sausage, fruit… you name it. By the time sophomore year of high school rolled around, my mom's Sunday breakfasts were legendary. My friends regularly showed up to eat with us, and it became somewhat of a weekly ritual. *"The more the merrier,"* my mom would say, happy to feed anyone who walked through the door.

So it's no surprise that, when I walk into my parents' house the next morning, I find Teddy flipping pancakes in the kitchen with my mom.

"Morning, honey!" my mom calls out over her shoulder. "Look who I found salivating outside the kitchen door this morning."

"You mean Teddy actually showed up for a free breakfast?" I say sarcastically. "That's shocking!"

Teddy grins. "I was just following the smell of bacon."

"You know you're always welcome here." My mom wraps an arm over Teddy's shoulder, giving it a squeeze. "I've missed all of my boys! With you and Dex gone, I hardly have anyone to feed anymore."

I pour myself a cup of coffee and give my mom a kiss on the cheek. "Don't worry, Mom. You still get to feed me."

"Thank goodness for that!" She pulls an egg carton out of the refrigerator and shoos us out of the kitchen. "You boys go on into the living room and relax. I'll call you in when breakfast is on the table."

I'm spoiled, I know. My mother is far too good to me. It's no wonder I stick around.

"I'm glad you decided to come by," I tell Teddy as I slump down onto the couch. "Where's Dex?"

"He had a big family breakfast at his grandparents' house," he says. "But he mentioned that he was going to stop by after."

"I'm surprised you both aren't sleeping in after leaving the bonfire with those girls. What happened? Don't tell me you guys struck out."

Teddy groans. "Don't remind me."

"That bad?" I ask.

"Nah, we were actually having a good time. This girl I met was really cool, and we were about five seconds away from climbing into her parents' hot tub, when Dex chimes in about how we need to get home and get some rest so we can squeeze in a morning workout."

"No way, did he really?"

Teddy nods. "Yup, and ten minutes later I was in his car driving home when I should have been in a hot tub driving my... well, you get the picture."

I shake my head, laughing. "That's pretty rough, dude. Though I must commend Dex on his dedication. That's devotion right there."

"I'll say," Teddy chuckles. "It's not even like I paired him up with the ugly friend or some shit like that. These girls were fuckin' smokin'!"

Both Dex and Teddy have been fully committed to the Marines since high school, and while they both take it very seriously, Dex's dedication is on a whole other level. I'm not sure that I've ever seen anyone with the kind of drive that he has. He's never let anything—girls included—get in the way of what he wants to accomplish. There's no doubt in my mind that he's going to do some amazing things.

"Even though I had to endure a wicked case of blue balls, I can't be mad at him," Teddy continues. "There's no one else I'd rather have watching my back or leading me into battle. That's a hell of a lot more important than one frisky night in a hot tub."

"Damn straight," I agree.

"How'd your night turn out?" Teddy leans back in the couch, narrowing his eyes at me curiously. "It was awfully nice of you to make sure Amy got home okay."

I don't miss the underlying suspicion in his tone, so I try and brush it off. "Yeah, well somebody had to, since her jackass of a boyfriend ran off and left her there."

"Didn't seem like she was too upset about it. In fact, some might even say that she was relieved when he left. Just saying."

"What are you getting at, Ted?" I say, eyeing him carefully.

He sighs. "Look, I saw the way that you and Amy were cozying up to each other last night, and I've seen the way she's always looked at you. It's obvious there's something going on there. I just want to make sure you know what you're doing."

I begin to search my brain for some kind of excuse, but I know that I can't lie to Teddy. "There's nothing going on with Amy and me. I mean, there was, kind of, but I put a stop to it. I'm not going there with her, I swear. Dex is my best friend and I won't let anything jeopardize that."

No matter how much I want her.

"You're a good guy, Nate. And you know Dex loves you like a brother, but Amy is his twin sister. He's been protecting her for as long as I can remember, and if things didn't work out between you two, or you did something to hurt her, it wouldn't matter how good of friends you are. I just don't want to see that happen."

Guilt rushes through me and I nod. "I know, and I promise I won't let that happen."

"Good, because we need you buddy." He grins briefly, and then his face turns serious. "Being away all the time… it's not easy, and it's only going to be harder once we ship out overseas for our first tour. It really means a lot to us to know that we have you here to keep an eye on things for us, and watch out for our families. Having someone here who we can trust and rely on makes it a whole lot easier to be away."

My throat tightens, not only because of what his words mean to me, but because I also understand the bigger meaning behind those words. Uncertainty looms in front of them with each step, reminding them that there's no guarantee for a future. I realize in this moment that the most important thing for me to do is to be there for them. Any way that I can.

"You know that you can depend on me," I choke out. "Anything you need, I'll be here for you. No matter what."

My mom yells in from the kitchen that breakfast is on the table, so we rise from the couches and awkwardly pat each other on the back.

Teddy looks at me with a wide grin. "Now that all the serious shit is out of way, let's eat some damn breakfast!"

chapter six

Amy

When I arrive back on campus after the weekend, life returns to normal. Well, almost normal.

Things with Duncan and me are still up in the air. When he came back to my parents' house on the night of the bonfire, he saw my tears and assumed they were for him. He was full of apologies and determined to work things out, but I told him I needed space to decide what I want. I don't know why I didn't simply end it right then and there, because no amount of time or space will change my mind about him.

Now I've spent the entire week avoiding him around campus; ignoring his calls and texts, pleading with me to talk to him so we can resolve things. I know that I should just deal with him and tell him it's over, but I don't have the energy or the strength to do it. My whole body feels drained. I barely leave my dorm room except to go to class, and even then, my mind is elsewhere. The rest of the time I stay curled up beneath my covers, wondering how everything in my life got so messed up over the course of one weekend.

It isn't until I wake up feeling nauseous and have to run into the bathroom to empty the contents of my stomach that I start to wonder if I might actually be sick. I've been sad and miserable ever since Nate ran off on me and crushed my heart into a million pieces—again—so I assumed that was the cause of it. After spending an hour curled over the toilet in the bathroom, I'm fairly certain that the flu is to blame. For most of my symptoms, anyway. I don't think a virus is responsible for how much my heart hurts.

Every time I think I'm feeling better and am finally out of the woods, I find myself rushing into the bathroom yet again without warning. By day four, I decide it's time to make a trip to Health Services on campus to see if they can give me some medicine or antibiotics to speed up my recovery.

The doctor jots down a few notes on her clipboard while I sit down on the examination table and describe my symptoms. She nods along until I'm finished, and then asks me questions.

"So, would you say that the nausea is persistent or intermittent?"

I bite my lip nervously. "It seems to come and go. One minute I feel fine, and the next I'm curled over the toilet."

She furrows her brow as she makes another note on her chart. "Are you sexually active? And if so, when was the date of your last menstrual cycle?"

Blushing furiously, I reply, "Um… well, I was, but I'm not anymore. And I guess my last period was…" I do some math in my head, trying to come up with the dates, but I can't remember. "I'm not sure, exactly. I've never been very good at keeping track of it."

The doctor looks at me with concern, and I get a terrible feeling in the pit of my stomach. "I'm going to have you take a pregnancy test, just in case, and then we'll go from there." She offers me a reassuring smile, but it does nothing to calm my nerves.

Fifteen minutes later, my worst fears are confirmed when I hear the words that I never could have prepared myself for.

"Well, Miss Porter, it looks like you're pregnant."

■　　■　　■

Duncan stares at me with wide eyes, his face frozen in shock as he tries to absorb what I just told him. I understand exactly how he feels, because I felt the same way when I found out, so I remain quiet and give the information a chance to sink in.

"You're kidding me, right?" His voice is full of disbelief, and his eyes are wide. "This must be some kind of sick joke."

Boy, do I wish this was nothing more than a joke.

The week following my doctor's appointment had gone by in a blur. I barely spoke to anyone, and the only time I even bothered to leave my dorm room was when I had a class. I didn't tell anyone about my situation. Just thinking about it is enough to make me burst into tears, or throw up. Or both.

I did everything in my power *not* to think about it. The semester is almost over, and then we have a month off for winter break. I figured that if I could just get through the final week of classes and exams, then I could go home and start to work everything out.

I tried to focus on my lectures and keep myself busy with studying, but nothing helped. It occupied a permanent spot in my brain, and nothing could keep me from thinking about it. My thoughts were consumed by a never-ending loop of questions: How it happened... what Duncan would say... how my parents would react... if I could even go through with all of this.

After a while, I couldn't take it anymore. I decided that I needed to get some answers, and telling Duncan was the first step.

I offer him a sympathetic look and shake my head slowly. "It's not a joke, Duncan. I went to the doctor last week because I thought I'd come down with the flu. She had me take a pregnancy test, and it was positive." My words sound calm and rehearsed, thanks to all the time I spent practicing what I was going to say, but on the inside, I'm barely holding it together. As it turns out, there's really no good way to inform someone that his life is about to drastically change.

"Are you sure it's even mine?" he asks, his mouth set in a cruel twist as he narrows his eyes on me. "I mean, I have no idea what the hell you've been up to. You've barely even spoken to me in two weeks."

"Of course I'm sure," I snap back. "I've never been with anyone else." His question isn't unreasonable, but it still infuriates me that he would ask. Up until our trip to my parents' house, I'd been the perfect girlfriend to him. It wasn't until he showed me his true colors and ran off on me that my feelings changed. Not that any of it matters anymore.

"How the hell did this even happen?"

"I don't know." I sigh, shrugging my shoulders. "I thought we were careful. You always wore protection, right?"

"Most of the time, yeah." He leans back, crossing his arms defensively. "I might have forgotten once or twice when we were drunk, but I figured it wasn't a big deal since you're on the pill."

"I'm not on the pill!" I hiss, trying to keep my voice down so that no one passing by can hear our conversation. "Why would you assume that I was?"

"I don't know! Because that's the normal thing for college girls to do when they're dating someone? I mean, we've been together for months now, and you're a smart girl. I would've thought you'd take some initiative."

My whole body sizzles with irritation, but I close my eyes and take a deep breath to calm myself down. Duncan might be an idiot, but getting angry about it now won't change anything. What's done is done.

He drags his hands through his hair, letting out a sharp breath. "Okay, well, it's not the end of the world. I have some of my own money saved up, so we can take care of it without my parents ever finding out, and with winter break coming up…"

"Wait a second." I hold up a hand to stop him, and my heart thumps anxiously in my chest. "What exactly do you mean, *take care of it?*"

"Uh, what do you think I mean?" he replies with a blank stare. "I'm not ready to have a fucking kid! My parents would kill me, and my life would be ruined. I didn't work this hard to get to where I am only to throw it all away. Don't tell me you're actually thinking about keeping it?"

Up until this very moment I hadn't made any kind of decision regarding my options. At least, I didn't think I had. The overwhelming sense of panic and anger that washes over me when I hear Duncan suggest getting rid of it makes me realize that I have my answer.

Maybe it's natural instinct, or simply a hormonal response, but in this moment I know that I will do whatever I have to do in order to protect this baby. *My baby.* I don't know how big it is, or whether it's a boy or a girl, or how the hell I'm going to handle all of this. There's about a million things that I *don't* know, but the one thing I do know is that I'm going to do this.

"What if I am?" My voice trembles, and I swallow nervously while I wait for a response.

He stares back at me in disbelief, pursing his lips together as he shakes his head slowly. I know what he's going to say before he says it.

"Look Amy, you're a great girl, and we had a good thing going. I want to be there for you, really I do…" He trails off, fixating on the ground beneath him before raising his stony gaze to meet mine. "But if you're determined to throw your life away, then you're going to have to do it on your own. I obviously can't force you to do something that you don't want to do, but I won't be any part of it. I just… I can't do this. I'm sorry, Amy."

I feel the tears pooling in my eyes, but I refuse to let him see me cry. Choking them back, I nod once and simply say, "I understand."

Duncan rises from the bench and stands over me, shifting his feet uncomfortably. "I really hope you know what you're doing. I'd hate to see you ruin your life because of a stupid mistake."

As he slowly walks away, a sob breaks free from my body, and tears begin to roll down my cheeks. The reality of my situation hits me like freight train moving at a hundred miles an hour, leaving me beaten, wrecked and ruined.

I may have made the decision to go through with this, but I'm still not ready for it to be real. I'm not ready for *this* to be my life.

My thumb hovers over the "SEND" button on yet another text to Amy. It's been almost three weeks since she went back to school, and despite the numerous text messages I've sent,

I haven't heard a thing from her.

My first few messages were basic apologies: "I'm sorry", "Please forgive me", "I never meant to hurt you." But the more time that's passed, the more desperate my messages have become, until they're basically begging her to speak to me.

I'm not sure why I'm so determined to talk to her. In the beginning it was simply about trying to earn her forgiveness, but somewhere along the way, I've become totally consumed with the need to make things right. I feel awful about what happened, and I hate myself for hurting her, but it's more than that. Everything feels... unsettled. The smart thing would be to let it go and accept it for what it is, since she clearly doesn't want anything to do with me. I can't do that, though. I have to know that she's okay. Otherwise, all I'll be able to think about is the way her eyes filled up with unshed tears and the crushed look on her face before she climbed out of my car.

My thoughts are interrupted when one of our regular customers arrives at the auto shop to pick up the 1966 Chevelle we've been working on for the past couple of months. I quickly send the message to Amy before stuffing my phone in my pocket and stepping out of the office to meet him.

"Hey, Mr. Connelly." I walk over and shake his outstretched hand. "You ready to see what we've done with her?"

"You bet I am," he responds with an eager smile as he follows me over to the car.

We've done a lot of work for him in the past, and he's one of my favorite customers. Not only does he bring in amazing cars for us to work on, but he's also a really nice guy. He used to be some kind of big-deal stockbroker type who made tons of money doing stuff that I don't understand. Now he's retired and spends most of his time hunting down classic cars to restore and add to his already-impressive collection. It's always exciting to get a phone call from him, because it means he has an awesome new car for us to work on.

I lean into the driver's seat and pull the lever to pop the hood. When I lift it up to reveal the engine we rebuilt, he lets out a low whistle.

"Damn, that looks good!" He bends forward to take a closer look. "Where'd you end up finding the SS 396 engine block?"

"I know a guy who runs a couple of salvage yards upstate, and he always hooks me up with the rare parts I need. If he doesn't have them, then he can usually find them for me. He had actually just gotten this beauty in a couple of days before I called, so it worked out perfectly. Six cylinders, three-hundred and fifty horsepower, immaculate condition... doesn't get much better than this."

We spend another half-hour looking over every inch of the car. I show him all the new parts that went in and describe all the work that was done while he admires the finished product, listening with rapt attention.

"You did one hell of a job on this," he remarks. "I've met a lot of so-called experts who have been doing this for a lot longer than you, but none of them could have pulled this off as well as you did."

"Thank you, sir. It's not every day I get to work on a car as amazing as this. I'm already looking forward to the next one you bring in for us."

"It might be a little while," he chuckles. "But I've met a lot of serious collectors out there who offer full-time gigs doing restorations, and they would pay top dollar to get someone like you on their payroll. They're people who would send you all over the country to find rare cars and parts for big-time rebuilds. If that's something you might be interested in, I could put you in touch with some of my contacts."

The idea of working on those types of cars—the ones that are so rare and valuable that most people only ever get to see them on the pages of a magazine—sends a surge of excitement through me. This is the kind of opportunity that car fanatics like me can only dream about. However, as thrilling as it might be, it isn't something that could fit into my life. I've had my future mapped out since I was twelve. Not only do I enjoy working in the shop with my dad, but he needs me. I can't just run off and leave him to handle everything on his own. I made a commitment, and I intend to stick to it.

"I appreciate the offer," I tell him, rubbing the back of my neck. "But as tempting as it is, I can't take you up on it. I've got a good thing going here with my old man, you know?"

He nods. "I totally understand. Family comes first, I get it. If you ever change your mind though, don't hesitate to call. I wasn't exaggerating when I said that you're better than a lot of the other hacks I've come across. You could do real well for yourself out there."

"I'll certainly keep that in mind."

"Good." He climbs into the car, his eyes full of excitement as he motions to the open seat next to him. "Now, let's get this thing out on the open road so we can really see what she's got."

■　■　■

I'm driving back from the auto supply store when I get stuck in traffic and notice a familiar figure walking out of the small corner deli up ahead. At first I think that I'm seeing things—since lately I've been imagining her everywhere—but when my car inches forward and I get closer, I'm certain that it's Amy.

I watch as she moves across the parking lot, carrying a brown deli bag at her side as her body sways with natural grace. My heart automatically lifts at the sight of her, but that feeling is soon eclipsed with anger. For weeks I've been trying to get in touch with her, only to be continuously snubbed. I didn't want to believe that it was intentional. I've managed to convince myself that she was probably busy with exams and school stuff, and that she would reach out to me when her schedule cleared up.

But here she is. Back in town for her winter break, grabbing lunch at the deli and continuing to act as if I don't exist. Meanwhile, I've been agonizing over what happened between us, beating myself up for letting things get out of hand that night. I can't blame her for being angry, and maybe I deserve this, but she could have at least given me some kind of acknowledgement after the dozens of apologies I made. Even a "Go to hell" or "Leave me alone" would've been better than no response at all.

The traffic remains at a standstill, so I pull out my cell phone and scroll through the list of contacts until I find her name. As I tap the call button, I stare through the window and raise the phone to my ear.

It rings three times, and I can pinpoint the exact moment she hears it because she halts mid-stride and begins digging through her purse. My heart thunders in my chest as I watch her retrieve the phone and examine the screen. Her mouth curves into a frown as she looks at it. I can see her thumb hovering over the button, wavering between whether or not to answer the call.

I'm holding my breath, silently begging her to answer and prove me wrong. After what feels like an eternity, her shoulders slump, and she shoves the phone back into her bag.

The voicemail greeting that I've become all too familiar with plays in my ear. I toss my phone into the passenger seat and grip the steering wheel until my knuckles turn white. As soon as the cars ahead of me start to move, I stomp on the gas pedal and surge forward.

I'm sick of these stupid games. I never would have thought that Amy was the type to pull this kind of shit. Unlike most girls her age, she's always been upfront and direct, and frankly, it pisses me off that she's turning out to be just like them. If she wants to hate me, that's fine, but I won't let her hide from me anymore. I'm going to make damn sure that she hears me out.

chapter seven

Amy

Being at home feels entirely different than it used to. Everything about it is so... definite. All the freedom and excitement that used to exist during any time off from school is painfully absent, replaced by a crippling burden of fear and uncertainty. When the month of winter break is up, I won't be returning to school and gearing up for the new semester. Instead, I'll be staying here. Living under my parents' roof as I gear up for motherhood.

I'd foolishly thought that I would be able to return for the spring semester to finish out my sophomore year, but after the fallout with Duncan, the idea of being on campus has lost its appeal. Before leaving, I spoke to my student adviser and came up with a plan to complete the required courses for my remaining credits online. Since I took such a heavy course load last year, I won't even fall that far behind. At least, not for this year. I haven't even thought about what I'll do when the baby comes.

It's all become real. Especially since I told my parents.

I hadn't planned on telling them right away. After worrying for weeks about what I would say to them, I'd decided that the best thing to do was to put it off for a while. Of course, I was barely three steps inside the house when I saw my mom and completely broke down, collapsing into her arms and spilling my guts.

There was a lot of hugging. Even more tears. My mom held me tight and told me that everything would be okay. That she and my dad would take care of the baby and me, no matter what. She assured me that they would support whatever decision I made and would be there for me through it all. Then she sat next to me on the couch, squeezing my hand tight while we told my dad and went through it all over again.

There was no anger. No sharp looks of disappointment or judgment. Only comfort. We huddled together on the couch, and they let me cry. I cried for the future I was letting go of. I cried for the baby who would grow up without a father. I cried for everything I was giving up.

It was emotional and exhausting. But at least the hard part's over, right?

Wrong.

As nervous as I was to confess my pregnancy to my parents, I'm far more terrified to tell Dex. I knew that my parents would be supportive, because that's the kind of people they are. They're kind, wonderful, caring and accepting, and they would do anything for their children.

Dex would also do anything for me. He's been looking out for me for our entire lives, doing everything possible to shield me from harm. Sure, he's overprotective and controlling, but it comes from a place of love. He wants the best for me.

Which is why it breaks my heart to know that I let him down.

I'm settled on the couch watching a marathon on Bravo when I hear the doorbell ring. Both my parents are still at work, and I haven't told anyone else that I'm home. I shouldn't even be here yet. Most other students are still on campus, finishing their final exams, but I took mine early so I could get out of there as soon as possible.

The knocking persists, and I consider ignoring it. The last thing I want to do is see anyone. But when the bell sounds again, I reluctantly lift myself off the sofa and make my way to the door.

Before answering it, I take a peek through the curtains. When I see who's standing on the front step I automatically jolt back, flattening myself against the hard wooden door. My chest rapidly rises and falls as I squeeze my eyes closed, holding my breath in a desperate attempt to silence my thundering heartbeat.

"I know you're in there, Amy," Nate shouts from the other side of the door. "I saw you pull back the curtain, and I can hear you shuffling around. Would you please just let me in?"

I gradually turn around, smoothing my hair and adjusting my rumpled clothes. Two hours of lounging in front of the television has me looking even more disheveled than usual. I remind myself that there's no point in trying to impress Nate anymore. Any hope that may have lingered after our last interaction had completely disintegrated with the words, "You're pregnant."

My hand twists around the doorknob, and I slowly pull it toward me, only opening it wide enough to peer around the edge.

"What are you doing here?"

He narrows his eyes at me, pressing his lips together in a hard line. "You've been ignoring me for weeks. I got sick of waiting for you to finally give me the time of day."

I stare down at my feet, fidgeting with the hem of my shirt to avoid his penetrating gaze. I hate that I'm acting like such a coward. I hear him sigh heavily, and when I glance up, he's dragging his fingers through his dark hair.

"Why are you hiding from me, Amy?" His expression is softer now, but tension lingers throughout his whole body. "I know that I messed up, okay? Whenever you're around I seem to forget all the reasons why I can't be with you. I let my attraction for you get the best of me, and I wasn't thinking straight."

My throat tightens painfully, my chest heavy. I desperately want to stop him from saying anything more, but my voice won't work.

He takes a hesitant step toward me, his eyes pleading as they stare down into mine. "I'm so sorry. You have to know that I would never intentionally hurt you. God, if things were different, I…"

"Nate, stop," I choke out, knowing that my heart can't bear to hear him finish that sentence. "Nothing can ever happen between us. I understand that now."

I can see it on his face that my sudden acceptance comes as a surprise to him. He probably expected me to put up a fight or disagree with him, because in the past, I almost certainly would have. There's no point in arguing now, though.

He frowns. "Right, uh… yeah. For now, anyway. Who knows, maybe someday Dex will be okay with it."

I shake my head. "It won't matter, Nate. We need to just let it go and move on." The words taste bitter and deceitful as they pour from my mouth, but I force them out. The hurt that appears in his eyes as he absorbs them is enough to break me, and I have to fight back the tears that are threatening to spill down my cheeks.

"Amy…" He slowly lifts his hand to my face, brushing his thumb across my jaw with a caress so light and delicate, I almost don't feel it.

The first tear breaks free, tumbling down my cheek. It's followed shortly after by another, and whatever was holding me together inside suddenly shatters.

"I'm pregnant."

Nate

Her words hit me like a knife to the gut.

I stare at her, blinking rapidly as I wait for her to tell me that she's joking, or that I misheard her. With each second that passes, the knife twists more painfully.

"How… are you sure?" It's all I can manage to say as I attempt to sift through the jumbled mess inside my head. My thoughts have been all over the place since the second I arrived on her doorstep. I came here with the intention of apologizing and making her understand why nothing can happen between us, but as usual, my heart betrayed me the second I laid eyes on her. I knew almost immediately that something was different. The subtle flicker of hope that I normally saw in her was gone, and instead of reiterating that we couldn't be together, I found myself basically trying to convince her not to give up.

It was in that moment that I realized how much I've come to rely on seeing that flicker of hope. I need it. Even though I've never allowed myself to feel any hope for us, I've always been able to hold on to hers.

Now, there's nothing left to hold on to.

Amy nods, causing more tears to fall from her sad hazel eyes. "I went to the doctor after my last trip home. I guess it must have happened a few weeks before that, when I was still with Duncan."

"You're not together anymore?" I ask, unable to stop myself. I know it's the wrong thing to be focusing on, but I can't help it. I can't think straight.

"No." She bites down on her bottom lip to stop it from quivering, staring at the ground to hide her face. "He doesn't want anything to do with this, or me. He told me…" A sob finally tears loose from her chest, and her voice becomes a strangled whisper. "He told me to get rid of it."

I have to fight to keep my feet rooted in place. Every cell in my body wants to rush out of here and hunt that worthless fucker down. I want to make him pay for all the fear and sadness that he put in her beautiful eyes. I want him to suffer for what he did to her. My arms are rigid at my sides, every muscle twitching with the impulse to take action.

Drawing in a slow and steady breath, I force back the anger that's thumping through my veins in an erratic rhythm. I push my own feelings aside and shift my attention to what's really important: Amy.

When the hazy fog of anger finally lifts, I notice that Amy has stepped out of the doorway and is sitting on the entryway floor with her back to the wall. Her knees are drawn up against her chest and she hugs them tightly, using them to muffle the sound of her soft cries.

My heart clenches, and I move inside, closing the door behind me. Sliding to the ground next to her, I wrap my arm around her and pull her close.

"It's going be okay," I murmur, pressing a soft kiss to her temple. "I promise, it will be all be okay."

We sit like that for a while, until her tears subside and I feel her body begin to relax into mine. She lifts her head, peering up at me with red, puffy eyes and tear-streaked cheeks. "I don't know how

I'm going to do this on my own."

I sweep back a piece of hair that clings to her wet face, tucking it behind her ear as I draw her closer with a reassuring squeeze. "You're not doing this on your own, Amy. You have a whole army of people behind you in this. Me, Dex, your parents. We're all here for you."

Her eyes fill with new unshed tears. "I haven't told Dex yet. He's going to hate me, Nate."

"You're kidding, right?" I glance down at her with raised eyebrows. "Your brother loves you more than anything. He could never hate you, babe. Not in million years."

"But… I've let him down. He's going to be so disappointed in me."

"Hey." I tilt her chin toward me, forcing her eyes to meet mine. "You haven't let anyone down, you got that? You're brave and you're strong, and Dex will be proud of you. All he's ever wanted to do is protect you, and nothing will ever change that. I promise." She offers me a weak nod, and my lips curl up in a half-smile. "However, I can't promise you that he won't hunt down that fucker Duncan and cause him serious bodily harm. He'll probably be sterile when Dex is finished with him."

"Oh, no…" Amy says with a groan. "I hadn't even thought about that part. What am I going to do?"

"That's easy. You let it happen," I tell her. "Maybe even tag along so you can get the whole thing on video and watch it over and over again. Or better yet, get a few punches in yourself."

"Nate!" she exclaims, her eyes wide with shock. "I can't just sit back and let that happen!"

"Why not?" I say, my voice dripping with contempt. "He deserves it. Dex knows how to control himself, so he won't let it go too far. Can you honestly say that it wouldn't make you the least bit happy if your brother taught that scumbag a lesson?"

A faint smile touches her lips, and for the first time since I arrived at her doorstep, I see a glimmer of life in her eyes. "Maybe just a little bit."

■　■　■

The whole time I'm with Amy I manage to hold myself together and suppress my violent feelings, but as soon as we say our goodbyes and she closes the door, they're right back at the surface. My hands are wrapped around the steering wheel in a death grip as I make the short drive home, speeding through the otherwise quiet streets until I pull into the driveway. Without even bothering to cut the engine, I throw open the door and run into my parents' house.

Going straight to the kitchen pantry, I begin sifting through the items on the shelves until I find what I'm looking for. I grab it off the shelf, spinning around to find my mother standing in the kitchen, watching me with a puzzled expression on her face.

"What's got you in such a hurry?" She glances down, noticing the box in my hand, and raises her eyebrows. "Is there a reason you're stealing my white rice? Because we both know you aren't planning on cookin' it."

"I, uhh…" I search my brain for an acceptable explanation and come up empty. "I just needed it for a little spur of the moment project I'm working on. No big deal."

"Do I even want to know?" she asks.

"Probably not." Leaning forward, I plant a kiss on her cheek as I move past her to leave. "I won't be home for dinner, but thanks for the rice. Love you, Mama."

"Be safe!" she calls out as the door swings closed behind me.

As soon as I'm settled back into the driver's seat, I stomp on the gas and drive toward the highway. I've never been to the USC campus, but I know the area well enough to get myself there without any complications. The real question is, what the hell I'm going to do when I actually get there. This isn't exactly something I was planning to do when I woke up this morning.

But I can't sit back and do nothing.

It's early in the evening by the time I get there. The campus is huge, even bigger than I expected it to be. The likelihood of finding one person among nearly thirty thousand is damn near impossible, but I refuse to give up. I have to at least *try*.

I drive around aimlessly for nearly an hour, my frustration rapidly mounting, when I see a sign for the Williams-Brice Stadium. Remembering that Duncan mentioned playing football, I make a sharp turn and follow the signs until I reach a huge parking lot with the stadium looming above. It looks deserted, but I can make out the glow of the stadium lights and the sharp sound of a whistle piercing through the twilight.

For the first time all day I feel a hint of a smile. Thank God for football practice.

As I come around the back of the stadium, I find a smaller parking lot reserved for players and staff. It doesn't take long for me to identify Duncan's black BMW among them. I pull into an empty parking spot a few rows down, taking a quick scan of the area to make sure there's nobody else around.

When I'm sure that the coast is clear, I grab the box of rice from the passenger seat and a piece of aluminum wire from the glove box before casually walking over to the front of his beamer. I twist the wire into a loop and stick it through the thin space underneath the hood, carefully hooking it on to the latch. With a slight tug the hood pops open, revealing the impeccably clean engine below.

I take another look around before reaching forward to unscrew the cap on the radiator. As I flip open the box of rice and hold it over the opening, I hesitate for a split-second. I hate the idea of destroying a car like this, and I know for a fact that as soon as I pour the rice in, it's as good as ruined. However, all my doubts vanish instantly when I remember the expression on Amy's face, and the absolute devastation in her eyes. With that image in my head, I tilt the box forward, spilling its contents into the radiator until not a single grain is left.

As I drive away I can feel the tension in my body beginning to ease. I know that what I did isn't significant, and it certainly doesn't solve anything, but doing nothing would've eaten me alive. I need Duncan to experience some form of suffering.

I know without a doubt that when Amy finally does tell Dex, he will punish Duncan in his own way—most likely by beating the shit out of him. Frankly, I was tempted to do that myself, but I couldn't take that away from Dex. He's going to need it when he finds out. The same way that I needed to destroy the car. It's the urge to do something—*anything*—to regain a semblance of control when faced with a situation that makes you feel utterly powerless.

chapter eight

Amy

"Are you okay?" Savannah asks, her eyes full of concern. "You look worried. I thought you'd be more excited about this."

I shift uncomfortably on the exam room table, keeping an eye on the door as we wait for my doctor to return with the ultrasound equipment.

"I am excited," I respond. "Just a little nervous, that's all. What if she finds out there's something wrong?" I fiddle with the hem of my shirt, resting my hands on the slight swell of my belly. "I drank a couple of times before I found out I was pregnant. What if my baby has fetal alcohol syndrome or some other awful thing because I was stupid?"

Savannah rolls her eyes. "I've seen you drink, Amy. There's no way that you could have drunk enough to do any damage." She reaches for my hand, giving it a reassuring squeeze. "I'm sure that everything is going to be just fine."

"Thanks for coming with me today. My mom offered to bring me, but I didn't want her to have to take yet another day off work because of me." I smile appreciatively. "I'm sure there are a lot of other things you'd rather be doing on your spring break than hanging out with your pregnant friend, but I'm really glad you're here."

"Girl, don't be ridiculous," she says, waving her hand dismissively. "There's nowhere else I'd rather be right now."

Having Savannah around makes life seem almost normal again. We've spent nearly every day together since she got into town, and it's been the only fun I've had in nearly three months. I'm dreading the end of the week when she returns to school, and I go back to moping around the house alone.

The door to the exam room is pushed open as Dr. Snyder returns with the ultrasound machine. She rolls it into position alongside the exam table, and after a few minutes of tinkering with the cords and buttons, she turns to me with a practiced smile. "Are you ready to take a look at your baby?"

I nod, sucking in a nervous breath as she carefully lifts up my shirt and tucks it underneath the elastic of my bra to keep it in place.

"This might be a little cold," she warns before squeezing a small amount of clear gel onto my skin. I watch nervously as she brings the small wand to my abdomen, moving it around against me as she studies a small screen.

For a while all I hear is the *click, click* sound of the keyboard as she captures the images she needs. It feels like an eternity before she finally looks at me and says, "Everything looks good here, Amy."

I breathe a small sigh of relief, and Savannah's fingers briefly tighten around mine.

"We'll know more once we get your blood work back," Dr. Snyder continues. "But from what I can see, you're right on track for sixteen weeks."

She shifts the ultrasound machine toward me so I can get a better look at the screen, and when she begins pointing out little fingers and toes, I nearly stop breathing altogether. With my eyes glued to the image on the screen, everything else fades into the background. Dr. Snyder is talking about measurements and fetal bones, but I'm not listening to a word she's saying. All I can do is stare at the tiny blur in front of me, my eyes filling with tears that I don't bother to wipe away.

"Are you interested in finding out your baby's gender?"

■　　■　　■

Turning the small envelope over in my hand, I run my thumb along the seal and tempt myself to open it.

When Dr. Snyder asked me about the baby's gender, I was hesitant to find out. Instead of telling me, she offered to write it down and seal it in an envelope for me to open when I was ready.

I managed to make it all the way home and up into my bedroom without tearing it open.

The only thing stopping me is the fact that I don't want to be alone when I find out, and there's only one person I want to have with me when I do. Unfortunately that person is halfway up the coast in the middle of training, with very few opportunities to make personal phone calls. I normally wait for him to call me, but I can't wait any longer.

Sitting down at my desk, I power up my laptop and open the application for Skype. There's only one phone number saved, because Dex is the only person I call on here, so I click on his picture and wait for the call to go through.

It rings four times, and I'm about to hang up when my

brother's face appears on the screen.

"What up, Ames?" he says with a goofy grin. "How's that baby you're cookin'?"

I'd confessed everything to Dex on the same day that I told Nate. As terrified as I was to tell him, it didn't seem right for Nate to know when my own brother didn't. Plus, Nate's pep talk made me feel a lot better about the whole thing. Of course, he'd been right, too. Dex was angry at first—which I'd expected—but the second I broke into tears, he was comforting me and assuring me that everything would be okay. Since then, he's become surprisingly excited about the idea of having a niece or nephew. He's constantly calling to check in and make sure I'm doing okay, and we've even spent some time discussing baby names. Now that I have him behind me, everything just feels... better.

"That's actually why I called," I tell him.

A concerned look crosses his face. "Is everything okay? Did something happen?"

I can't help but smile at his protectiveness as I shake my head. "No, everything's fine. I just got back from the doctor, and she said we're right on track." I reach for the card, holding it up in front of the screen. "She also learned whether it's a boy or a girl, but I wouldn't let her tell me. I wanted you to be with me when I found out."

His face softens in the way that it only ever does for me, and his eyes light up. "So it's right there in that envelope?"

"Yup."

"Well, what are you waiting for? Open it up and tell me if I'm going to have a niece or a nephew!"

"I'm nervous!" I exclaim in response. "Can you read it for me?"

Dex chuckles. "I'd love to, sis, but I'm kind of in another state right now."

"I know that, doofus." I roll my eyes. "I'll hold up the card to the screen, and you can read it and then tell me. Okay?"

"Okay," he grins.

I rip open the envelope, closing my eyes as I position it in front of the camera so Dex can see it. "Got it?" I ask in a shaky tone.

"Got it," he says.

I wait for him to tell me, frozen in place with my eyes squeezed shut. When he doesn't say anything, I lower the card and open my eyes, glaring at his smirking expression on the screen. "Well, are you going to tell me? Spit it out!"

His grin widens. "Looks like we're going with 'Sadie' for a name after all."

I stare at him, openmouthed, as my eyes well up with tears. "Sadie?" I repeat in a choked whisper. "It's a girl?"

Dex nods. "It's a girl. Congrats, Mama."

Over the next several months, I watch Amy's belly grow. It's the only indication I have of her progress anymore. After finding out she was pregnant, I made it a point to be there for her as best I could—calling her to check in, and stopping by her house with her favorite desserts—but even though she tried to hide it, I could tell that my calls and visits were hard on her. After a short time, she confessed that as much as she appreciated it, my presence was a constant reminder of what she was giving up, and the best thing I could do for her was to give her space. The last thing I ever wanted to do was upset her, or make things harder for her, so even though it killed me, I agreed.

Since then, I've stayed away. No matter how badly I'm itching to check in with her and make sure she's doing okay, I'm respecting her decision and keeping my distance.

A while back, she got a job at the bank across the street from the shop, and every day at noon I stand in front of the window and wait for her to appear outside for her lunch break. She walks from the bank to the deli next door, gets a sandwich, and sits alone at one of the picnic tables outside while she eats.

Every day it breaks my fucking heart, and I have to fight against myself to keep from going over there. The only thing stopping me is knowing that she doesn't want to see me.

So all I do is watch. Every day at noon.

By now my dad has figured out my routine. He used to give me a hard time about it, but lately all he does is squeeze my shoulder and shake his head as he walks by.

I'm not sure what I'm trying to accomplish by doing this. It's my own personal form of torture, and yet I keep coming back for more like some kind of masochist.

According to Dex, she's doing really well. He doesn't talk too much about it, but I try to get as much information out of him as possible without seeming too interested. He did call me after she finally told him the news, and I did my best to act surprised about the whole thing. I'd never heard him sound as angry as he was that day on the phone. It didn't come as a shock to hear from Teddy that Dex had jumped in the car and driven all night to find Duncan in his hometown of Winnsboro.

I can only imagine what he did to him when he got there. Whatever it was, I'm sure it wasn't pretty, but that little shit deserved every second of it.

Shortly after that, Dex made me promise to keep an eye on Amy, since he wasn't around to do it himself. Naturally, I agreed. I didn't tell him that I was planning on doing that anyway.

I also found out from Dex that Amy is having a baby girl. God, I smiled so wide when he told me that. I know that her little girl will be just as sweet and wonderful as she is.

I'm flat on my back staring up at the engine of an old Ford truck, finishing a standard oil change, when my internal clock alerts me to the fact that it's almost noon. After so many months of the same routine, my body has become attuned to the time.

After screwing on the new filter, I climb out from underneath the truck and pull a few quarts of oil from the shelf. Once I've poured it in, replaced the oil cap and closed the hood, I grab a bottle of water and move to stand in the doorway where I have a clear view of the bank across the street.

It's an unusually hot day in June, and after a brief moment of standing in the sun, I already miss the cool cement floor of the garage. I take a long swig of water, keeping an eye on the front door of the bank so I won't miss seeing Amy when she leaves for her lunch break.

When there's no sign of her for nearly fifteen minutes I start to worry. I didn't see her yesterday, either. I hadn't thought anything of it at the time—everyone misses a day of work now and then—but now I'm concerned that something might be wrong. What if something happened to her?

I'm debating whether or not to call Dex and find out, when the sound of my ringtone breaks the silence and interrupts my thoughts. Seeing Teddy's name on the screen, I answer it immediately.

"Hey, Ted, what's goin' on?"

"Not much, man," he responds. "I haven't had a chance to talk to you for a while, so I figured I ought to check in and see how you're doin'."

"Can't complain, just work as usual. I was actually about to give Dex a call. I haven't seen Amy at work for the last few days, and I wanted to make sure everything is okay. You know anything about that?"

"You're worryin' about Ames, eh?" Teddy comments, his voice full of amusement.

I mentally curse myself for mentioning anything to him. He's way too perceptive about this shit, and I should've known he'd see right through me.

"Well, Dex asked me to keep an eye on her," I remark in a feeble attempt to suppress my obvious curiosity.

"Yeah, I bet you are." Teddy chuckles into the phone, making it clear that he isn't buying it. Fortunately, he leaves it alone, and instead says, "I overheard Dex on the phone with her a few days ago, and she mentioned that she was done with work. Something about needing to take it easy during the last month of her pregnancy, or whatever."

I let out a small sigh of relief when I hear that everything is okay. However, the tightness in my chest lingers. Has it really been almost nine months? I was able to see from the size of her belly that she was far along, but I guess I never really thought about what that meant. Soon she'll have a baby. She'll be a mom. The realization comes as a shock, and I'm silent for a long moment while I let it sink in.

"You're a good guy, Nate," Teddy says, all traces of humor gone from his voice. "Amy is really lucky to have someone like you looking out for her. As overprotective as Dex is, he knows that, too."

The line goes quiet as I let his words float around in my head, trying to grip their meaning. He can't possibly be suggesting that Dex would be okay with Amy and me... could he?

Dragging a hand through my short hair, I let out a frustrated breath. "I appreciate you sayin' that, Ted. You know I'd do anything for you guys." Unsure what else to say, I decide to switch to another topic of conversation. "How's Camp Lejeune?"

After completing nearly two years of extensive, specialized training for the Marines, Dex and Teddy were recently stationed at a military base in North Carolina.

"Well, that's actually the real reason I called you," Teddy says. "We're not going to be here much longer. We, uh, got our orders today. Our unit is being deployed next week."

"Next week?" I repeat, a sudden coldness hitting me in the core. "You've only been there for, like, a month. How can you be shipping out already?"

"That's just the way it works sometimes," he explains. "Sometimes it's a month, sometimes it's a year. You never really know."

"Well, shit." I shake my head in disbelief. "Where are they sending you?"

I hear his small exhale of breath as he replies, "Iraq."

My heart sinks in my chest. Feeling unsteady on my feet, I lean up against the doorframe and grip the edge for support. I've been dreading this moment ever since they enlisted. I knew it was coming—it's what they've been training for—but it doesn't make it any easier.

chapter nine

Amy

The mood at home is noticeably somber after getting the news that Dex will be shipping off to Iraq. He leaves in less than a week, and until then he's here with us in Charleston. We've been trying to stay positive and supportive around him, but it hasn't been easy. I barely made it five minutes before bursting into tears after he first walked through the door.

I blame the damn pregnancy hormones. They've turned me into a weak, emotional mess.

Of course, Dex remains his usual calm, steady and confident self; comforting the rest of us when we need it. I should have known that, even though he's the one risking his life, he would be the one to ultimately hold us together. He's always been the strong one.

This visit is noticeably different than all the others. Rather than going out to party and meet up with his friends, Dex has been content to stay close to home and spend time with our family. Taking Mom to the flea market, fishing with Dad... he hasn't even missed a single dinner with us. I should be happier about getting all this extra time with him, but it's just another reminder that he's leaving. In the back of my mind, there's the nagging thought that this could possibly be our last chance to spend time with him.

Since day one, Dex and I have been a team. No matter how much we fought while we were growing up, or how much we teased and annoyed each other, there was never a single moment that he wasn't my best friend. There were times that we drove each other crazy to the point where we couldn't stand to be around one another; but if a nasty storm rolled in during the night, I could still count on Dex to climb into bed with me and hold my hand until I fell back asleep. He's always been there for me when I need him.

Even when he was off at training, I could take comfort in the fact that he was only a phone call away. That's all going to change. While he's in Iraq, I'll be lucky to get an occasional call or letter. I won't know what he's doing, or even where he is most of the time. I won't know if he's safe.

Just the thought of something happening to Dex is more than I can bear. I can't lose him. He's my other half, and I can't imagine my life without him. No one could ever take his place.

"Enough with the depressing thoughts, sis." Dex flashes me a warning look through the mirrored lenses of his sunglasses. "I can see your mind going a mile a minute, and I know what you're thinking. Now knock it off with that shit so we can enjoy this beautiful day."

We're at the swimming hole behind our house, floating side by side on inflatable rafts while the sun beats overhead. Dex has a cold beer in his hand, and I have a sweet tea balanced on my huge belly.

"Is it that obvious?" I respond.

Dex grins. "To me it is."

"Sorry," I sigh, swirling my fingers in the cool water. "I can't help but worry about you."

"Yeah, I know." He offers me a sympathetic smile. "I wish I didn't have to put you through all of this. I knew what I was getting into when I signed up for this. I chose it. You never had a choice. I don't want you to waste time worrying about me, especially now. I want you to live your life and focus on that little girl of yours. That's what's important."

"I still can't believe you're not going to be here when she's born. I really wanted you to meet her first."

"So did I, Ames." A flash of disappointment crosses his face, and for the first time ever I see his confidence falter, making me instantly regret bringing it up. The last thing I want to do is make him feel guilty.

"Well, you'll just have to spoil her a little extra when you finally do meet her," I say, putting on my most convincing smile. "I'll try not to worry too much. Just... promise me you'll be careful, okay?"

"I promise." All traces of uncertainty vanish, replaced by his typical cocky grin. "I got mad skills, sis. Nothing can take down Dex Porter."

I flick my hand into the water, splashing him in the face. "Smug bastard," I tease, rolling my eyes.

Beads of water cover his sunglasses and drip down his face, but all he does is laugh. As he looks back at me with my favorite goofy smile, all I can do is hope that he's right.

Nate

The sun is barely peeking over the horizon when I go outside and take a seat on my front porch step. The air is quiet and still, providing a sense of calm that can only be felt in the early morning hours before the rest of the world is awake. Inside I feel anything but calm, and my stomach churns in nervous anticipation of what's about to come.

It's not long before a green SUV turns into the driveway, breaking through the glassy silence as it comes to a stop in front of the house. Dex climbs out of the passenger seat wearing his camouflage utility uniform, and I let out a breath before rising from the step to meet him.

We're both quiet for a moment, until a small grin appears on Dex's face. Shaking his head, he mutters, "I fucking hate goodbyes."

I can't help but chuckle. "Me too, man. Can we agree to skip over all the sappy shit and just say… see ya soon?"

"Hell yes," he agrees. "I can't handle any more tears right now. Amy almost broke me already, and I still have my mom to deal with later on at the airport."

Glancing into the car I see his dad in the driver's seat and his mom in the back, both wearing the same somber expression. They seem to be holding it together fairly well, considering they're sending their son off to Iraq in a few short hours. I offer them an understanding smile before turning back to Dex.

"Amy isn't going with you?" I can't believe that she would miss seeing Dex off at the airport.

He shakes his head. "I wouldn't let her. She's about ready to pop, and I didn't want to put her through the whole scene at the airport. She's supposed to be taking it easy and staying relaxed. I've put her through enough as it is, and I would never forgive myself if something happened to the baby. Obviously she's not too happy about it, but I couldn't take the risk."

I nod in agreement. "Good thinking."

"I was actually hoping to ask you a favor," Dex continues. "Would you mind stopping by the house to check on her? She's having a tough time with all this, and I'm worried about her being there all alone until my parents get back. I know it's a lot to ask..."

"It's no problem at all," I quickly respond. "Of course I'll check on her."

"Thanks, I really appreciate it." Dex glances over his shoulder to where his parents wait in the car. "I guess I better get going. Teddy should be dropping by any minute to say goodbye to you, too."

I step forward and grab his hand, pulling him in for a hug. "Stay safe over there, okay?"

He nods, squeezing the back of my neck before stepping back. "You know I will. See you soon, buddy."

With a heavy heart, I stand in the driveway and watch the car as it pulls away. I can't help but think about Amy, and wonder how she's doing. Considering how close she is with her brother, I'm sure she's a wreck right about now. I hate that she's home by herself. We haven't spoken in months, so I don't know how she's going to react to having me check on her today, but frankly it doesn't matter. There's no way I'm going to let her go through this alone.

Before I can give it much more thought I hear the sound of tires on the gravel as another car turns into the driveway. This time it's Teddy.

I fucking hate goodbyes.

■ ■ ■

I take the front steps two at a time when I get to the Porters' house. Pausing on the stoop, I stare at the door for a brief moment before finally reaching up and gently tapping my knuckles against the wood.

When no one answers I knock harder, and when I hear nothing from the other side of the door, I hesitantly reach for the knob and twist it slowly, pushing it open when I realize it's unlocked. I'm met with silence as I walk inside, and I'm about to call out for Amy when I hear the soft, muffled sounds of crying from upstairs.

I tread softly up the stairs and down the hallway to her bedroom. The door is slightly ajar, and through the opening I can see her curled up on her bed, facing the windows on the other side of the room.

"Amy?" I say quietly, stepping inside her bedroom. "It's me. Nate."

She doesn't turn to face me, and all I hear in response is the sound of her soft cries. As I move closer, she whimpers. "He's gone." Her body collapses into another round of sobs.

Immediately I rush toward her, kicking off my shoes and climbing into the bed behind her. Drawing her against me, I bring my mouth to her ear and murmur, "Shhh, it's okay. It's gonna be okay."

I can feel her body shudder in my arms. Pulling her close, I rest my chin on her shoulder and softly try to soothe her.

"I—I can't lose him, Nate." Her voice trembles with each word, and it nearly breaks my heart.

"You're not going to lose him," I tell her. "Dex is smart, he's strong, and he's a damn good Marine. He knows how to take care of himself."

In a feeble whisper, she says, "I'm scared."

"I know, baby." My heart clenches as the urge to protect her burns hot and fierce inside me. Unable to stop myself, I press my lips to the slope of her neck.

Amy tenses slightly, and I hear her sharp intake of breath. Goosebumps pebble her skin beneath my lips, and I'd be lying if I said I didn't fucking love that. I'm trying to comfort her, but there's a part of me that can't stop thinking about how incredibly good it feels to have her in my arms.

"Why are you here?" she asks, as if only now realizing that I'm lying in her bed next to her.

"I was worried about you. I wanted to make sure you're okay."

"I don't want you to see me like this," she groans, burying her face in her pillows. "I'm such a mess. Please don't look at me."

Lifting myself up on my elbow, I reach over and gently grab her chin, tilting her face toward me. For the first time in months, her beautiful eyes rest on mine.

"You're gorgeous," I tell her, brushing my thumb across her damp cheeks. "You're always gorgeous, Amy. This is no exception."

And it's true. Her hair is mussed up from sleep, her eyes red and puffy from crying, and there's not a stitch of makeup on her face, but she still takes my breath away.

Her bottom lip quivers, and a tear escapes down her cheek. "I'm a whale."

I have to suppress a grin at how adorably self-conscious she is, despite the fact that she's nowhere close to resembling a whale. If not for her very round midsection, you wouldn't even know that she's pregnant. I lower the blanket and rub my palm over her swollen belly. "You're perfect."

A weak smile touches her lips as she turns and nestles her head back into the pillows, finally relaxing against me. I lie back down and curl her body into mine, spreading my fingers across the curve of her stomach. It feels harder than I expected as I absentmindedly rub lazy circles over the surface.

I'm drifting between awake and asleep, exhausted after having such an early morning, when I suddenly feel a flutter beneath my hand.

"Whoa." I jerk back, staring at her belly with wide eyes. "Are you okay?"

Amy giggles. "It's just the baby kicking. She moves around a lot when I'm trying to sleep."

I carefully put my hand back and resume the motion. Within a few seconds I feel it again.

"This is crazy," I declare in amazement, completely absorbed in the tiny, gentle movements happening inside her. "She's a little acrobat."

Half asleep, she utters drowsily, "She likes you."

That casual declaration hits me with such force it sucks the air right out of my lungs. It burns through all the other bullshit occupying space in my head until only one thought remains, and I'm left with a sense of absolute clarity.

In this moment I know that I want her to be mine.

I want *them* to be mine.

I want to protect them and take care of them. I want to make them smile and laugh, and hold them when they cry. I want to be there to revel in the good times and help them through the bad. I want to be the one by their side in life, not looking in from the outside.

I don't care that she's my best friend's sister, or that Dex will probably kick my ass. It doesn't matter that she's pregnant with someone else's baby, or that I don't know a damn thing about having a kid.

None of that matters.

Because the one thing I do know is that there will never be anyone else like her. No one else will make me feel the way that she does. She's it.

No matter how much I've tried to deny them, or bury them, I've always had those feelings for Amy. But the second I felt that tiny flutter beneath my fingertips, a second string wrapped itself around my heart and tied me to someone else. Someone who I could love just as fiercely, but in an entirely different way.

As my tired eyes float closed and I fall into slumber, I breathe into her ear, "Let me take care of you."

chapter ten

Amy

I open my eyes to the mid-afternoon sun pouring in my bedroom window. As I shift to glance at the clock, Nate's arms tighten around me, drawing my body against his warm, broad chest. I let myself sink into him, enjoying the comfort and protection of his embrace, and when I feel the hardness of his arousal pressing against my bottom, a gasp slips out of my mouth.

"Sorry," Nate chuckles, his voice low and heavy with sleep. "I told you that you're gorgeous."

I remain frozen in place as heat floods through me, igniting my body with lust. My breaths start coming in faster and faster, and my nipples pebble beneath the thin material of my shirt. It was difficult enough to control my body's reaction to him before, but now that I'm pregnant and full of hormones, it's damn near impossible. Over the past couple of months, when they've gotten more and more intense, Nate has starred in more late-night fantasies than I care to admit.

Stupid hormones.

"You okay?" Nate asks, running his nose along the shell of my ear and making me shiver.

I take a deep breath, attempting to get my body under control, but when his hand skates over my hip and up my rib cage, I let out a breathy moan and reflexively arch my body into his.

"Tell me what you need, Amy." He brushes his thumb along the side of my heavy, sensitive breast, just inches from where I desperately crave his touch. "Tell me what you need and I'll take of you. I promise."

His voice is thick with desire, but his words remind me of the softly spoken declaration I heard through the cloudy haze of sleep.

"Let me take care of you."

I thought I'd been dreaming those words. They were full of passion and promise, and spoken with such certainty and determination that they seemed too perfect to be real.

But they were real.

I heard it in his voice as he comforted me. I felt it in the way he held me like I was something to be cherished. I saw it in his eyes when he told me I was beautiful.

Nate wants to be with me.

And I want him, too. God, I want him so badly. I've been wishing for this—for him—since the moment we met. It would be so easy to say yes, and fall into him.

But I can't.

Even through the thick fog of my feelings and desire for Nate, I can see how selfish that would be. As easy as it would be let him take care of me, and be there for me, and maybe even love me... I know, deep down, that it's not fair to him.

Nate is generous, thoughtful and kind. He cares so much for others, and has such a big heart. I've never met anyone like him. He's different and amazing… and truly one of the good ones. He deserves someone who can offer her whole heart to him, not just a piece of it.

That's not me anymore.

In a few short weeks I'm going to welcome a tiny human into the world, who will undoubtedly claim my heart. She will become the center of my universe, and all of my time and attention will belong to her. I won't be able to put both of them first, and Nate deserves to come first. He's worthy of so much more than what I'll be able to offer him.

I can't belong to him when, in a short weeks, I'll belong to someone else.

Everything in my life is about to change. I'm no longer merely responsible for my own life, but for someone else's, too. It's my job to care for her, and protect her from harm. I'm responsible for her. Not my parents, not my brother, not Nate.

Me.

It's going to be hard. It'll be exhausting, demanding, and full of challenges. There's no shortcut, or simple solution, and it's time for me to stand on my own two feet. No more relying on other people to help me, or fight my battles for me. It's up to me to become a person that my child can depend on.

I need to be able to take care of *me*.

I take a brief moment to memorize the way it feels to be in his arms, and then I pull away from him. "I can't do this, I'm sorry. I don't know what came over me."

Nate sits up next to me, drawing his eyebrows together as he looks at me. "Did I do something wrong?"

"No, of course not," I reply, shaking my head. "It's my fault. I wasn't thinking straight."

Frowning, he runs his hand through his hair. "But Amy, I—"

"I know you're just trying to help," I say, interrupting him before he has a chance to say anything else. "You've always been here for me, Nate, and I'm so thankful for that, but... everything's different now." I offer him a sad smile. "This is something that I have to do on my own."

"Why should you have to do this alone?"

"Because I need to know that I can." He doesn't seem satisfied with that answer, and I don't know what I can say to make him understand. If I tell him that he deserves better, he'll only try to convince me otherwise, so I try a different approach. "I have to focus on being a mom. I can't have any... distractions."

It feels utterly wrong to suggest that Nate is nothing more than a distraction, because it couldn't be further from the truth, but I stand my ground nonetheless. It's important for him to let me go, and he won't do that unless I can prove to him that it's what I actually want.

A shadow of disappointment crosses his face, and I know that I was successful. Part of me is screaming at myself to take it all back, but I swallow it down and force a smile.

He nods tightly, avoiding my eyes. "I get it."

My heart sinks as he turns to sit on the edge of the bed, hunching over as he grabs his boots and pulls them on. His back remains to me as he crosses the room, but when he reaches for the doorknob he hesitates, glancing back over his shoulder.

"I'll always be here for you, Amy." He pulls the door open, his gaze briefly meeting mine once more. "All you have to do is say the word."

Watching as he swings the door closed behind him, I stare after him from where I remain motionless on my bed. I listen to the sound of his footsteps as he descends the stairs, and it's not until I hear the roar of his engine that I curl up under my covers and burst into tears.

Nate

Walking away from Amy isn't easy. I keep pulling my car off to the side of the road to turn it around, debating whether or not I did the right thing by leaving, or if I should have done more to try and change her mind. As much as I want to go back, I know that I have to respect her decision. Beneath all the pain and disappointment, I can understand where she's coming from, and I admire her for wanting to do it on her own. I know she thinks that she's always been dependent on others, and I wish that she could see how strong she really is. There's no doubt in my mind that she'll be an amazing mom.

So instead of turning around to go back, I just sit here, cursing to myself for a few moments before pulling back onto the road and continuing home.

I'm left with a knot in my stomach that, days later, hasn't gone away. I return to my normal routine of working in the shop and eating dinner with my folks, but everything still feels… off. A sense of discontentment has settled over me that I can't seem to shake. It's more than just the situation with Amy. It's the monotony and predictability of my life as a whole. I've been doing the same thing since I was fifteen years old—working on cars, helping my dad with the business, family dinners every night—but it doesn't feel like enough anymore. There's no excitement, nothing to look forward to for the next thirty years except more of the same. It was easier when I had my friends around, but now Dex and Teddy are halfway across the world, and Amy is having a baby. I feel like everyone around me is moving forward while I stand firmly in place and watch them go.

For the first time I want more in my life.

However, wanting something and actually *doing* something are two very different things. I can't abandon my job and my family when they need me. This is my home. This is the life that I signed up for, and I won't just pick up and leave it. When I commit to something, I'm all in. That's how my mama raised me.

Throughout the next week I make an effort to conceal all my inner turmoil, but it isn't long before my dad realizes that something's bothering me. I should have known that it was pointless to try and hide anything from him.

"You ever plannin' on tellin' me what's goin' on with you?" he asks during our short afternoon lunch break. "Or are you gonna keep plasterin' that phony smile on your face and pretendin' like everything's A-okay?"

I brush off his question with a shrug, hoping to avoid the topic. I don't lie to my old man—it's not my style—but I don't want to talk about this either.

"Are you missin' the boys?" he says, referring to Dex and Teddy. "It must be weird not havin' them around."

"Yeah, I guess it's just a little lonely around here. You'd think I'd be used to it by now, since they were hardly ever in town during training, but somehow it's different with them being so far away this time. I'll get used to it, though. I need to find new ways to keep myself occupied, that's all."

"Well, maybe you ought to go off and have some adventures of your own," he suggests, taking me by surprise. "You've barely been out of this state, except maybe once or twice in your whole life. Maybe it's time for you to go off and explore the world, and see what else is out there. Take a chance and experience somethin' new."

I shake my head. "I couldn't do that to you. What about the shop? You can't run this place on your own, you need my help."

My dad chuckles. "Son, I was runnin' this place on my own long before you ever came along. As much as I appreciate your help and enjoy workin' beside you, I can still do it without you." He slaps a hand down on my shoulder and gives it a squeeze. "I love that you and I share the same passion for fixin' cars, and you know how much your mama and me like havin' you around, but I never wanted it to feel like an obligation. You should enjoy bein' young, kiddo."

"But there's so much work," I say, glancing around the shop at the scattered tools and abundant amount of paperwork strewn all over the small desk in the office.

"I can handle it, no problem." He waves his hand dismissively. "I still got quite a few good years left in me, and if I need to hire an extra hand, I will. Stop worryin' over things here and just go out there and have some fun. I got this place covered."

Later that night I lie awake in bed for hours, contemplating what my dad said, going back and forth about what I want to do. I feel guilty for even thinking about leaving my dad here on his own, despite his assurances, but I can't deny that there's a part of me that really wants to take him up on his offer. I feel stuck here, and the idea of experiencing something new and different lights a tiny spark of excitement inside me that I haven't felt in a long time.

When I wake up the next morning, I've made my decision. Before I have a chance to change my mind, I pull out my phone and make the call. He answers on the third ring.

"Hey, Mr. Connelly. It's Nate Miller, from the shop. I've been thinking about what you said, and I was hoping you could put me in touch with one of your contacts about a full-time job doing restorations."

part three

. . .

four years later

chapter eleven

Amy

Sunshine pours down from a clear blue sky, twinkling through the lush green leaves of the tree above us, and casting the moment in a captivating glow that none of us feel. It's the kind of day that should inspire hope and signify promise, but instead it mocks us, as we stand gathered around the deep mahogany box, watching as it slowly descends into the ground.

Teddy's mom grips the folded American flag in her hand like a lifeline, staring with hollow, vacant eyes as they bury her only son. A single tear falls down her cheek, and it amazes me that she has any tears left at all. It's been almost a month since we got the news that Teddy had been killed in Iraq, but it took weeks for his body to finally return home.

It's strange to say goodbye after so many days have passed. You'd think that the added time would have given us a chance to heal, but instead it seemed to put our hearts in a state of limbo; stuck in a place between grief and acceptance. Normally a funeral is a final goodbye, and a celebration of life. For us, it feels more like a confirmation of our loss; proof that Teddy is really gone.

Even now, none of it seems real. There's a part of me still hoping I'll wake up from this.

Dex and Teddy were nearing the end of their second tour in Iraq when it happened. Their convoy hit a roadside bomb, and as they were doing a sweep of the area to search for additional devices, a second IED went off unexpectedly. Dex suffered major head trauma and hearing loss, but he still managed to pull several members of their unit to safety. Unfortunately, by the time he got to Teddy, it was too late. He'd been closer to the blast than the others, and his injuries were too severe. There was nothing Dex could do to save him.

Dex was transported to the military hospital in Germany, where he was treated and closely monitored for the next few weeks. He was lucky. Really, really lucky. His only lingering injury is partial hearing loss in one ear. It may be temporary, but most likely, it's permanent. He was supposed to stay in the hospital for another couple of weeks, but he discharged himself so he could escort Teddy's body back to the States for the funeral. According to the Marine who accompanied him for the trip, Dex sat next to the casket the entire way, refusing to leave his best friend's side until he was ordered to.

He's barely said a word to anyone since he arrived home two days ago. When I saw him step out of the car in my parents' driveway, I smiled for the first time in nearly a month. I've never felt such relief as I did in that moment. He looked a bit battered and almost fragile, so unlike the brother I've always known, but he was there and he was alive. Tears poured down my cheeks as I ran over and flung my arms around him, holding him close to reassure myself that he was here with me in one piece. Dex was stiff and silent, placing a gentle kiss on my forehead before stepping out of my grasp and walking into the house.

Since then he's stayed in his room, closing himself off to the rest of us while he deals with his grief alone. My parents keep reminding me that he's still healing from his injuries and he needs time to recover, but we all know that his real wounds go far deeper than the physical trauma. What he's really dealing with… I'm not sure he'll ever recover from.

I glance over to where he's standing with the other men from his unit, all fully clad in their blue dress uniforms. They look so impressive all grouped together in the elaborate blue, red, gold and white, it's almost dazzling. They stand at attention, stiffly frozen in place with their hands clasped in front of them as they stare straight ahead with stoic faces; expressionless masks that hide everything brewing beneath the surface. One of them clutches a cane at his side, and I can see how tired he is from the simple act of standing, but he never once falters. Another one of the men has burn scars peeking out from his collar and up to his ear. This is a group of men who have been to hell and back. They're fighters and survivors. True heroes.

I can't help but wonder if any of them will go back and continue to fight. How many of them will return safely? It's heartbreaking to think of them surviving such horrible circumstances, only to have their lives cut short regardless.

Dex has always told me that being a Marine isn't what you do, but who you are. It's someone who charges headfirst into danger and chaos without a second thought, or a moment's hesitation. Someone who sees fear, feels it, and tastes it, but pushes through it in order to do what is necessary. Rather than running away from danger, he runs straight toward it, plunging into its violent grasp and fighting back with everything he's got.

Someone like my brother, who barely escapes death's grip one minute, only to rush right back into it the next.

It takes an extraordinary kind of person to do what they do. That's how I know that the group of Marines in front of me are probably not done fighting yet. If any of them can go back, they will. It's who they are.

Dex's future with the Marines remains uncertain. It all depends on his injury, and whether or not he regains the partial hearing that he lost. If he does, and they clear him medically, then there's no doubt he'll eventually return to active duty. However, if his hearing *doesn't* come back, he'll have no choice but to retire with an honorable discharge.

I'm ashamed to admit there's a part of me that secretly hopes Dex will have to retire. I know how selfish that is—especially considering how badly Dex wants to go back—but I can't help it. More than anything else, I want him to be safe. The thought of losing Dex is unbearable. The fear that lived inside of me during the time that he was overseas is not the kind that ever goes away; it takes root and only grows more potent as the time passes. During the time he was on his first tour, I woke up with that fear every single morning. I didn't feel at ease until he came home, and the moment he left for his second tour, it was back.

I'm sick of missing my brother, and living with the fear that, at any moment, I could get a phone call to inform me that he's gone. If that makes me selfish, then so be it.

Throughout my life, my brother and I have been lumped together as a pair. We've always been known as "the twins". While I was growing up I frequently resented being part of a set, wanting nothing more than to be an individual for once, to stand out as my own person. But when Dex went overseas, all I could think about was how terrified I was to lose my other half.

I suddenly feel the faintest tingle creeping up my spine, snapping me back to reality and shifting my attention away from the spot on the ground I've been staring at. When I look up, my gaze immediately locks with a pair of green eyes that I haven't seen in nearly four years.

Nate

It's been close to four years since the last time I saw her. The day I walked away.

I almost don't recognize her at first. I half expect her to still have a big pregnant belly, even though it's obviously long gone. She looks older, more grown up. Her brown hair is sleek and glossy, falling just beyond her shoulders and tucked behind one ear. She has the same slender figure, but with added curves that she didn't have before—fuller breasts with a slim waist that tapers down to slightly rounded hips, and legs that look a mile long.

Amy is definitely not a teenager anymore.

When she glances up and her eyes meet mine, it feels like someone attached jumper cables to my chest and revved the engine, igniting my heart from its dormant state. I can't look away, I can't even move. I feel like I should smile, or nod, or do something… but I can't. All I can do is stare.

Her whole body is tense as she watches me from the other side of the crowd. It's not until her focus shifts to something beside her that I finally tear my eyes away from her face. As I follow her gaze downward, I notice the tiny hand she's holding, and the little blonde girl standing next to her.

Holy shit.

All the air is sucked out of my lungs. I stand motionless, observing the two of them together and studying the child who is clearly her daughter. Aside from the blonde hair, she looks like a miniature version of Amy.

It shouldn't come as such a surprise to see her with a child—it's not as if I didn't know she had a baby—but witnessing them together is something else entirely. She must be almost four years old by now, and she stands quietly next to her mom as the service comes to an end. There's a black bow in her wispy, light blonde hair, and she's wearing a velvety black dress with black tights. When I notice the sparkly red shoes on her small feet, a grin automatically spreads across my face. It's the first time I've smiled since hearing about Teddy.

I was in Arizona when I got the phone call. I'd been there for almost a week, sifting through various junkyards and bartering with different collectors, trying to find a part for a rare Pontiac GTO. I'd finally found it when I saw my mom's name appear on the caller ID. I was so anxious to get the deal done and get out of there, that I almost ignored it. It was a weird gut feeling that made me answer, and a few seconds later my mom gave me the news that rocked my fucking world.

No one ever wants to get that call.

What happened after that is a bit hazy. I don't remember leaving Arizona, or smashing my cell phone, but both of those things happened at some point.

All I know is that I hopped a flight back to Kentucky, packed up the stuff from my small apartment there, dropped my keys off to my landlord, picked up my car from the garage, and drove straight back home to Charleston.

It was surprisingly easy to leave it all behind. I'd been living in that apartment for nearly four years, but it wasn't much of a home. I was rarely ever there. Most of the time I was traveling around the country—sometimes even Europe—to find rare parts for antique or classic rebuilds. These weren't your typical restorations. I was working on the kind of valuable, one-of-a-kind cars that I'd only ever dreamed about, for serious collectors with *seriously* deep pockets. It was an unbelievable experience; one that took me to a lot of amazing places and showed me some incredible things.

But I was ready to get back to my life. Teddy's death just brought me home a little bit sooner than planned.

I've missed my parents, and it's time for me to return to my dad's shop to help out. Most importantly, my best friend needs me. Home is where I belong.

I'd made a few short visits over the last four years, mostly for holidays or when I was picking up parts nearby. Dex and Teddy had been around during a couple of those trips, spending time with their own families in between tours. They were happy to see me doing my own thing, and we spent time exchanging stories about some of the places we'd been and the things we'd seen. It was like it had always been with the three of us.

Now Teddy's gone.

All I can do is thank my lucky stars that I still have Dex. I easily could've lost both of them, and I don't know what the hell I would've done if that happened. It breaks my fucking heart to think that I'll never see Ted again—with his goofy smile and easygoing personality—it's a loss that I'll feel for the rest of my life. But I'll always remind myself that it could have been worse.

I haven't seen or spoken to Dex since it happened. The only contact I've had is with his mom, who called me a few days ago to let me know that he'd arrived home safely and would be attending today's funeral. I could hear it in her voice how concerned she is about him, and frankly, so am I. Dex and Teddy were as close as two people could possibly be. They weren't just best friends; they were brothers. I've always been slightly on the outside, and while I used to envy the friendship they had, I grew to admire it. The bond between them was deep and permanent, the kind that doesn't ever go away, even in death. And because of that, I'm certain that Dex is taking this harder than anyone and will probably never be the same.

A gunshot rings through the air as part of the rifle salute, signaling the end of the service. The crowd begins to disperse, following behind the uniformed members of the honor guard and Teddy's family as they lead us away from the gravesite. I search for Dex among the large group of people assembled in the cemetery, hoping to catch him before he leaves, but he blends into a sea of dress blues that are impossible to distinguish from one another.

I visited Teddy's family as soon as I arrived home, but I seek them out to offer my condolences nonetheless. When I catch a glimpse of Dex a few minutes later, all I see is his back as he slowly retreats from the crowd and disappears at the other end of the cemetery. I'm still staring after him, debating whether to follow him or simply let him be, when I hear a soft voice behind me.

"He's barely spoken to anyone since he got back."

I spin around to find Amy standing there, a troubled expression on her face as she looks in the direction that he went. I catch the slight tremble of her lip when she turns toward me and says, "I'm really worried about him."

"Me, too." I shove my hands into my pockets, shifting uncomfortably on my feet, suddenly feeling tongue-tied.

"How are you doing?" Amy asks, concern filling her beautiful eyes.

I shrug slightly, reaching up to rub the tense muscles at the back of my neck. "I, uh… I'm doing okay, I guess. I've had a month to process it, but it's still hard to believe that he's really gone." I offer a small, hesitant smile. "I'm getting through it, though. I'm just thankful that we didn't lose both of them, you know?"

She lets out a huge breath. "Yeah, I think about that every day." Her eyes shine with unshed tears that she quickly blinks away before offering me a relieved smile. "It's really good to see you, Nate."

"It's good to see you, too." I gaze down at her, fighting the urge to wrap my arms around her and tell her how much I've missed her. I hate that we're acting like strangers. Granted, it's been a long time since we last saw each other, but I foolishly crave the ease and familiarity that used to exist between us.

"How long are you staying in town?"

"I'm back for good," I tell her. "As much as I enjoyed what I was doing, this is where I belong. I never intended to be gone for as long as I was. It was time for me to come home."

A tiny smile plays at her lips. "Well, I'm glad you're back." As soon as the words leave her mouth, a faint blush appears on her cheeks, and she stumbles to correct herself. "I mean, it will be good for Dex to have you around."

Knowing that Amy is happy for me to be home—for whatever reason—is enough to deliver a surge of excitement through me. Five minutes with Amy and I'm already right back to where I was when I left.

"How's everything with you?" I finally ask. "I saw you with your daughter earlier. She's beautiful, Amy."

Her face instantly lights up at the mention of her daughter;

beaming with obvious pride and joy. "Thank you. We're doing really well. Sadie is… incredible."

Right on cue, Amy's little girl appears at her side, gently tugging at her mother's dress to get her attention.

"Mommy?" Her small, sweet voice chimes out. "I'm hungry."

"I know, baby girl. You've been very patient." Amy reaches down and gently brushes her wispy blonde hair out of her face. "We're going home soon, okay?"

Sadie tilts her head back, looking up at me with a curious expression. "Hi."

"Sadie, this is my friend, Nate," Amy says, motioning to me.

"Hi, Sadie." I crouch down to her level, offering what I hope is a reassuring smile. "It's nice to finally meet you."

"Hi," she says again. "You know my mommy?"

"Yup," I tell her. "And your Uncle Dex."

She smiles widely at me, showing off her small, uneven teeth. "I love Uncle Dee, he's my best friend."

"Oh, yeah?" I can't help but grin at how adorable she is. "He's my best friend, too. Do you think I could hang out with you and Dee sometime?"

She bobs her head up and down. "You can come to my birthday party!"

"Wow, you have a birthday coming up?" I glance up at Amy, who's observing us with an amused smile.

"She sure does," Amy confirms. "It's on Saturday."

Sadie grins proudly. "I'm gonna be four."

"Well, if it's okay with your mom then I'll definitely be there."

"Can he come?" Sadie looks up at Amy expectantly.

"Of course he can come," she answers. "It's your birthday."

"Yes!" she exclaims, jumping into the air.

I hold my up hand for a high-five, and she smacks her tiny palm against mine. "I'll see you on Saturday, birthday girl."

"Sadie, why don't you go over to the car with Grammy and Papa?" Amy says, pointing to where her parents are standing. "I'll meet you there in a minute."

With a quick wave goodbye, Sadie runs over to them. Straightening out of my crouched position, I turn to Amy with a grin. "She's totally awesome. Sorry for putting you on the spot about the birthday party. I hope it's okay for me to come."

She laughs. "Don't be silly, of course it's okay. Don't feel like you have to, though. I'm sure a four-year-old's birthday party wasn't part of your weekend plans."

"Are you kidding?" I cock my head to the side, raising my eyebrows. "I can't wait. I happen to love birthday parties. Besides, it will give us a chance to hang out and catch up some more." I quickly add, "And Dex, too."

chapter twelve

Amy

On the morning of Sadie's birthday, my parents take her to the aquarium while I set up everything for the party. We're having it at their house, since they have more space than I do in my two-bedroom apartment.

Sadie and I moved out of my parents' house a little more than a year ago. From the day she was born, and every step of the way, both my mom and dad have been a hugely important part of Sadie's life. Not only have they helped me raise her, but they also provided us with a roof over our heads, meals to eat, and most importantly, took care of Sadie on a regular basis so that I could finish the courses I needed to earn my degree. They've done it all willingly, without a single protest or complaint, and as much as I loved living with them, it was time for me to be out on my own.

We didn't go far—only about three miles—and the house we moved into is one of two properties that my grandparents left to us when they passed away. It's right on the edge of a small inlet off

Lighthouse Creek, looking out across the water and fields of marsh. My parents thought I was crazy at first, when I chose to live there rather than in the oceanfront cottage on Folly Beach; but this has always been my favorite of the two. It's beautiful here, and peaceful. There's a small dock with a raft to swim off of, when the tide's high enough, and I don't have to be concerned about Sadie running into the ocean. Plus, at some point the house was divided into two apartments, one on each floor, so I'm able to rent it out for additional income.

It took me a while to adjust to being on my own, without having my parents around for constant backup, but it's better for us. I hated the thought of being a burden to my parents, and relying so heavily on them in so many aspects of everyday life. It's always been important to me to know that I can do this on my own, without becoming too dependent upon anyone else to handle my responsibilities. After moving into our own place, I finally feel like I'm in charge of my own life.

Of course, my parents are still a huge part of our lives—frankly, they wouldn't have it any other way—but it's nice to no longer rely on them for quite so much.

After picking up the birthday cake and a bunch of balloons, I drive over to my parents' house to start setting it all up. As I climb out of the car and attempt to carry everything inside in one trip, I begin to lose my grip on the cake box, and the ribbons for the balloons start slipping through my fingers. Before I let go, and accidentally send fifteen pink and yellow balloons floating into outer space, they're taken out of my hands.

"Let me get those for you," Dex says, coming up beside me.

"Dex!" I exclaim, as a gigantic smile appears on my face. I was so distracted that I didn't even notice his truck pull up behind me. "I'm so glad you're here. I wasn't sure if you were going to make it."

Dex decided to move into the beach house last week, and I've barely seen him since then. I was starting to worry that he would isolate himself completely, so the fact that he's here is a relief.

"I couldn't miss my niece's birthday party. It's the first one that I'm actually around for." His eyes darken momentarily at the inadvertent reminder of *why* he's here for this one, but he shakes it off and continues, "Besides, I figured you could use a hand with the party setup."

With Dex's help, it doesn't take long for us to decorate the house with birthday banners, streamers and balloons. We set the table with paper plates and cups featuring the Disney princesses, and order more than enough pizza to feed Sadie's friends from daycare and the other various adults who are coming. We stack the boxes inside the oven to keep it warm until the guests arrive, and then we wait.

Even after we're finished decorating and setting up, I can't seem to shake the nervous, uneasy feeling from the pit of my stomach. It's the same dull twinge I've been fighting all week, but it's morphed into a steady, vibrant pulse that resonates from my head to my toes. It has little to do with my daughter's birthday party, and everything to do with the fact that Nate's going to be here.

I'd be lying if I said that I haven't thought about him over the last few years. No matter how hard I've tried to push those thoughts away, he's always hovering at the edge of my mind; tugging at the seams of my thin veil of denial, threatening to tear the whole thing down and expose the truth hidden behind it.

Fortunately, my life has been hectic enough to keep those thoughts at bay, and the more time that passed without seeing him, the more firmly the veil was kept in place. But the second I locked eyes with him at the funeral, I felt the pull of the first thread. Now the fabric is worn, the edges are frayed, and the whole thing is in danger of unraveling.

Dex and I settle into the rocking chairs on the front porch as we wait for my parents to return with the birthday girl. I perch my feet up on the railing, relishing in the rare moment of peace and quiet, when I notice how uneasy my brother seems.

Sitting rigidly in the chair next to me, his whole body appears tense and stiff. His hands are clenched into fists as he drags them up and down his legs, staring straight ahead to the entrance of the driveway.

I realize just how big of a step it is for him to be here. Since arriving home, he's almost completely shut himself off from everyone around him. He's barely seen or spoken to anyone and has avoided any and all conversation about what happened. I think he's terrified to talk about it, and by coming here today he's opening himself up to the kind of unwelcome attention he's so desperately trying to escape.

Despite all of it, he showed up for Sadie. It goes to show just how much he loves his niece and how far he'll go for the ones he loves. He may seem battered and broken, but underneath it all, he remains the strongest, bravest person I've ever known. I want to jump out of my seat to hug him, and thank him for being here and still being *him*. I don't though, because I know he needs space. Instead, I decide to do everything in my power to make him feel comfortable during the party.

"Nate told me that he would try and stop by today," I mention. I don't know how he's going to react to that, and I feel the need to warn him so he won't be caught off guard if Nate does in fact show up.

"Good," he nods. "That's good. I'd like to see him."

I'm not sure if he's trying to convince me, or himself, but the most important thing is that he's willing to try.

A few minutes later, my dad's car pulls into the driveway. After emerging from the front seat, my parents open the back door to help Sadie out. She comes running toward us with a huge smile on her face, towing a giant stuffed penguin along behind her.

Grinning, I turn to Dex. "Ready to get this party started?"

His whole demeanor softens when Sadie rushes up and throws her small arms around him, and for the first time since he's been home, a genuine smile appears on his face.

"Let's do it," he says.

Nate

I arrive at the Porters' house a little bit later than planned, thanks to a guy who called the shop for a last minute tow. I didn't have the heart to turn him down, and after being gone for such a long time, there was no way I was going to ask my dad to take care of it. Then, I got covered in grease so I had to shower—again—and dig through my drawers to find suitable clothes to wear to a four-year-old's birthday party. By the time I found a pair of jeans with no holes in them and threw them on with a plaid collared shirt, I was already fifteen minutes late.

The sound of voices and high-pitched laughter leads me to the backyard, where a group of adults are mingling together, keeping an eye on Sadie and the handful of other young kids who are happily playing around in the grass. I don't see Amy or Dex, but Mrs. Porter quickly comes over to me.

"It's so nice of you to come!" She gives me a quick hug and a kiss on the cheek before leading me across the yard to where everyone is gathered. "Dex had to run out to buy some birthday candles, but Amy should be in the kitchen."

When I walk inside and discover Amy bending over to retrieve a stack of pizza boxes from the oven, my eyes automatically settle on her perfect round ass. I can't help it. Her snug jeans mold to every curve, and all I can think about is grasping my hands around it and hauling her against me.

I'm frozen in place, still staring, when she turns around and notices me standing there.

"Oh, hi!" she exclaims, sounding breathless. "I'm glad you made it."

"Hey, umm... hi, yeah." I stumble over the words, flustered. Warmth spreads to my ears when I see her coy smile, and I clear my throat. "Can I, uh... help you with anything?"

"Think you can handle making some lemonade?" she asks, her eyes gleaming with amusement as she holds up a container of powdered mix.

"That's probably within my skill level," I say with a chuckle, taking the mix from her hand, and then reaching into the top shelf of the cabinet for a pitcher. After filling it with water, I move to stand next to her at the counter, where she's combining the ingredients for a salad into a large bowl. "So, Amy," I begin, "tell me a little more about what you've been up to over the last few years. Aside from raising a kick-ass little girl, of course."

"There's not much to tell," she replies, shrugging her shoulders. "After Sadie was born, I finished the online classes that I needed for my degree, and then got a full-time teaching job shortly after that."

"What grade?"

She smiles fondly. "Kindergarten. I hadn't originally considered teaching such young kids, but having Sadie changed my mind about it. Watching her learn and grow, I realized how significant those early years are to a child's education."

"That's really great, Amy. I always knew you'd be an amazing teacher."

It's clear to me that she loves working with kids, and there's no doubt in my mind that she's great at her job. She's so caring, patient, and kind; I've never met anyone else quite like her.

I stare down at the pitcher of lemonade, stirring it excessively as I gear myself up to ask the one question I really want the answer to. As casually as possible I ask, "Is there anyone… special… in your life?"

Sneaking a sideways glance in her direction, I watch her body tense briefly before she shakes her head slowly. "I don't have much of a social life these days. Between Sadie and teaching, I barely get a moment to myself." Her mouth curves into a lackluster smile, but there's sadness etched in her features. "Besides, most men aren't interested in dating a single mom with zero free-time."

I want to kick myself for asking. As relieved as I am to know that she's not seeing anyone, my chest aches to think of Amy being lonely or unhappy. And does she seriously believe that having a child makes her any less desirable? I'd like to beat the crap out of whoever put that ridiculous idea in her head, because it couldn't be further from the truth. Child or not, Amy is gorgeous and remarkable, and Sadie only adds to that. Any guy would be lucky to have them. *Both* of them.

"You just haven't found the right one." I lean forward, holding her gaze. "None of that matters to a real man."

Her lips part slightly as she stares back at me. I can see the subtle rise and fall of her chest with each shallow breath she takes, and all I can hear is the sound of my own racing heart. The heat and hunger between us is palpable, seeping into my pores and consuming my every thought. The years that have gone by are irrelevant; vanishing in a cloud of dust and bringing us right back to where we were before.

My gaze falls to her mouth, watching eagerly as her tongue darts out to moisten her lips. She stands frozen in place, and my body shifts forward, instinctively gravitating toward her.

"Got the candles!"

Dex's voice booms through the kitchen, immediately causing me to shift backwards and put space between us. Hurt floods her hazel eyes, and I feel a pang of guilt for reacting the way that I did.

Clearing her throat, she forces a smile and looks past me to her brother. "Thank you, Dex. You're a lifesaver."

I turn toward Dex, and he grins when he notices me standing there. Stepping toward him, I don't hesitate to pull him in for a hug. "It's damn good to see you, man."

"You too, buddy. I'm glad you came."

We grasp each other tight for a long moment as a variety of emotions pass through us. Relief... pain... joy... regret. Words aren't spoken because we don't need them. Instead, we take a quiet moment to mourn our best friend and welcome each other home.

■　■　■

After the birthday party, Dex and I head over to one of the local bars for a drink. We didn't have much of a chance to talk at the party, since our attention was devoted to Sadie, but I don't think it would have mattered either way.

Although Dex appears to be doing a lot better, he's still closed off to everyone around him. There are moments when he's almost cheerful, but other times he's very quiet, and seems to be lost inside of his own head. I don't doubt that there's a hell of a lot more going on beneath the surface than he lets on. I think he pretends to be better than he really is, because it's easier to act a certain way than to admit what's really going on.

Despite my concerns, I let him be. He's been through hell and back, and the last thing I want to do is push him away, or force him into anything he's not ready for. Instead, I've decided to just be here for him while he gets through this. Which I have faith that he will.

He's already unsteady on his feet as he tips back yet another shot of whiskey. I've lost count of how many he's had, but I refuse to act like a babysitter for a man who's fought in a war and saved countless lives. That's not what he needs. What he needs is a friend, and as his friend, I'm sitting beside him, drinking beer instead of whiskey, and making sure he gets home safely at the end of the night.

When Dex starts talking to a woman at the bar, I take the opportunity to pay our tab and use the restroom. Dex has been popular with women for as long as I've known him, but his focus was solely on the Marines. He put his heart and soul into it. Being a Marine is so much more than what he does... it's who he is. It's how he defines himself. If he doesn't have that anymore, I don't know what he'll do.

My leisurely stroll from the bathroom turns into a mad dash when I emerge to find Dex at the center of a brawl on the other side of the bar. He's fighting two or three guys but easily holds his own. With his skills and training, he's capable of inflicting serious damage on these idiots, and I can't let that happen. Pushing my way through the crowd that's gathered around to watch, I make my way over to them as fast as I can.

"Okay, that's enough. Break it up!" I scream at no one in particular. When I get no response, I reach down to grab one of the guys' arms and start to pull him back. "Come on, man. Back off. Time to go."

Before I have a chance to react, he swings his arm around and clocks me in the jaw. I stumble back a step, caught off guard, and rub a hand over the spot where he sucker-punched me. It was a weak-ass punch, so it's not even that sore, but now I'm fucking pissed off.

He comes at me again, but this time I'm ready for it. Clenching my muscles, I rotate my arm back and then bring it forward, slamming my fist into his nose. He drops to the ground, clutching his face as a steady stream of blood pours out of his now-broken nose.

"Fuck you!" I yell down at him. "Next time, just back off when I tell you to, asshole!"

Dex is still at it with one of the guys, but someone has stepped in to pull the third one out of there. I grab Dex with both arms and start to drag him away. "All right, Dex, that's enough." I tell him as he struggles against my hold. "You've made your point, now let's get the fuck out of here, okay?"

He finally stops resisting, and I manage to get him outside of the bar. It's dark, and the late night air is cool against my heated skin. Dex has a bloody lip, and there are a few red streaks on his white shirt, which I'm guessing are from the other guy. He'll likely have a few killer bruises, but he's relatively unscathed. We perch on the hood of my car, catching our breath, and after a while, I turn to Dex. "What the hell happened in there?"

"That fucking asshole came over and started talking shit." He spits blood from his mouth onto the gravel of the parking lot and turns to me with a satisfied grin. "He wanted a fight, so I fucking gave him one."

The manager of the bar steps out the back door and makes his way toward us, looking drained and weary. "I don't allow this bullshit in my bar, do you understand?"

"I'm sorry about all of this," I start to explain. "I promise to pay for any damages—"

He waves a hand, cutting me off, and narrows his steely eyes on Dex. "If this were anyone else, I'd be having you arrested and hauled off in handcuffs right about now. Fortunately for you, kid, I have an enormous amount of respect for what you do, so I'm giving you a pass this time." He lets out a heavy sigh, and some of the anger disappears from his features. "I have a brother in the Corps, and I watched him struggle for years after he was done. I get that sometimes you need an outlet for all that anger, but this ain't the place for it." He hands Dex a piece of folded white paper with what looks like a phone number written on it. "This is your only pass. If you ever pull this shit again, I'll let the cops deal with you."

The manager walks away, and I breathe a sigh of relief to know that I won't be spending the night in a cell. The short drive to Dex's house is filled with empty silence, but when I come to a stop in his driveway, I hear him let out a long breath.

"They won't let me back in," he mutters in a pained voice. "The hearing loss is permanent, so I'm done. Officially discharged. That's it."

"Fuck," I breathe, feeling the enormity of his loss. The Marine Corps is everything to him, and even though we understood this was a possibility, I know what a tremendous blow this is. He's barely hanging on as it is, trying to deal with Teddy's death and the accident, but now… shit.

"Look, man," I continue, "if pounding the shit out of some guy or draining a bottle of whiskey is what you need right now to help get through this, then I'll have your back. Always. I'll be there to fight beside you, and then haul your bloody or drunken ass home afterwards. You won't get any judgment from me. We all deal with shit differently, and I'll never pretend to know what you're going through." I pause for a moment, firming my gaze on his. "But at some point, if I have to, I'm going to pull you out of it and do whatever it takes to help you. I won't let you throw your life away. All I ask is that, whatever you're doing, you're cautious and you stay safe. Because we can't lose you too, Dex."

He nods tightly, and as he opens the door to climb out, he glances back. "Thanks, Nate."

chapter thirteen

Amy

Over the next few weeks, we settle into a new kind of routine. Dex and Nate spend a lot of time together, and since Dex found out that he won't be able to return to active duty, they've even started working together at Nate's auto repair shop.

They spend time with Sadie and me, too. We often eat dinners together at my house or go to the beach on the weekends. It's nice, until the two of them head out to the bar at night for a drink, or to see a band, and I'm the one who gets left behind. They invite me along, of course, but it's mostly just to be polite. They know that I have responsibilities. When you have a child, you can't go out for a spur-of-the-moment good time. So, instead I hang back, plaster on a smile, and send them off to have a good time without me.

I allowed myself a brief second of hope, of longing, when I shared that moment—or whatever it was—with Nate at Sadie's birthday party. I thought that maybe this time it would be different. Maybe this time we could have a real chance.

But then Dex came in, and Nate couldn't get away from me fast enough. In that instant I realized that even though we're older and lead completely different lives than we did before, nothing has really changed. Dex will always be the obstacle that stands between us.

So now, things have returned to the "new" normal. Dex and Nate are best friends, and I tag along when I can. I'm right back to being the tomboy, twin sister who's friends with all the boys, but nothing more.

It may not be turning out the way I'd hoped, but it's for the best. I feel as though I'm finally starting to get my brother back. He's acting a lot more like his old self, and I know that his progress is due in large part to Nate. I can't begrudge their friendship when it's helping Dex get better. If burying my feelings for Nate means getting my brother back, then I'll gladly do it. That's the most important thing to me.

He needs Nate far more than I do right now.

Not that I'm actually giving Nate up or anything. You can't give up something you never had.

■   ■   ■

I pull into my driveway after a long day of wrangling a bunch of five- and six-year olds, followed by an additional two hours of parent-teacher conferences. It amazes me how uptight and overbearing some of these parents can be. I recognize how important early education is, but come on… it's kindergarten for God's sake! Most of the time I consider it a success when all of my students make it through the day without any tears or temper tantrums.

Thankfully, it's Friday, which means I have two full days to spend with my *own* little munchkin. Dex volunteered to pick Sadie up from daycare today and stay with her while I was enduring parent meetings, so I know she's been in good hands. Those two have a special relationship, which I love, and in a lot of ways it seems as though Dex is more comfortable with Sadie than he is with anyone else. Perhaps it's because he can let his guard down around her. Children accept people for who they are, with no added expectations or complications. I suppose that's what Dex needs right now.

I notice Nate's car parked next to Dex's, which means that Sadie is having a blast with the two of them. She has those boys wrapped around her little finger, and she loves every second of it. She may be only four years old, but she's already learned how to use her cuteness for extortion purposes. Dex and Nate are absolute suckers when it comes to her.

I find them all in the backyard, Nate and Dex pushing Sadie on the swing as she giggles hysterically. Dex gives her another big push while Nate chases her back and forth, causing her to squeal happily every time he gets within reach.

When she notices me approach she smiles widely. "Hi, Mommy!"

"Hi, baby girl. Are you having fun?"

Dex grabs a hold of her mid-swing and helps her to the ground. She runs right over to me and jumps into my arms. "Yeah! Dee and Nate push me soooo high! And they took me to get ice cream!"

"Wow, lucky girl!" Lowering her back to the ground, I gesture to the boys. "Now, go thank Nate and Uncle Dee for taking such good care of you today."

She scampers over to them, throwing her arms around Dex, and then Nate. "Thank you, Dee and Nate."

"Anytime, Sadie girl," Dex says with a smile, rumpling her blonde hair. "We'll see you soon, okay?"

Sadie nods before running over to her sandbox, clearly bored with this part of the play date.

"Thanks so much for watching her," I say to both of them, holding Nate's gaze a few seconds longer than I should. "Do you want to stay for dinner? I was planning to grill up some hamburgers, and there's going to be way more than we need for the two of us."

"Appreciate the offer, Ames," Dex says, "but me and Nate already have plans. There's a band at the Seaside tonight, so we're going to grab a bite there beforehand."

I do my best to hide my disappointment behind a forced smile and a casual shrug. "No problem. It is Friday night, after all. Of course you have plans."

"You should come with us," Nate says, sounding hopeful. "The band is pretty good, and if you want to do burgers here with Sadie, you could meet us there afterward."

"I wish I could," I say with a frown. "I don't have a sitter."

"Ask Mom and Dad," Dex suggests. "I'm sure they'd be happy to do it."

"I feel bad asking them on such short notice." My eyes shift to Nate, who smiles sadly. "Maybe next time?"

Nate nods. "Yeah, next time."

■　■　■

After talking myself into, and out of, going to the Seaside at least a dozen times throughout dinner and Sadie's bath time, I finally make the selfish decision to call my mom and beg her to come pick up Sadie for the night. She's happy to do it and even commends me for taking a night to enjoy myself and have a little fun. I still feel guilty, but for the first time, the guilt doesn't outweigh my desire to go. It was painful to watch Nate and Dex walk off, knowing that they were heading out to have a good time while I spent another night at home alone. It's different when Sadie's awake to talk to and keep me company, but she goes to bed early and the rest of the night I'm all by myself. It's lonely.

Plus, I could have sworn that Nate looked disappointed when I turned down their invitation. He seemed almost irritated that I wasn't making more of an effort to meet up with them. Had I imagined that? Was I seeing what I *wanted* to see?

That's what I need to find out. If there's a chance that Nate wants me there as badly as I want to be there, then my foolish heart wants to know. He either shares my feelings, or he doesn't, but I'm sick of wondering. Tonight, I want the truth.

I rarely spend time on my appearance—because I rarely *have* time—but tonight is different. I do my hair and makeup to perfection, and even put on a slinky black dress with some high-heeled pumps.

Nate definitely won't mistake me for "one of the guys" tonight.

I pause outside the entrance to the bar, taking a deep breath as I prepare myself to go in there and get the answers I came for. After tonight I'll finally be able to determine if Nate and I have any kind of future, or if it's time to finally close the book on us. I can hear the band's music pumping through the air, and I can't keep the smile off my face as I pull the door open and step inside.

I'm in the bar for less than thirty seconds when I get my answer.

My heart sinks to the floor, any trace of a smile quickly fading. All I can do is stare.

Nate is leaning against the bar, grinning at the woman beside him. Her back is to me, so I can't see her face, but I can see his. And he looks… happy. Every ounce of his attention is focused on her, as though no one else around him matters.

She casually rests a hand on his chest, and he bends down to whisper something in her ear, causing her to giggle and throw her head back. Tears prick at my eyes, threatening spill over, but I'm frozen in place.

How could I possibly be so stupid? To think that Nate would be pining away, wishing for me to be here with him. What a stupid, naïve thought! He doesn't care that I'm not here. He's not thinking of me. He was never *upset* that I wasn't coming. The only reason he invited me in the first place is because he felt sorry for me. What I thought was disappointment on his face was nothing more than pity. Once again, I've managed to completely misinterpret him, seeing what I *want* to see, and conjuring up feelings that don't really exist.

At least now I have my answer.

When the woman grabs his hand and starts to pull him in my direction, I finally manage to lift my feet off the ground. The last thing I see as I slink out the door is their arms wrapping around each other on the dance floor.

My eyes continuously dart to the bar entrance, waiting to see Amy walk through the door to meet us. Despite the fact that she insisted she couldn't come, I can't stop myself from hoping that she'll change her mind and show up anyway. She had to have seen how badly I want her here tonight; my eyes were practically begging her to say yes. Doesn't she realize how much I crave her presence? How often I insert myself into her life merely for the chance to be around her?

I've always believed us to be on the same page, feeling the same things. The attraction between us is palpable—crackling and burning in the air whenever we're in the same room—but what we have goes so much deeper than that. There's a pull between us, a cord fastened from her heart to mine that perpetually connects us. It tugs and strains to draw us closer, stretched tight as we both struggle at each end to resist its force. We've ignored it and fought against it because the timing wasn't right. But it never went away, and I've always thought— or hoped—that Amy was right there with me, waiting for the moment when we can stop running away from each other and finally run toward each other. Let the cord snap us into place where we belong.

Now there's a part of me that wonders if Amy no longer feels that connection between us. She's never accepted an offer to come out with us, despite the fact that I always make it a point to invite her. Obviously her obligations as a mother come first, so I understand that it's not easy for her to leave Sadie or make arrangements for someone else to watch her, but could there be more to it than that? Have I misread her completely?

The thought is only in my head for a split second when I see a familiar woman standing near the entrance of the bar. It's fairly crowded, and her back is to me, but she has the same slender build and long dark hair. It has to be Amy.

My heart begins to race as I watch her from the opposite side of the bar, eagerly waiting for her to turn around and find me. I move toward her, grinning widely, and when I'm within a few feet of her, she finally spins around and latches her eyes on mine.

She looks at me with confusion, but a smile quickly appears as she says, "Um, hi."

I stare at her face blankly without speaking. She tilts her head questioningly when I don't respond, and finally I blink. "I'm sorry, hey," I mumble quickly. "I thought you were somebody else."

She has the same dark brown hair and slim figure that Amy does, but instead of whisky-colored hazel eyes, her eyes are brown, and she wears heavy makeup to accentuate her features. She doesn't have the same natural beauty as Amy, who can make jaws drop without a speck of makeup on, but she's still pretty.

With a cautious smile she asks, "Can I assume you're waiting for someone, then?"

Am I waiting for someone? Or am I just wasting my time?

I'm not even sure if there's a place for me in Amy's life. What do I have to offer her? She's probably looking for someone stable and reliable who has his shit together, and can provide for her. Someone who can give her the life that she deserves. Maybe I'm not that guy for her.

Maybe it's time for me to move on.

I want someone special to share my life with. Someone who I can bring flowers every Friday for no reason other than to see her smile. I believed that Amy was that person, but what if I'm wrong? She's clearly not interested in spending time with me, or else it would have been *her* walking through the door to meet me instead of someone else. There's an attractive woman right in front of me, who's clearly interested in me, so why shouldn't I take a chance with her?

"Nope, not meeting anyone," I say with a lazy grin, stepping toward her.

"Good," she smiles, extending her hand to me. "I'm Kelly."

"Nate." I shake her hand, bending forward to speak in her ear so she can hear me over the music. "Can I buy you a drink, Kelly?"

Her breath quickens at my nearness and a soft giggle escapes her lips. "I'd love that."

We stand at the bar and start chatting as we sip our drinks. I find out that she recently moved here from Florida and is living in an apartment in downtown Charleston. She's working at a clothing store while she figures out what she wants to do with her life.

The band starts playing a song that I recognize from the radio, and Kelly lets out a squeal as she grabs my hand. "I love this song. Come dance with me!" She starts pulling me toward the dance floor, and I obediently follow behind.

I instinctively glance toward the entrance of the bar as we pass, catching a glimpse of another Amy look-a-like turning to leave. Shaking the image out of my head, I focus my attention on Kelly as she tugs me onto the dance floor and winds her arms around my neck.

Time for me to stop chasing the past.

■ ■ ■

"Are you sure about this whole thing?" I ask Dex, eyeing the dark building suspiciously.

He climbs out of the car behind me, slamming the door. "Yeah, it's totally legit. I asked around, and one of my Marine buddies told me he's heard about it. We're good."

After the fighting incident at the bar, the manager gave Dex a piece of paper with a phone number on it for a man named Reece. As it turns out, Reece is a former Marine who now coordinates some kind of underground fight club for off-duty and retired military as a way for them to let off steam while adjusting to civilian life. It's a controlled environment where they can set up fights without having to worry about getting into trouble, and since all the fighters volunteer, there's no risk of innocent bystanders getting hurt. The whole thing is incredibly secretive and strictly invite-only. I'm not even sure if I'm supposed to be here, seeing as I'm not military, but Dex assured me that it's okay as long as I'm with him.

I still don't know how I feel about all of it. Granted, I'm the one who told Dex he needed to find a more suitable outlet for his anger, but it seems so… dark. However, I have no right to make judgments. I have no idea what it's like to go from a war-zone where I'm fighting for my survival to suddenly being back in ordinary life. I've never experienced the fear and adrenaline that goes along with being a soldier, so I don't understand how it feels to have that taken away. All I do know is that if Dex needs this, then I'll be here. I'm not going to let him do this alone.

"Okay then, let's do it," I respond. We venture toward the heavy warehouse door and pause in front of it. "Did you tell anyone else about this, or should I start working on an elaborate story to explain why your face looks like Rocky Balboa after nine rounds with Apollo Creed?"

"Nope, this is our little secret." His mouth twists into a smug grin. "So, I'll just have to knock them out before they can touch me."

Chuckling, I shake my head. "There's the cocky bastard I know and love." I reach for the cold metal handle and pull open the door. A dark, desolate industrial space looms in front of us. Huge steel beams are covered with colorful graffiti, and debris is littered across the concrete floor. Moonlight pours in through the broken panes of the small windows along the top of the outside wall, letting in enough light for me to make out a figure standing in front of another door on the opposite side.

Dex lets out a long breath. "Here we go."

chapter fourteen

Amy

I don't see much of Nate over the next couple of weeks. I try to tell myself that it's merely by chance and I'm not intentionally avoiding him, but I know it's a lie. Ever since I saw him at the bar with that woman, the idea of being around him churns my stomach. The sting of rejection is fresh, and I don't know how I'm supposed to act normal with him. He's always been able to take one look at me and really *see* me. I'm worried that it will be written all over my face, giving me away. With one glance, he'll read the unmistakable pain and longing inscribed in my eyes when I look at him.

It doesn't help to know that he's actually *dating* her. The few times I expected him to come around with Dex, I let my curiosity get the best of me, and Dex explained that Nate was out with the new girl he's seeing.

I felt the cut of those words like a sharp knife in my gut.

I managed to plaster on a smile and act like I was happy for him.

Until Dex plunged the knife in deeper by saying, *"Yeah, I'm just glad he's finally getting laid!"*

I had to excuse myself after that one.

As awful as it was to hear about Nate's new relationship, it gave me the push I needed to start moving on. My personal life for the last four years has been basically non-existent, and I decided that it's time for me to explore the dating world again and see what else is out there.

So, I agree to a blind date. It's the younger brother of another teacher at my school, and she's been trying to get us together since I first started working there, saying how amazing David is, and what a perfect match we would be.

David brings me to a trendy restaurant in downtown Charleston that I've always wanted to visit, but never had the chance. It's the first time in years that I've dined at an establishment that doesn't hand out crayons and paper placemats at the beginning of the meal, and I'm not sure how to act.

"You're even more beautiful than my sister described," he says once we're seated. "I'm glad we finally had a chance to meet."

My cheeks flush at his compliment, and I offer him a small smile. "Thank you. I'm glad, too."

And I am. David is handsome in a very clean-cut kind of way, with perfectly combed brown hair and deep blue eyes. He wears an impeccably tailored suit, but leaves his shirt collar unbuttoned and doesn't wear a tie, giving him a casual yet stylish look. He's polite, confident and charming without being arrogant, and doesn't seem put off by how nervous I am.

I'm grateful when he orders a bottle of wine, and by my second glass I already feel more at ease with him. We talk about our jobs, and he tells me about what he does as a real estate developer. He smiles warmly across the table while I talk about my group of kindergarteners, listening intently even when I ramble on a bit.

"I'm sorry, you don't want to hear all this," I murmur, dipping my chin down and tucking my hair behind my ear.

David reaches for my hand, giving it a reassuring squeeze. "Of course I do. I want to hear all about you," he says, leaning closer. "I think it's sweet how much you care for those kids. They're lucky to have you."

I'm surprised by how comfortable he makes me feel, like I can be myself without constantly worrying about saying the wrong thing. His eyes shine with obvious interest when he looks at me, and I enjoy knowing that I'm the cause of it. After spending so much time trying to interpret Nate's feelings, sorting through the haze of ambiguity, it's nice to be in a situation where I don't have to question it. He's here with me because he *wants* to be.

"Tell me about your life outside of work," he asks, focusing his gaze on me as he rests his elbow on the tabletop. "What do you do for fun?"

"Um, I guess I haven't really had all that much time for fun." I admit with a shrug. Normally I wouldn't mention my status as a mom on a first date, but I'm assuming that his sister already filled him in. Besides, David seems so open and understanding, that it makes me want to be honest with him. "My daughter, Sadie, is four years old. She's wonderful, but I don't get a whole lot of time to myself."

I focus on his hand, still resting on top of mine, but when he remains quiet after several seconds, I glance up at him. He gapes back at me with wide eyes, unmoving, and my stomach sinks. I sense what's coming before it happens.

David blinks once, twice, and then clears his throat. "Gosh, I'm sorry, I totally spaced out on you. I just remembered that I left the iron on in my apartment, and I have this horrible vision of the whole place going up in flames."

His hand slips away from mine as he reaches into his back pocket to pull out his wallet. "I feel awful, but I need to get home. This should cover the meal, so feel free to stay and enjoy it." He throws a couple of hundred dollar bills on the table. Standing, he offers a deep sigh, his expression conflicted. "It really was nice to meet you, Amy. I'm sorry."

I nod without glancing up. I don't bother saying a word or wasting my breath trying to convince him to stay. Instead I stare down at the napkin in my lap, cursing myself for my own stupidity.

I can't regret telling him about Sadie, because it wouldn't matter if I'd told him now or waited until our fifth date. His opinion isn't going to change over the course of a few dates, and it's better to know now, before I've wasted more time and become emotionally invested. I feel like an idiot because I actually convinced myself that he might be different. I thought he could be someone who would accept the fact that I'm a mother, without sprinting from the restaurant in terror. I completely misjudged him, and it's discouraging to realize that I could be so wrong about someone.

How am I supposed to meet anyone when I'm totally naïve about all of this?

I slowly rise from my chair, wanting nothing more than to get the hell out of this restaurant without drawing attention to myself. I've almost made it to the door when a voice stops me in my tracks.

"Amy?"

Cringing, I spin around to see Nate—and *her*—sitting across from each other at a cozy table against the wall next the door I'm trying to escape through.

"Uh, hi," I mumble, blushing furiously. A fresh knot twists in my stomach as I take in the sight of the two of them together.

"Were you here for dinner?" Nate asks, scanning the restaurant for any sign of my dinner companion.

"Excuse me, miss!" my waitress calls out to me as she approaches. "I saw your friend leave. Is he planning on coming back, or should I wrap your food up for you?"

My cheeks flame and I feel my throat tighten. Shaking my head I respond, "No, he's not. No need to wrap it up, though. I'm on my way out."

She nods, her eyes full of pity as she turns away.

"He?" Nate questions, raising his eyebrows. "Who are you here with?"

"Well, no one anymore." I've never been so humiliated in my life, but it can't possibly get any worse at this point. "I was here on a date, and I made the mistake of telling him that I have a daughter, and well..." I shrug. "He couldn't get out of here fast enough."

"Oh, honey, that's just awful!" Nate's girlfriend exclaims, reaching her hand across the table to grab his.

I don't miss the possessive gesture. She may feel sorry for me, but she also wants me to know that Nate is with her.

"He just fucking left you?" Nate grumbles through gritted teeth.

I shift my eyes away from their joined hands, finding Nate's gaze locked on mine. His handsome face is tight, and those gorgeous green eyes are brimming with barely contained fury.

All of a sudden I feel like bursting into tears. About my failed date, my hopeless personal life, and most of all... Nate. It's agonizing to see him with someone else when being with him is all I've ever wanted since I was a teenager. Tears burn behind my eyes, and I know that any second the floodgates will open. I won't let them see me fall apart.

"I think my cab is here," I lie, struggling to keep it together for just a few seconds longer. "I better get going. Enjoy your evening."

I race for the door before they even have a chance to respond. I only make it to the end of the block before my first tears fall. Dipping down a quiet side street, I collapse against the wall of a building and slide to the ground as I sob into my hands, giving in to my misery.

Nate

I want to cringe when Kelly grabs my hand over the table, staking a claim on me in front of Amy. We've only been together for a few weeks, and the idea that she's already acting so possessive is irritating. It doesn't sit well with me. I have to fight the urge to pull away from her, especially when I see the forlorn look on Amy's face as she fixates on our hands. Unfortunately, Kelly's hand on top of mine is the only thing holding me in place at the moment. Otherwise I'd already be out the door in search of the lowlife who ran off on Amy.

I want to fucking kill him.

What kind of a man could leave this beautiful, amazing woman sitting alone in a restaurant? How dare he make her feel like any less than she is, all because she was open and honest with him about her life when most people wouldn't be?

Amy's eyes glisten with unshed tears before she spins toward the door and runs out of the restaurant. I automatically stand up to go after her.

"What do you think you're doing?" Kelly hisses, clenching my hand to hold me in place.

"She's obviously upset. I want to make sure she's okay." I forcefully wrench my hand away from hers. "I'll be right back."

"Nate!" she barks after me a low voice as I hurry to the exit.

Ignoring her, I fling the door open and step onto the sidewalk. I glance down the street in both directions, searching for any sign of Amy, and when she's nowhere to be seen, I start running. When I can't find her after several blocks, I turn around and go back the other way, searching for her face among the crowded downtown streets.

When it's clear that I'm not going to find her, I slip back inside the restaurant. Kelly is fuming as I return to my seat, despite the fact that I wasn't gone for more than five minutes.

She glares at me across the table, her lips pursed and her face stretched in a scowl. "Want to explain what *that* was all about?"

I stare back with raised eyebrows. "You tell me," I counter, no longer hiding my frustration. "First, you go out of your way to claim me and rub our relationship in her face, as if she's not feeling bad enough, and then you make a huge fuss when I try to check that she's okay. Amy is a good friend of mine, and I would think you might have a little more empathy for her."

"Friends?" Kelly snorts. "Yeah, right. Do you really expect me to believe that?"

At this point I don't care what she believes. I'm more worried about the possibility that she may have some kind of multiple personality disorder. Whatever side of her I'm seeing now, I don't like it.

"Listen, Nate," she breathes, flipping her brown hair over one shoulder. "I'm not trying to make a big deal of this, but I don't like the idea of you hanging around with a girl who *obviously* has a thing for you. You know?"

"Uh, no, actually. I don't." I frown, dragging a hand through my hair. "Amy's one of my oldest friends."

"But I'm your girlfriend."

I look at her. I mean *really* look at her.

Seeing her next to Amy has put our relationship under a microscope, making it impossible for me to continue to ignore all the signs that we don't fit. Kelly is a very pretty girl, but I can't deny that what initially attracted me to her was her resemblance to Amy. As we started talking, she made it clear that she was interested in me, and I enjoyed the attention she gave me. She was fun, flirty and affectionate, and I thought to myself, *"Why not give it a shot?"*

As I spent more time with her and got to know her better, I began to pick up on aspects of her personality that I didn't like so much. She could be shallow, vapid, and judgmental at times. The attentiveness that flattered me in the beginning grew to be irritating, and she became needy and clingy.

But despite it all, I've stayed with her. Not only because I like having someone in my life, but also because I hoped that I could find happiness with someone other than the one woman I haven't stopped thinking about since I was eighteen. A woman who makes me feel like no other but is surrounded by complications and doubt and may not share my feelings. I was so desperate to believe there was someone else out there for me that I've been forcing a relationship that isn't meant to be. When it's right, you shouldn't have to force it or pretend. It should come naturally and be the most real part of your life.

I thought that also meant it should be easy. Uncomplicated. Straightforward.

Those words have never applied to my relationship with Amy. There have always been obstacles between us and instead of clearing a path, I let them stand in the way while I searched for a different route or an easier way around them.

But nothing good comes easy. And easy isn't always good.

Of all the obstacles that have kept Amy and me apart—Dex, pregnancy, bad timing, and miscommunication—there's only one still standing in my way. Unfortunately, it's the biggest hurdle of them all, because if Amy doesn't feel the same way, then none of this even matters.

I can't force her feelings any more than I can force a relationship with Kelly. Or anyone. I don't know where Amy stands, but if I've realized anything over the past few weeks, it's that no one else can take her place.

And that terrifies me.

It wasn't fair of me to try using someone else as a replacement for Amy. Despite Kelly's faults, she's a decent person, and she's been good to me during the time we've been together. She didn't deserve to be led on by me, even if it was never intentional. There's only one person to blame here, and that's me.

Kelly looks at me expectantly, waiting for me to say or do something, but I don't know how to say what needs to be said.

"Well?" she prompts.

"I'm sorry," I say, shaking my head. Her lips curve into a pleased smile, assuming that I'm giving in to her demands, but it quickly fades away when I continue. "This isn't going to work, Kelly. You're great, and we've had a lot of fun together, but I think we rushed into this."

"You're *kidding* me, right?" Her mouth falls open and she stares at me with wide eyes.

"I'm really sorry." I feel awful for telling her this over what was supposed to be a nice dinner. I wish I could have done it privately, but with the way the conversation was going, I knew it couldn't wait.

The awkward moment is interrupted by the appearance of our

waiter, who arrives at the table with the food we ordered before all of this shit happened.

"Can I get you anything else?" he says, oblivious to the uncomfortable situation he just walked into.

Clearing my throat, I glance up with a tense smile. "Just the check, please. Thank you."

After he walks away, I wait for Kelly to start yelling at me or storm off, but she calmly picks up her fork and starts eating her salad.

"Should we, uh, get the food wrapped up so I can take you home?" I ask, puzzled by the idea that she would want to eat a meal together after breaking up.

Kelly waves me off, shaking her head. "This is so silly, Nate. Let's just calm down and talk about this later. No need to make any rash decisions, okay?"

I want to tell her that this isn't a rash decision, and there's nothing left to talk about, but I'm too stunned to respond. She went from seething with anger one minute to suddenly acting like nothing happened. I don't know how to make it clear that we're over without being rude.

"Look, Kelly, I can't do this with you anymore. I'm sorry. We can talk about it if you want, but I'm not going to change my mind."

Ignoring me completely, she squeals, "Oh my god, this dressing is *amazing!*"

I let out a heavy sigh, sagging against my chair in defeat.

This is going to be harder than I thought.

chapter fifteen

Amy

I devote the rest of the weekend to Sadie, doing my best to keep from dwelling on my disastrous date with David. Every time I think about what happened, I get the same heart-sinking, gut wrenching feeling that I did in that moment.

As upsetting as it was for David to run out on me, the most painful and humiliating part of it was seeing Nate and his girlfriend together. That was the real torture. There's a part of me that desperately wants to meet someone else, just so I can finally move on, but after what happened with David, I know it will be a long time before I have the courage to date again.

I'm dreading the moment when I have to see David's sister at school and discuss what happened. I'm sure she had no idea that her brother would be such an inconsiderate jerk, but I don't want to hear her make excuses for him, or attempt to rationalize his behavior. Frankly, I'd prefer to never mention it ever again. The whole night was a complete failure, and all I want to do is forget about it.

Thankfully, it's spring vacation, so I have the entire week off from teaching and don't have to face her right away.

Toward the middle of the week, I'm eating breakfast with Sadie when I get a call from a woman who's interested in renting the first floor apartment of the house. I've been advertising it for months, but until now the only inquiries I've gotten are from single men, and I'm much more comfortable with the idea of having a woman in there. Dex also made it clear that a woman is the *only* option. I don't bother to argue with him because I know he's right. It would be nice to finally have someone living there, though, so I really hope it works out with her.

It's almost noon when I see a beat up old sedan pull into the driveway. I carry Sadie with me down the outside steps as we go to greet her.

"Hi, you must be Olivia!" I extend my free hand out to shake hers. "I'm Amy, and this is my daughter, Sadie."

"It's so nice to meet you," she says with a shy smile. "Thank you so much for seeing me on such short notice."

Olivia appears to be about the same age as me, with a perfect figure, long blonde hair and blue eyes. She's absolutely stunning, but also looks thoroughly exhausted. Based on her rumpled clothing and the dark circles under her eyes, I'm guessing that she drove all last night, maybe even longer. I can't help but wonder what brought her here.

"It's no problem at all," I tell her, lowering Sadie to the ground so she can play in the yard. "We live in the upstairs apartment, so we're here anyway. You're the first person to inquire who isn't a creepy middle-aged man. It's just the two of us, so I really wanted it to be a woman downstairs. Ready to take a look around?"

Olivia nods, and I lead her over to the front door of the

downstairs apartment. I quickly bend down to pick up some of Sadie's toys that are strewn across the walkway, glancing up at Olivia apologetically. "Sorry about the mess. She's usually better about picking up after herself. I promise that she won't be in your way if you move in."

"I don't mind at all. Really." She glances toward Sadie, watching her as she plays off to the side. "She's adorable. How old is she?"

"She just turned four," I answer, relieved to know that Olivia isn't put off by the idea of a little kid running around all the time. Reaching into my back pocket for the key, I unlock the door and let Olivia inside.

Her eyes light up as she looks around the apartment, which I take to be a good sign. Aside from a little dust in the corners, it's in great condition. The furniture is practically new, and we had the whole place repainted a few months ago. It's not huge, but it's bright and open with sliding glass doors that look out to the water of the inlet. If she doesn't mind hearing the pitter-patter of Sadie's busy feet coming from above, then this could be the perfect place for someone like her.

After giving her all the necessary information, I let her explore the apartment on her own for a few minutes. When she comes back, I glance nervously in her direction, clutching my hands together in front of me. "So, what do you think?"

"It's perfect," she declares, smiling widely. "Is there an application I can fill out, or...?"

"That won't be necessary," I quickly respond. "It's yours if you want it, and you can move in as soon as you'd like."

"Really?" Her shoulders sag slightly, as though a weight has been lifted from them, and her face softens with obvious relief. "Are you sure?"

"I'm sure." I nod. I'll likely get a lecture from Dex if he ever finds out that I let someone move in without getting a lifetime's worth of background information beforehand, but I don't really care. I have a good feeling about Olivia. I heard such desperation in her voice when we spoke on the phone this morning, and when she first walked in here, she looked at it almost as though it was her salvation. I get the sense that, for whatever reason, she *needs* this and that she's someone who hasn't had it easy in life. I want to help her. I also want to get to know her better. Since Savannah moved to California after graduating from college, I've been seriously lacking in the friend department. I hope that maybe, eventually, Olivia and I could be friends.

"Sadie, this is Olivia," I announce as she tugs impatiently on my shorts. "She's going to be living here, too."

Sadie peeks up at her. "Hi, Oleeva."

We both laugh at her four-year-old pronunciation and Olivia bends down next to her. "Hi, Sadie. It's nice to meet you."

Sadie quickly becomes infatuated with our new neighbor, asking her all sorts of questions while I grab the lease from upstairs for Olivia to sign. She eagerly hands me a check for this month's rent and the security deposit, and then I hand over the key.

Olivia doesn't have much stuff with her, and when I ask her if she's having more sent later on, she says no. I don't pry. Instead, I help her unload what little she does have from the car. I'm anxious to get to know her and spend time with her, but I can see how tired she is. She probably wants to be alone while she gets her bearings. As I exit the apartment, I tell her to come by for a glass of wine once she gets settled in, which she happily agrees to.

Nate

I'm in the shop earlier than usual, replacing some parts in my old Ford Mustang. It's been sitting idle ever since I found and restored the vintage Camaro I drive now, but I couldn't bear to sell it. It's the first car I restored, and it's a classic. I'm hoping that someday I'll be able to pass it on to my kids.

I hear the side door of the garage swing open as Dex arrives for work. He's always here first thing in the morning, usually before anyone else, and I suspect that he's having difficulty sleeping. I know it's a common side effect of PTSD, which Dex is likely suffering from. Not that he ever talks about it, but after all he's been through, it wouldn't surprise me. He seems to appreciate having the quiet time in the morning to focus on work, so I just let him do his thing.

"Hey, man. Don't you ever sleep?" he calls out to me.

"I'm avoiding the house," I explain, rolling out from under the car. "I ended it with that girl Kelly I was seeing, and now she won't leave me alone."

She's been calling and texting me nonstop all week, despite the fact that I made it clear we're over. When I stopped responding to her yesterday, she showed up at my house to "make sure that I was okay," and claimed that she was only trying to be friends. I reiterated to her once again that our relationship—friendship and otherwise—is over, which made her storm off angrily. I haven't heard from her since, but I'm not taking any chances. I figure I'll hide out at work for the day until I'm certain she got the message once and for all.

Dex raises his eyebrows questioningly. "What are you, scared of this girl? Tell her to get lost."

I wish it were that simple. "She's a little… unpredictable. I figured I'd give her some time to cool off."

"You mean bat-shit crazy," he concludes. "I'm surprised you stayed with her as long as you did. Although, the crazy ones are usually pretty wild in bed, so I get it."

"You're such a dog," I chuckle, shaking my head. "Kelly and I didn't click, that's all. I was trying to force something that wasn't there."

Because I'm completely hung up on your sister.

"Whatever, I'm just glad you're single again," he says. "I've been stuck without a wingman for over a month while you experimented with a relationship. It's seriously affecting my game. Last weekend, I had a hot chick on the hook, all ready to go, but she wouldn't leave the bar without her damn friend."

"So you had to go home all alone, eh?"

"Hell no, I took them both home." He grins devilishly. "Turned out to be a pretty great night, actually, but you're missing the point."

I laugh. "Oh, you poor thing… and I'm supposed to feel sorry for you, why?"

"Dude, it's not easy handling two girls at the same time. It's twice as much ground to cover! Do the math… it's a lot of work. I've only got two hands, and although my dick is incredibly efficient, I still only have one."

"Yeah, until it falls off." I cringe. It's too early in the morning to be discussing another man's junk. "Considering all those dirty skanks you go home with, I'm surprised it hasn't shriveled up and died already."

"Are you kidding?" he says, pulling on his coveralls and zipping them up. "I love my dick way too much to let that happen. I'm always careful. In fact, careful is my middle name. I'm clean as a whistle over here, don't you worry."

I pour myself a cup of coffee from the fresh pot in the workbench. The machine is ancient and covered in a thin layer of dust, but it still brews a decent cup.

"Okay, but I still think you need to get yourself a girlfriend," I say to Dex. "Not one of those dumb bar sluts that you seem to love so much, but a nice girl you can actually have a conversation with."

"Thanks, but no thanks," he responds with a frown. "I'm not built for monogamy. Why be with one woman when you could be with lots of different woman... sometimes at the same time? Relationships are nothing but a headache."

"Okay, Dex," I chuckle to myself. "But one of these days, you're going to eat your words."

Although Dex may be playing the field—quite extensively—right now, it's not who he really is. Deep down, beneath the cocky, insensitive player, is a guy who is devoted and determined. It's the way he was with the Marines, and the way he is with his family. There's no doubt in my mind that when he meets the right person, nothing in the world will get in the way or stop him from fighting for her.

Maybe it's time for me to start acting more like him.

chapter sixteen

Amy

After leaving Sadie with Dex while I go to the grocery store, I come back to find him standing with Olivia in the driveway, waiting for me.

"What's going on?" I ask, climbing out of the driver's seat.

"Olivia's car won't start," Dex explains, motioning to her old Honda. "I'm going to give her a lift to work at the restaurant and then stop by the shop to pick up the parts I need to get it running. I'll be back for dinner, though."

I glance curiously between them, wondering when they got so familiar with each other. Olivia's working two jobs and is barely around, so I haven't had a chance to introduce them yet. Apparently, I won't have to.

"I don't want to interrupt your plans," Olivia says. "I don't mind walking. It's not far to the Seaside, and I already called to inform the other waitresses I'm running late."

"Don't be silly," I assure her. "Dex is here all the time, scrounging for meals. He's useless in the kitchen, though, so you'll be doing me a favor if you get him out my hair." I turn to Dex. "Get the girl to work, would you?"

"Yes, ma'am," he laughs, opening the passenger side door of his truck so that Olivia can climb in. Once he's in the driver's seat, he rolls down the window and calls out to me, "See you soon, sis! Don't act like you don't love having me around."

He knows that I do. Especially when he's being the goofy, loveable brother who I absolutely adore. I've been seeing that side much more often lately. I know he's still working through his issues—mainly by sleeping with a lot of woman and fighting—but I have faith that he'll get past it. I only hope that he won't add my new neighbor to his list of conquests.

He seems different with her, though. I haven't seen him interact with many women, but I can sense that he's intrigued by her. Not that I blame him. I've hung out with Olivia a few times since she moved in downstairs, and there's definitely something special about her. She's smart and strong, but also caring and compassionate. Way too good for a casual hookup.

Exactly the kind of woman that my brother needs.

My mind is still thinking up ways to get the two of them around each other again, when I hear Dex's truck pull up in front of the house. He unloads numerous boxes of car parts from the back, and I smile, knowing that he's going to do a lot more than just get Olivia's car running again.

A little while later, once the lasagna is in the oven and Sadie is on the couch watching a show, I bring a beer out to him. "Got a little crush on my new neighbor, Dex?" I tease him playfully, handing him the cold bottle.

"Yeah, right." He smirks, lifting the bottle to his lips and taking a long pull. "You know I don't do the girlfriend thing. I'm just trying to be a Good Samaritan over here."

"I wouldn't blame you if you were interested in her. She seems really great, and in case you haven't noticed, she's drop dead gorgeous."

He shrugs, feigning disinterest. "She doesn't seem like the one night stand type, and that's all I'm good for."

"That's a load of crap, and you know it." It breaks my heart that my brother thinks of himself that way, that he can't see what everyone else sees in him. "I wish you would let other people in, Dex. It's impossible not to love you when you do. You don't need to isolate yourself so much. You deserve to be happy."

He goes back to working on Olivia's car, giving me no indication that he's even listening to what I'm saying. I let out a frustrated breath. I can't force him to see himself differently, no matter how much I want to. He's going to have to learn to forgive himself all on his own.

"I already have a reason to be happy," Dex says, glancing up from Olivia's engine.

I tilt my head and look at him with narrowed eyes. "And what reason is that?"

He rests his hip against the hood of the car, a pleased smile forming on his lips. "Now that Nate's single again, I finally have my wingman back. Together we'll be able to pick up twice as many girls."

Nate and his girlfriend broke up? When did that happen?

My heart pounds in my chest. I want to ask Dex to give me the details, but I stop myself. This doesn't change anything. It's not as though Nate pursued me before they got together, and he certainly didn't come running to me when they broke up. *She* isn't the reason that nothing is happening between us.

Any excitement I felt is fleeting. However, when I process the rest of what Dex said, dread quickly fills its place. The prospect of Dex and Nate picking up girls together is more than I can stomach. It's bad enough that Dex has turned into a womanizing man-whore, but I won't allow him to transform Nate into one as well.

It makes me more determined than ever to try and drive Dex and Olivia together.

■　■　■

By the time the weekend arrives, the temperature in Charleston has climbed to new heights. It's not even summer yet, but the sun burns down from the blue sky above, invading the air with blazing heat. The only sane place to be is at the beach.

I pack a bag with sandwiches and snacks, loading it into the car along with Sadie's beach toys and our huge umbrella. Sadie runs around in the yard in her bathing suit, already wearing her bright yellow water wings. "Almost ready to go, baby girl?"

"Yup!" she shrieks, practically jumping with excitement.

Olivia pulls up in her car—which is now running great, thanks to Dex—and steps out wearing the uniform from her second job at the aquarium.

"Hey!" I call out to her. "I was hoping you'd be back before we left. We're heading to the beach. Want to join us?"

She looks tired, but her eyes light up at the mention of the beach. "I'd love to! I'll go change. Just give me ten minutes."

"Take your time," I tell her, pleased that she decided to join us. It will be nice to have someone there to talk to while Nate and Dex do their guy thing, which is likely to hit on every female within a mile-wide radius. Although I still hold out hope that there's something between Dex and Liv.

There's no sign of the boys as we settle into our spot on the beach. Olivia doesn't waste any time before jumping into the ocean, while I set up the umbrella and lather Sadie with sunscreen so she doesn't get burned.

Nate and Dex arrive, huge cooler in hand, just as Olivia steps out of the water. Dex's eyes are glued to her as she makes her way over to us, his mouth falling open as he examines her skimpy bikini. Olivia hesitates when she sees him standing there, and I feel guilty that I didn't let her know that he was joining us.

After introducing Olivia to Nate, I leave her standing with Dex while Nate and I begin unpacking the food. I've barely seen him since my humiliating date, and things are a little tense between us.

"So, Olivia and Dex," I mention casually, gesturing to where they stand nearby. "What do you think?"

"Are you playing matchmaker?" His eyes twinkle conspiratorially, making my pulse flutter.

"Maybe just a little bit." I smile. "She's really great, and I want to see my brother happy."

"Yeah, me too." He leans forward with a wink. "Maybe I can help you."

My smile widens. It feels good to have Nate as my partner in crime. Our friendship used to be easy and effortless, but lately the air between us has been riddled with things left unspoken. I've missed being able to talk to him without the constant undercurrent of tension. It's a relief to know that even if nothing happens between us romantically, there's still hope for us to remain friends. Because as much as I'll hate losing him to some other woman someday, it would be even worse to lose him altogether.

Nate

Amy hasn't brought up what happened the other night at the restaurant. As much as I want to ask her how she's doing and make sure that she's okay, I get the sense that she doesn't want to talk about it. I'm not sure if she knows that I ended it with Kelly. I definitely *want* her to know, but it's not the kind of thing I can blurt out randomly.

There seems to be an awful lot of things that I *can't* discuss with her, and I hate that. I'm so desperate to talk with her—about anything—that when she mentions trying to get Dex and Olivia together, I jump at the opportunity. I have no clue whether or not there's actually anything between them, but I love that she cares so much about her brother. There's also a small part of me thinking that if Dex were to find happiness with someone, then maybe, just *maybe*, he'd be more open to the idea of Amy and me together.

I wonder if Amy's thinking that, too.

I've told myself over and over again to let her go, but I can't do it. She's all I've been able to think about. No matter how much I try to convince myself that we're not meant to be, I'll never believe it. I can't let her go. Not yet. Not until she looks me in the eye and tells me that she doesn't feel what I feel.

I'm finally prepared to fight for her.

I'll make Dex understand. I realize that he needs me right now, but I can be there for both of them. It doesn't have to be a choice between one or the other.

My gaze continues slipping toward Amy, watching as she dives gracefully into the small waves and disappears beneath the ocean's surface. When she emerges a moment later, she smoothes her hands over her hair, slicking back the long, wet tresses. Everything else blurs out of focus. Beads of salt water glisten on her bare skin, sliding down her body as she steps onto the sandy beach. My eyes follow the gentle sway of her hips as she walks, mesmerized by the innate sexiness that radiates from her every move. She doesn't even realize it. She has no idea the effect she has. It's just *her*.

She lights me up. She awakens my senses and stirs a carnal desire inside me like nothing ever has before. I feel myself harden just from watching her. All I can think about is peeling that tiny bikini off her body and running my hands over the swell of her hips. I want to feel the weight of her full breast in my hand as I cover it with my mouth and suck on her pert nipple. I can picture the look of pure lust on her face when I sink deep inside her.

"Nate, you stink at this." Sadie's tiny voice instantly breaks me out of my fantasy.

Dex and I are supposed to be helping her build a sandcastle. While I was busy visualizing all the naughty things I want to do with her mom, my section completely collapsed.

"Are you firing me, Sadie girl?" I ask with an exaggerated pout, pretending to be deeply offended.

She smiles sweetly. "You can still watch if you want. Just sit over there." She points her tiny finger to a spot a few feet away.

I do as I'm told, glancing at Dex as I move off to the side. "She's ruthless."

"No kidding," he says with a laugh, putting the finishing touches on his castle. "You don't want to mess with this one."

"More seashells!" Sadie barks out orders to Dex. "And a moat!"

I chuckle to myself. I love watching Sadie boss Dex around. Not that I can talk, because I'm just as willing to do anything she tells me. When someone is that adorable, how could you not?

"Okay, boss," he tells Sadie. "Why don't you go find some seashells, and I'll work on the moat?"

"Mmmkay!" She hops up, grabbing her bucket to collect more shells in.

I keep an eye on her as she moves closer to the shoreline, crouching down to sift through the sand. Each time she finds a shell, she holds it up, furrowing her eyebrows as she examines it closely. I love watching the way she goes about every task, taking it so seriously, as though it's the most important thing in the world. She's curious about everything around her, finding beauty and fascination in things that others see as ordinary.

"Cute sandcastle."

I glance up and see two girls standing over us. They're young— probably eighteen or nineteen—with huge sunglasses, fake tans, and bathing suits that leave nothing to the imagination.

Dex barely acknowledges their presence. "Thanks."

"Looks like you're really good with your hands," she continues, smirking at her friend and clearly not getting the hint. "Maybe we could… help you out somehow?"

I shake my head, fighting back a grin as I watch them shamelessly seek out our attention. It blows my mind that they can act so brazen. I normally find confidence to be attractive, but this is just desperate.

"We're all set," Dex retorts, his voice cold and dismissive.

His reaction comes as a surprise to me. Lately, these are exactly the type of girls that Dex is drawn to: easy and cheap. I was sure that he would be all over these two, but he's not showing them the slightest bit of attention. Perhaps Amy's right about him being interested in Olivia.

Once they're gone I turn to him. "Wow, Dex, I think that's the first time I've ever seen you turn down a willing female."

"Way too easy," he clarifies. "This place is flooded with easy college chicks looking for a good time. They'll give it up to anyone with a six-pack."

He's right about that. I don't pay much attention to those kinds of girls. Or *any* girls, really. Except Amy. My eyes automatically drift over to where she's sitting, and when I see that she's not alone, I frown. "It's not just the girls."

Amy and Olivia are no longer alone. A couple of guys are standing next to their beach chairs, trying to chat them up. They look like typical dumb college frat boys, strutting around the beach with their shirts off and acting as though they're God's gift to woman.

I despise them already.

"Who are those assholes?" Glancing over at Sadie, I quickly realize my mistake and stumble to correct myself. "Uh, I mean those *guys*."

I really have to stop swearing.

"I don't know. Who cares?" Dex shrugs, trying to act unconcerned, while at the same time staring at them with a hard, narrowed gaze.

"Sure you don't care. That's why you keep glancing that way with a murderous look in your eyes like you want to kick someone's ass." Half a second later I stammer, "Uh, I mean *butt*."

Dex just shakes his head. At this rate, I'm going to have Sadie cursing before she starts kindergarten.

"Why don't you ask Olivia out?" I ask, focusing on him rather than on how much these idiots are pissing me off.

"Because we're just friends," he says with irritation. "Amy's the one I'm worried about. She has a tendency to attract assholes."

That's the damn truth. First that useless prick Duncan, and then the idiot who ran off on her in the middle of the date. Neither of them were even close to being good enough for her.

As I continue watching these two random clowns trying to hit on Amy and Olivia, every cell in my body demands that I go over there and stop them. But that would require explaining to Dex why I have such a problem with it. Telling him that I can't stand the thought of anyone other than me with his sister would probably not go over too well.

I have to do something. I won't sit around and watch while some jackass tries to charm his way into her life. I've done too much of that already.

Standing up, I say to Dex, "I'm going to grab another beer. Want one?"

"Nah, I'm good."

As I stalk over to where they're standing, the guys quickly become aware of me. "You boys lost or something?" I snap, glaring at them flatly. "Move along now."

They both stiffen, scowling at me with their jaws clenched. At first I think they're going to try and say something to me, but instead they turn and walk away, muttering under their breath.

"I thought they were never going to leave!" Amy says with a laugh, flashing an appreciative smile my way. "Thanks, Nate."

Relief floods through me when she makes it clear that she *wasn't* interested in those meatheads. I was so focused on getting rid of them that I never gave much consideration to the possibility that Amy or Olivia might actually want them around.

"Any time," I grin back at her.

chapter seventeen

Amy

"What's the story with you and Nate?" Olivia asks once he's gone back over to Dex and Sadie. "Are you together or something?"

Boy, is that a complex question.

"No, there's nothing going on with Nate and me," I answer simply. That's the truth, when it comes down to it. Anything else is my unrealistic expectations. "He's just protective because I'm Dex's sister. I used to think that there might be something more between us, but then he was dating someone else, and nothing ever happened."

"Was?" she questions, raising her eyebrows. "So, they're not together anymore?"

"No, Dex mentioned they broke up a couple of weeks ago."

She looks at me hopefully. "Well, maybe now something will happen with you two."

"I don't think so," I sigh, twisting my hands together in my lap. "Nate is really sweet and funny—and cute—but we'll never be more than friends. He and Dex are so close that he probably just thinks of me as a sister."

Okay, maybe not a sister. More like the off-limits sister of his best friend.

"Those looks definitely didn't seem brotherly," she points out.

I'm surprised she noticed them, too. I assumed that I was so desperate for him to look at me that way that I'd imagined the whole thing. Not that it makes a difference. I've misinterpreted his feelings before, and I'm not going to do that again.

"If not Nate, is there anyone else? I don't suppose those two chumps from earlier are your type?"

"Definitely not!" I answer with a laugh. "My 'relationships'—if you can even call them that—typically only last a couple of dates. As soon as the guy figures out that I have a kid, they tend to bolt." I shrug, trying not to let on how much that hurts.

"What about Sadie's dad?" she asks in a tentative voice. "Is he around at all?"

"Nope, he was out of the picture before she was born. I met him in college, and we'd only been dating for a few months when I found out I was pregnant. He totally freaked out, said he couldn't handle it, and that was it. Haven't heard from him since, which is fine by me. We're better off without him."

The best thing Duncan ever did for me was signing over his parental rights.

There's a thoughtful expression on Olivia's face, like she understands. I'm accustomed to people feeling sympathy toward my situation and pitying me, but that's not what I see. It makes me curious to know more about her.

"What about you?" I ask. "Is there anyone in your life?"

"Not anymore," she says, a hard edge to her voice. Sighing, she glances sideways with an irritated smirk. "I moved down here after I caught my fiancé cheating on me."

I suck in a breath. "Wow. Men are scum."

"Yes, they are! Which is exactly why I've sworn them off. They bring nothing but trouble."

"So, I guess it's pointless for me to try to get you together with my brother, then?"

Olivia laughs. "I hate to break it to you, but Dex and I will only ever be friends." Her eyes shift toward him, lingering there thoughtfully. When her gaze snaps back to mine she says, "Besides, he doesn't seem like someone who's interested in any relationship that lasts longer than twelve hours. No offense."

"None taken." I smile, making it obvious that I'm not bothered by her accurate assessment of my brother. "Believe it or not, he wasn't always like this. In high school, he was so focused on joining the Marines that he didn't really have time for anything else. He enlisted right after he graduated, started boot camp, and went overseas to Iraq. He was... different... when he came back. Iraq changed him."

I explain what happened overseas, how he saved three men despite his injuries, and earned a Silver Star but is no longer able to serve because of his hearing loss. I don't mention Teddy, though. That's something he needs to disclose to her on his own.

I notice a slight change in her expression when I reveal some of his past, as though something clicked in the back of her mind, and she finally solved a puzzle. I'm not sure why I feel the need to tell her this. I suppose I want her to know that there's more to him, and that this cocky womanizer isn't who he really is. Part of me wonders if she might already see that. There's something in the way she looks at him, with such consideration and perception, as though she's glimpsing beneath the surface.

It's enough to make me hold onto the hope that maybe she's the one who can help him heal.

■　■　■

Later that night, once I've put Sadie to bed, I pour myself a glass of wine and curl up in my usual spot on the couch. I'm restless and uneasy as I start flipping through the television channels, sick and tired of the same old routine, night after night.

Most of all, I'm lonely.

Olivia, Dex and Nate all went out for dinner and drinks after leaving the beach. They invited me along, but once again I had to decline.

I love spending time with my daughter. She's the most important thing in my life, and I wouldn't trade her for anything in the world. I feel guilty and selfish for even *thinking* that there's somewhere else I'd rather be right now, but I can't help it. I hate sitting at home alone, while my friends are out having fun without me. I hate wondering if, while I'm parked on my couch watching HGTV, Nate's at the bar flirting with some woman. A woman who, unlike me, actually has a life.

By the time ten o'clock rolls around, I'm ready for bed. After cleaning the kitchen and loading the dishwasher, I slip on my flip-flops and take out the garbage. As my feet hit the bottom step, the beam of headlights burst across the yard, slicing through the darkness. I recognize the orange paint of Nate's Camaro immediately and wonder what he's doing here.

I take a few steps forward, but when Olivia pops out of the passenger side, I freeze. I'm anxiously waiting for Dex to appear behind them, and when he doesn't, I'm hit with the agonizing realization that they're walking into her apartment alone.

Nate's going home with Olivia.

My chest constricts painfully, making it hard to breathe. I feel like I just got the wind knocked out of me. My mouth falls slowly open as I watch them, all the color draining from my face. The trash bag slips from my trembling hand, causing Nate to glance up and notice me standing here in the shadows. His eyes are filled with concern as they lock on mine for a long moment before he mumbles something to Olivia, sending her inside.

He studies me carefully as he approaches, his brows knit together in a frown. "Amy?"

"Olivia?" My voice is weak and shaky. A tear sneaks down my cheek, but all it does is ignite my anger. I hate him for making me cry. "How could you do that?"

"Amy—"

"No!" I cut him off. "You told me that you would help me get her together with Dex, and then *you* go home with her?" My pulse is pounding as the words continue to pour out of me. "I can't believe you would do that!"

He takes a cautious step toward me. "Amy, I—"

"Don't you ever stop to think about how anyone else feels?" Wetness pools in my eyes. "Do you have any idea how much it hurts to watch the person you care about with someone else? To know that their arms are wrapped around someone who isn't you, but there's nothing you can do about it? To want someone so desperately, knowing you'll never have them?"

I'm not talking about Dex and Olivia anymore.

A huge smile spreads across Nate's face, and the next thing I know he's closing the space between us. I frown, "What?"

His hands come up to cup my face, brushing my tears away with his thumbs. "You do feel what I feel," he murmurs, crushing his lips against mine.

Nate

Amy's lips are stiff and motionless at first, but it only takes a split second for her to respond to me. Her body melts into me at the same moment her lips do, moving with mine as I gently coax them apart. A faint whimper escapes her throat when I sweep my tongue against hers, tilting her head back to devour the sweet taste of her mouth. As she loops her arms around my neck, I bring my hand down to her hip, dragging her body against mine until no space remains between us.

Everything about her feels perfect. The way her body aligns with mine... the soft press of her lips... the gentle tug of her fingers as they weave through my hair. I've been waiting so long to feel this again, to feel her again. It's even more amazing than I remember.

After a while the kiss becomes less demanding, less feverish, until my lips make one last delicate brush with hers before pulling away.

She looks up at me with wide eyes, breathless. Her cheeks are flushed, and her lips are slightly swollen. "Wh—what was that for?"

"Because I've been waiting forever to know how you feel about me, and I needed you to know that I feel the same way," I explain it the easiest way I can. "I didn't want there to be any more questions between us."

"But, I didn't tell you—"

"You didn't have to tell me," I answer. "I could see it written all over your face. I could hear it in your voice."

She frowns. "You came home with Olivia."

"I *drove* Olivia home," I clarify. "Dex was on the verge of doing something stupid, and I didn't want him to ruin his chances with her. So, I offered to give her a ride home, and I walked her to the door. That's *it*."

When I saw Amy standing there, watching Olivia and me with that inconsolable look on her face… God, it gutted me. It didn't take long for me to realize what conclusion she'd drawn. When she started yelling at me, I couldn't control the smile that appeared on my face, because even though it broke my heart to see her like that, it allowed me to *finally* see how she really feels.

Her shoulders sag with relief, and I lean toward her. "How could you think that I want Olivia?" I ask her softly, grazing my thumb along her jaw. "How could you think that I want anyone other than you?"

"I thought you'd moved on," she says in a shaky voice,

"I've never moved on," I tell her. "You're the only one I want."

She bites her lip, looking down at the ground. "How do I know that you really mean that, and that you're not going to come to me tomorrow and tell me that it was a mistake?" She glances up, her eyes glistening as they meet mine. "How do I know that it's real this time?"

In that moment I realize just how much my past actions have affected her. All the back and forth between us, when I was too weak to control myself around her and yet too scared to admit my true feelings… it was cruel and selfish. I was careless with her emotions—with her—and she has every right to doubt me now, even though it hurts.

"I'm going to prove it to you." I rest my forehead against hers, leaning in close enough to feel her breath against my lips. "There's a lot of things I should have done differently, but not a single moment I spent with you was a mistake. I'll do whatever it takes to show you that this… us… is as real as it gets."

I place another soft kiss on her lips, and then slowly pull away. I feel the loss of her contact instantly, but I know that I need to leave her so she has a chance to absorb everything that I'm saying. I have a lot to prove to her, and this isn't something that's going to happen overnight.

Grinning, I keep my eyes locked on hers as I back toward my car. "Good night, Amy."

■　■　■

Over the next couple of weeks, I do my best to make sure that Amy knows I'm not changing my mind or backing down. Little things, like sending random text messages to her throughout the day and calling her every night before I go to sleep. It's crazy how, in such a short time, those messages and nightly phone calls have already become the best part of my day. I smile every time her name pops up on my phone, and I look forward to hearing her voice on the other end of the line at night.

We talk about everything and nothing. We fill each other in on what happened during the years we spent apart and about what we did during the day. Sometimes we chat about stupid stuff, like what we're watching on television or what we're listening to on the radio.

It's mostly friendly, but the important thing is that we're growing closer and getting to know each other better. I don't want to rush into anything. We need to take it slow for now and reestablish our friendship so we can start this thing off right. I have to prove to her that I'm serious about her and that she can trust me. That takes time.

But good things come to those who wait… and Amy Porter is definitely worth waiting for.

■ ■ ■

I'm at the gym with Dex, getting an early morning workout in, when he brings up the fact that he won't be in the shop this weekend because he's watching Sadie while Amy's out of town.

I'm surprised that she never mentioned anything to me about going away. Frowning, I ask, "Where's Amy going?" I try to hide my interest, since Dex doesn't know that there's anything going on between me and his sister. "Who's she going with?"

I don't have any claim on Amy. Not really. I don't expect that she'd be seeing anyone else, but it strikes me as odd that she didn't talk to me about going out of town for the weekend. I'm also disappointed that since she's going to be away, I won't have a chance to see her.

"I don't know. She has some work thing." Dex narrows his eyes at me curiously, and I decide that it's best for me to put an end to this line of questioning before I give myself away.

"How did you end up with babysitting duty?" I say, adjusting the weights on the bar. "Don't your parents usually take Sadie?"

He shrugs. "It's their anniversary tonight, so I offered."

"That was unusually considerate of you." I glance sideways at him. "This act of kindness wouldn't have anything to do with the person who just happens to live below your sister, would it?"

Dex and Olivia have been spending a lot of time together lately, but he insists that they're just friends. I'm fairly certain that there's more to it than that, so I'm just waiting for *them* to figure it out, or at least admit it.

He takes a swig from his water bottle, tossing an aggravated look in my direction. "Olivia and I are just friends. You know that."

"Yeah, but in all the time I've known you, I've never once seen you be just friends with a girl. So what's different?"

"I don't know," he says. "Olivia's cool. She's fun, smart, and she's never afraid to say what she's really thinking. She doesn't pretend to give a shit about what I'm saying just so I'll spread her out on the mattress."

"You're not biding your time to eventually get with her?"

Dex purses his lips, ignoring my question completely as he goes back to lifting weights. "Yeah, that's what I thought," I say with a smirk.

"I would only find a way to fuck it up with her if I did, so no, I'm not." He finishes his set, letting the bar fall onto the floor with a bang. "She's too good for a cheap fuck, and I don't do more than that."

It kills me that my best friend could think so poorly of himself. I wish I could make him see that someone like Olivia would be lucky to have him.

"Maybe not," I finally say. "But the Dex Porter I know doesn't back down when things get tough. He fights for what he wants."

"Not anymore," he grumbles to himself.

chapter eighteen

Amy

I had trusted Dex to look after Sadie while I went out of town to a teaching symposium in Columbia. I was skeptical at first, but when Olivia offered to help him out, I eventually agreed. Not that I had much of a choice, considering I had completely forgotten about the event until the very last minute. I could've asked my parents, but I didn't want to disturb them on their anniversary, and there was no way I could get out of the symposium. It's an event that most of the teachers at school attend every couple of years, and this was my first chance to go along with them. Spending two days with my fellow teachers, attending sessions for "career advancement and education" wasn't exactly my idea of a perfect weekend, especially considering it's summer vacation, but I didn't have much of a choice.

It turned out to be better than I expected it to be. However, the one disappointing aspect of it was that I couldn't talk to Nate while I was there. We were busy all day with lectures and various events, and I was sharing a hotel room with one of the other teachers. It was the first night in weeks that I hadn't spoken to Nate before bed.

With each night that passes, I keep thinking that Nate will forget, or eventually just stop calling. But he hasn't. Like clockwork, he calls me as I'm climbing into bed, and we talk until I can't keep my eyes open any longer. I'm trying not to get my hopes up, but it's hard not to. So far he's shown no signs of backing down, and I really, *really*, want to believe that he's serious about giving us a chance.

Then there's the pessimistic side of me that wonders if, after having no contact with him for the last couple of days, the whole thing will taper off. What if he decided that we're a mistake after all?

I try not to think too much about it during the drive home from Columbia. Dex and Olivia took Sadie with them to my parents' for dinner, so I stop there to pick her up before going home.

I stay there for a little while, but when Sadie starts falling asleep at the table, I decide that it's time to get her into bed. Not to mention that I'm exhausted, too.

"Do you want a ride home, Liv?" I ask, standing up from the table.

Dex quickly jumps in and offers to drive her home himself after dessert, giving me an angry look from across the table for asking her. I smile to myself, enjoying the fact that my brother is all tied up in knots over this girl. I don't know how much longer he'll be able to pretend that they're just friends.

By the time I pull into the driveway, Sadie is fast asleep in the backseat. I'm so preoccupied with how I'm going to get her inside without waking her up, that I almost don't notice the bright orange Camaro parked outside.

Nate climbs out of his car when he sees me pull up. I park alongside him and get out, smoothing my wrinkled clothes as I walk over to him.

"Nate?" I look at him curiously. "What are you doing here?"

"I came to see you." He ambles forward, raking his eyes over me. "And to deliver an important message."

"What is it?"

A slow and sexy smile appears on his lips. "I wanted you to know that I've been thinking about you." He pulls a dark pink rose from behind his back and hands it to me. "And that I missed you."

My heart flutters in my chest. "I missed you, too."

"How would you feel about having dinner with me tomorrow night?"

"I would feel very good about that," I say with a smile. "I'll ask my mom if she can watch Sadie for me."

"Actually, I was hoping that she could join us," he suggests, shifting his feet nervously. "I thought that, if it's okay with you, I could cook dinner at your house, for both of you. Unless that's too much."

"That's perfect," I say, my smile widening. "Totally perfect."

He lets out a huge breath. "Okay, great."

"I should get Sadie to bed," I say, pulling away from him, even though I'd rather move closer.

"Can I help you get her inside?" he asks, glancing toward her sleeping form in the back seat. "It can't be easy to carry her up those stairs by yourself."

"Would you mind?"

He grins. "Of course I don't mind."

Nate easily carries Sadie up the stairs and into the apartment. I lead him into her room, where he gently places her in bed and covers her with the blanket.

As he stands to leave, he gazes down at her with a smile, tenderly sweeping the blonde hair out of her face. That simple gesture is so unbelievably sweet that I feel like I'm going to melt into a pool on the carpet. Before I have a chance to recover, he drops a soft kiss on my cheek.

"Good night, beautiful," he says, his eyes flashing with desire. "I'll see you tomorrow."

■   ■   ■

The next day, I spend part of the afternoon with Olivia, Dex and Nate at my house. When dinnertime approaches, Dex and Olivia show no signs of leaving anytime soon, and I start to worry that my plans with Nate are totally ruined. There's no way for me to clear them out of the house without garnering suspicion; especially since Olivia lives right below me. They'll immediately know something's up.

While Dex is distracted with his phone, I exchange a look with Nate, unable to hide my irritation. As if he can read my mind, he offers me a reassuring smile and silently mouths, *"It's okay."*

Dex suddenly bursts out in a small cheer, turning to Nate. "You feel like going to a fight with me tonight?"

My heart sinks.

"I can't," Nate says, surprising me. He glances in my direction, stumbling to find an excuse. "I, uh… I have to work."

Warmth radiates through me, and I have to look away to hide my pleased smile. I was certain that Nate would back out of our plans so he could go with Dex to the fight. Not necessarily because he *wants* to go, but because of his loyalty to my brother. Nate cares so much about him and has been trying so hard to look out for him. I should probably feel guilty for stealing Nate when my brother may need him, but right now I'm too happy to care.

Nate finally chose *me*.

Nate

"Are you sure you don't want to go with Dex?" Amy asks once Dex and Olivia have left us alone.

"Hmmm, would I rather spend the night here with you or surrounded by a bunch of sweaty guys…" I pretend as though I have to think about it.

"It's a tough one, I know." She smiles, but her eyes are clouded with uncertainty, suggesting that she may still be wondering if I'm here by choice.

"It's not even a question." Pulling her into my arms, I lean forward and whisper, "There's nowhere else I'd rather be."

She tilts her head up to meet my gaze, her lips parting slightly. "I'm glad."

I hadn't even considered going to the fight with Dex. It was never even a possibility. There was no way in hell I was going to miss spending time with Amy tonight. I would've found an excuse to get Dex and Olivia out of here, but fortunately they decided to go to the fight together, so I didn't have to.

I've gone with him enough times to know that Dex is more than capable of handling himself. I mainly go along so that he has someone to drive him home after the fight when he's battered and bruised. Because even though Dex has never lost, it doesn't mean he comes out unscathed. I feel better knowing that Olivia will be there, and I know that Dex will keep her safe.

"Mommy!" Sadie comes barreling out of her room. "I'm hungry. What's for dinner?"

"How about we order a pizza?" I suggest, giving Amy's hip a quick squeeze before putting some distance between us.

"I love pizza!" Sadie exclaims. "Are you going to eat with us, too?"

"I was hoping to. Is that okay with you, Sadie girl?" I ask her.

"Yes!" She grins, jumping off the ground before scampering into the kitchen.

I can't help but smile, and when I turn to Amy there's a matching one on her lips. "I hope you don't mind pizza," I say, wrapping one arm around her slim waist. "I promise to cook dinner for you next time, when Dex and Liv aren't around to hijack our date."

Her face lights up, and she nods. "Pizza is great."

Once the pizzas are delivered, I bring them outside to the deck and place the boxes on the table. We have a perfect view across the river and fields of marsh, and as the sun begins to set, it casts an orange and yellow glow on the surface of the water.

"Mmmm… this pizza is reeeally good," Sadie says between mouthfuls. "It's even better than the pizza Uncle Dee brings!"

"Only the best for my favorite girls," I say, winking at Amy across the table.

Sadie tilts her head curiously. "How come Dee isn't eating with us? Or Oleeva?"

Amy clears her throat, looking to me for an answer before she finally says, "They had something else to do, so we thought it would be fun for the three of us to eat dinner together."

"Cool," Sadie responds. "I think it's fun, too."

I breathe an internal sigh of relief. I didn't want to make a big deal out of being here, but it's nice to know that Sadie's okay with it. It's important to me that Amy understands I'm here for *both* of them, which is why I insisted that Sadie be here tonight. Being a part of Amy's life also means being a part of Sadie's life. I don't want there to be a shred of doubt in her mind that I am fully, completely, one hundred percent on board with that. Sadie is an amazing little girl, and I would be *lucky* to be a part of her life. Not the other way around.

Once we've finished eating, Amy takes a very tired Sadie into her room to put her to bed. I use that time to clear the dishes and put them in the dishwasher and tidy up the kitchen so that Amy doesn't have to do it later. I carry the empty pizza boxes to the trash outside, making a quick stop at my car to grab the bottle of wine I brought with me.

By the time Amy returns, I have the outdoor table set up with a citronella candle, two wine glasses, and soft music playing.

"Wow," she says, sliding the door closed behind her as she joins me outside. "This is really nice."

She moves to sit down in the chair next to mine, but I grab her by the hips and pull her into my lap. "I saved this seat for you," I tell her, winding my arms around her waist as I breathe in her sweet scent. "It's all warmed up and everything."

"Even better," she giggles, settling sideways against my chest. "Best seat in the house."

I hand her a glass of white wine and watch as she takes a long swallow "I can't believe I finally have you all to myself," I murmur, fixated on her wet lips.

She drapes her arm over my shoulder, placing her hand at the back of my neck as she winds her fingers into my short hair. "Well, now that you have me... what are you going to do with me?"

"What I really want to do is drag you inside, spread your naked body across the bed, and kiss every inch of that smooth skin until you beg me to stop." I watch as her mouth falls open slightly, and her breathing gets heavier. I was already getting hard just from thinking about it, but seeing how turned on she is by my words makes me stiffen completely. Her eyes widen, and I know she can feel it. Leaning in close, I whisper, "But I'm not going to do that."

"You're not?" she says breathlessly.

"Not tonight." There's a flash of disappointment on her face, and I run my hand up her thigh until I reach the frayed hem of her jean shorts. "Because as much as I want to… I mean, *really* want to… I don't want us to rush into anything."

"You're right," she nods. "And there's Dex. What should we do about him?"

"Eventually we'll have to tell him," I say. "But right now, this is about us. Not him. I don't want to sneak around behind his back, but I think that we should take some time to enjoy each other and explore what this is before we add the Dex factor. What do you think?"

"I think I like the sound of that," she smiles, resting her head in the crook of my neck as she nestles against me.

"Besides, there's a good chance you'll get sick of me after a week," I tease, drawing her tightly against me, unable to get close enough to her.

"That's true, you're pretty intolerable…" she hums against my neck, pressing her lips to my throat.

I suck in a breath as she continues trailing kisses across my skin, blazing a path along my flesh. When her tongue dips out to taste me, I groan loudly and bring her face to mine, sealing my mouth against hers.

Her lips part easily, and I don't waste any time before plunging my tongue inside and moving it feverishly with hers. Without breaking the contact, I grab the wine glass from her hand and place it on the table next to us. She instantly reaches up to grip my jaw, smoothing her fingers across the stubble and whimpering into my mouth.

Any control that I have left snaps. Digging my fingers into her hips, I lift her up and arrange her legs on either side of me so she's straddling my lap. She sinks down on the firm ridge of my arousal, allowing me to feel the warmth radiating from her.

When she rocks against me, I let my head fall back against the chair. "Fuck, Amy..." I thrust my hips up, causing a breathy moan to escape her lips. I slip my hand underneath her shirt and run it up the slope of her back, pulling her toward me as I start kissing her neck.

She rubs herself against the hard length of my cock, and I bring my hand around to her stomach, sliding up to palm her heavy breast. "You feel so good," I breathe against her skin. "So damn good."

"Oh my god, Nate..." she cries, arching into my touch. Her body trembles with need, and I can sense that she's close. Yanking her bra down, I run my thumb over her taut nipple, tugging it gently at the same time I thrust my hips up, making her body go still as she shudders with her release.

I adjust her bra so it's back in place, and wrap my arms around her while she catches her breath. When she finally sits back to look at me, her cheeks are flushed pink. "You're so incredibly beautiful," I tell her, cupping her delicate jaw in my hand. "I love watching you come."

Her cheeks redden even more, and she looks down to hide her face. "I'm sorry, I didn't mean to lose it like that. I don't know what came over me."

"Don't even think about apologizing." I turn her around so her back is resting against my chest, and I place a soft kiss on the curve of her neck. "That was by far the sexiest thing I've ever seen."

"What about you?" she twists her head to the side, frowning.

I chuckle. "Don't you worry about me. I'll be picturing your face in the shower tonight. You've provided me with enough material to last a lifetime."

"Nate!" She slaps me playfully on the arm. Laughing, she cuddles against me, laying her head back. "You're such a pervert."

I coil my arms around her. "Yeah, and I'm all yours, baby."

We spend the next few hours curled up in the chair, gazing up at the stars as we fall into easy conversation. When we both start yawning more frequently, I walk her to her bedroom and give her a kiss good night.

chapter nineteen

Amy

On Friday night, we make plans for a group of us to go out in downtown Charleston. In addition to our usual foursome of Nate, Olivia, Dex and me, we're also joined by Olivia's college roommate, Nora, her fiancé, Jake, and two of their friends, Susie and Ethan.

My parents take Sadie to their house for the night, so I'm looking forward to having the night off from being a mom and simply enjoying a carefree night with friends. And, of course, Nate. We can't exactly be open with each other when Dex is around, but I'm anxious to spend time with him regardless. He always finds ways to steal a few kisses or subtle touches here and there when no one is paying attention. As much as I hate hiding our relationship from my brother, it's nice to be able to enjoy each other without the added pressure of worrying what Dex will say, or how he'll react. I know it can't last forever, but at least it gives us time to concentrate on *us* and figure out what *we* are before we share the news with Dex.

The sneaking around part is kind of fun, too.

Olivia and I get ready together in my apartment. We make margaritas and help each other apply makeup and pick out what to wear. The whole time we're chatting and giggling hysterically, like two teenagers getting ready for a school dance.

It's the most fun I've had in a long time.

It only gets better from there. We all go to dinner at a trendy restaurant downtown, and although most of us have just met, by the time our food comes it feels as though we've known each other for years.

Nate claims a seat next to me at the restaurant and frequently sneaks his hand up my thigh and under the hem of my dress throughout the night. Not that I mind it. Dex and Olivia are so focused on flirting with each other that they probably wouldn't notice if we started making out right here at the table.

After dinner, we head to a club right down the block. It's packed by the time we walk in, and while the guys go straight to the bar, the other girls and I don't waste any time before heading onto the dance floor. We're all a bit tipsy, dancing and laughing without a care in the world. This whole experience is completely new to me. I rarely go out drinking, and I've never even *been* to a club before tonight. Although I keep a constant eye on my phone in case my mom tries to get in touch with me, I can't remember the last time I had this much fun, felt this relaxed, or laughed this much.

Nora is soon joined on the dance floor by her fiancé, Jake, who comes up from behind and wraps his arms around her. They quickly float into their own world, nuzzling and whispering in each other's ears, clearly over the moon in love with each other. Susie's husband, Ethan, appears shortly after that, leaving Olivia and me on our own to fend off the guys circling around us.

Dex's eyes are glued to Olivia from across the room, watching her every move as he drinks a beer at the bar. Considering the way the two of them have been acting with one other, I won't be surprised if tonight is the night that the just friends façade finally goes out the window.

I'm so busy waiting for Dex to make his move, that I don't notice Nate come up behind me until he places his hands on my hips.

"I'm going to try to keep an appropriate distance between us," he breathes into my ear, loosely holding my waist. "But considering the way you're dancing, and that sexy dress you're wearing, it might be impossible."

I slant my head around to meet his eyes. "I love a challenge."

We manage to keep our contact to a minimum, knowing that Dex is probably watching, but it's not easy. My entire body screams to melt against his, to fall into his warmth and fit our bodies against each other in the perfect way that we know they do.

By the time a new song comes on, Dex is dancing with Olivia. With his focus completely on her, and no one else, we're able to close the distance between us. Nate clutches my hips, pulling my back against his firm chest as we move to the beat of the music.

He slopes his mouth to my neck, brushing his lips against my skin. "Thank God, I don't think I could've waited another minute to feel you like this." His warm breath causes goosebumps to surface across my skin, and I shudder slightly, feeling dizzy from his proximity.

"If Dex weren't around…" His voice is heavy with lust. "I would drag my hand up your stomach and graze the side of your breast with my thumb, teasing you just enough to make your nipples hard." My nipples instantly respond to his words, pebbling beneath my dress.

"Then I'd wind my arm around your waist and haul you against me, so you could grind your gorgeous, round ass into my stiff cock until I can't take it anymore." He briefly presses his hips forward, allowing me to feel his considerable erection before pulling back to restore the space between us.

My entire body hums with arousal, desperately aching for his touch. There's a constant throbbing between my legs, and my panties are already soaked. I'm not sure I can wait any longer. When I glance around, I realize that Dex and Olivia have already disappeared somewhere.

Reaching up, I pull his face toward mine. "Let's go somewhere," I urge softly into his ear. "I want you, Nate."

Without a second's hesitation, he tows me off the dance floor, stopping only to offer a hasty goodbye to Jake and Nora on our way out. It's late, and the downtown area is practically empty, aside from a few people walking to their cars. Nate leads me down a quiet side street that goes past a small park and then finally ducks into a dark, narrow gap between two stone buildings.

"I'm so fucking glad you got us out of there," he says, pushing me up against the side of the building and crushing his lips against mine.

My arms wrap around his neck, and I mumble into his mouth. "I couldn't wait any longer." When he grabs my breast, fondling my nipple through the layers of clothing, my head spins with desire. Reaching down, I start rubbing his thick, hard length through his jeans. He lets out a sexy, guttural groan and thrusts into my hand. It's an unbelievable turn on, and it makes me eager to satisfy him.

"This time, it's your turn," I demand, urging him to lean back against the side of the building. My impatient fingers make quick work of unbuttoning his jeans and lowering the zipper before I drop to my knees in front of him.

"Amy, you don't have to—"

Ignoring his protests, I wrap my fingers around his silky length and cover him with my mouth.

"Oh, fuck yes," Nate says, relaxing against the building. "Just like that."

I massage the tip with my tongue as I work my fingers at the base. I've only ever done this a couple of times—and Duncan was nowhere near as big as Nate is—but it feels natural with Nate, and I find that I actually enjoy doing it. It turns me on to make him feel good.

As I take more of him into my mouth, I remove my hand so only my lips are moving over him. I trace my tongue along the ridge of his vein, taking him so deep that I feel him at the back of my throat.

"Holy shit, that's amazing," he groans. He weaves his fingers into my hair and gently thrusts into my mouth. "You're gonna make me come, baby. If you don't want me to come inside that sweet mouth, you better stop now."

I suck him harder. I work my lips and tongue over him until I feel him jerk in my mouth and taste the warm spurt of his release. I mop up every drop with my tongue, and his whole body shudders when I trail it along the swollen head.

The next thing I know, Nate heaves me to my feet and presses me into the wall. He yanks up my dress and grabs my ass, hitching one of my legs around his hip so he can position himself between them.

"I can't wait to make you come as hard as you just made me." Kissing me furiously, he reaches between my legs and rubs me through my panties. "God, you're so fucking wet for me." His hand slips under the edge of the material and comes into contact with my bare, slick flesh. He teases my opening with his finger, dipping it partway inside before drawing it back out. "And so damn tight."

"Oh God," I moan, cinching my leg tighter around his waist as I writhe beneath him, ready to explode at any moment. Using his other hand to lower the straps from my shoulders, he tugs down the front of my dress until my breasts spring free.

"Fucking perfect," he says, staring hungrily at my bare chest. Lowering his head, he draws my nipple into his hot mouth as he caresses the other with his large palm.

He's everywhere, all at once, and I'm on sensory overload. "Nate, I need…"

He plunges two fingers inside me, making me cry out. "Is that what you need?" he asks, looking up and circling his thumb over my clit while sliding his fingers in deep. "I want you to come all over my hand."

"Yes!" I gasp, firmly gripping his biceps to hold myself in place as my body climbs higher and higher. I love the dirty, sexy things he says when he starts to lose control. I love making him go a little bit wild.

"I can't wait to bury myself inside you," he says in a low, strangled voice. "I've never wanted anyone the way I want you."

My body flies over the edge, shaking and shuddering with the most intense orgasm I've ever experienced. Nate holds me securely as I collapse into his arms and catch my breath. When I'm finally able to stand on my own two feet, he tenderly puts my dress back in place to cover me up.

When he looks at me now, the wildfire in his eyes has dimmed, but what's left in its place is tender adoration that fills me with warmth from head to toe.

He brushes a sweet kiss across my lips. "I will never get enough of you, Amy Porter."

Nate

I'm on cloud nine when I wake up the next morning. Last night with Amy was nothing short of un-fucking-believable, and it's left me with a ridiculous smile on my face that I can't seem to contain.

I take my time getting to work, whistling to myself as I walk into the garage and see Dex there. "Getting an early start?"

"Couldn't sleep," he grumbles.

"Considering the way you and Olivia were dancing last night, and then ran off on us, I'm not surprised you didn't sleep," I say, directing his attention away from any discussion of Amy and me. "Did you two finally hook up?"

His silence confirms my suspicion.

"No shit, really?" I ask, lifting my eyebrow. "It's about time. Good for you, bro."

Dex rolls out from under the car, wiping his hands on a rag. "Don't get too excited," he scowls. "It was a mistake, according to Olivia. She wants to pretend it never happened."

"What about you?" I glance at him questioningly. "Did you think it was a mistake?"

"I didn't before, but now I don't know what the fuck to think." He tosses the rag aside. "I thought she was on the same page as me. Clearly, I was wrong."

I think back to some of the stuff Amy has mentioned over the past few weeks, like the fact that Olivia seems to have fled here after breaking off her engagement. "She's probably confused about the whole thing. I mean, she just got out of a relationship and totally uprooted her life. Maybe she's scared to make another big change." Dex glares down at the ground with a pinched expression. "It's obvious she has feelings for you though, anyone with eyes could see that. It's a matter of getting her to admit it… which won't be easy because she's determined to be on her own."

He nods, glancing up at me with narrowed eyes. "When did you get so damn smart?"

"Some of that may have come from Amy," I admit with a grin. "We've spent some time discussing your situation."

When we're not making each other come.

"Figures," he chuckles.

"So the real question is how you feel about *her*," I ask seriously. "Are you ready to give up all the casual sex and random woman, and be there for Olivia the way she would need you to be? 'Cause, if you can't do that, then the rest of this shit doesn't matter."

He's quiet for a moment, but when he finally answers, he doesn't waver. "Olivia's different from anyone I've ever met. She makes me want to be different. Better." There's honest, fierce determination in his eyes. "No one compares to her. I know that she deserves better than me, but the idea of her being with anyone else rips me apart. I would do anything for her."

"Well, there ya go. I guess you are ready."

"How do I get her to admit she has feelings for me?"

"Give it time," I suggest, giving him a pat on the back. "She'll come around."

"What if you're wrong, and she doesn't have feelings for me?"

Shrugging, I lean back against the work bench. "That's a risk you're going to have to take. Is it worth the risk?"

He doesn't have to answer for me to know that it is. I can see it in the determined set of his jaw and in the way his eyes are alight with renewed intensity. I recognize the passion that existed in him before the accident.

I can't help but think about the risk looming in front of me. The risk of what will happen when I inform Dex about my relationship with Amy. I want to believe that he'll find a way to be happy for us, but what if he can't? I don't want to lose Amy—I won't—but I also can't imagine my life without my best friend.

We need to tell Dex... and soon. Not only because it's not fair to hide it from him, but also because we've agreed that he needs to know before we take things to the next level. Considering what happened last night, and what seems to happen every time I'm alone with Amy, I'm not going to be able to control myself around her much longer.

The sooner he finds out, the better.

■   ■   ■

A few days later when the four of us, along with Sadie, are all at the beach, it's clear that Dex and Olivia haven't resolved anything. Olivia seems to be doing her best to ignore him completely, while Dex looks completely miserable. When the tension in the air becomes unbearably thick, I drag Amy and Sadie away to go for a swim.

I watch Sadie, noticing the timid way she stands at the edge of the water, wearing bright yellow inflatable water wings that are three times as wide as her tiny arms. There's an adorably determined look on her face, as though she's eager to jump right in but doesn't know if she can do it. Smiling, I ask her, "Want to climb up on my shoulders, Sade?"

Her eyes light up, and she nods. I easily lift her over my head and set her on my shoulders, holding her legs securely while she hangs onto my neck. "You ready?"

"Ready!" she squeals.

I run into the cool ocean water, going deep enough that the gentle waves lap around my shoulders and Sadie's feet are submerged. She giggles uncontrollably as I inhale a deep breath before dunking my head under, dipping her lower half in the water.

When I emerge, I tilt my head to glance at her. "I think we need to get your mom in here with us, don't you think?"

"Yeah!" she grins, giggling as we march toward the beach where Amy is watching us from. When we're waist deep, she calls out, "Mommy! Nate wants you to come in the water with us!"

Amy smiles, quirking an eyebrow at me. "Oh he does, does he?"

"He sure does," I wink, letting my eyes travel up and down her body. "So you better get your butt in here before we drag you in!"

She throws her head back, laughing, and warmth floods my chest as I observe her. I don't think I've ever seen anything more beautiful than this. I wish I could freeze this moment in time and remember it forever. Her happy, carefree smile... the bright sound of her laughter... her long, dark hair gently blowing in the breeze. More than anything else, I want her to always be as happy as she is right now.

Amy sprints into the water and dives below the surface. When she comes up a few feet away from us, Sadie is cheering from on top of my shoulders, urging me to follow Amy farther out.

Once we're chest deep, I use one hand to grab Amy's waist and drag her toward me. "You look good wet," I say, my voice quiet enough that Sadie can't hear me.

I hear her breath hitch in her throat, and I know that she's just as affected as I am. Water droplets bead down her wet skin as she gently traces her finger along the ridges of my stomach. "Mmmm, so do you."

"Do you what?" Sadie's voice pipes out.

I chuckle, taking a step back from Amy. "Do you… want to jump off my shoulders?" I ask, steering her attention elsewhere.

For the next twenty minutes, Sadie jumps off my shoulders into Amy's arms, and then swims the short distance back to me. Each time we move a tiny bit further apart, and by the last jump, Sadie is proudly grinning from ear to ear as she easily swims several feet between us.

As we climb out of the water, heading back toward our spot with Dex and Olivia, Amy turns to me with a frown. "I really hope they sort things out soon, or this whole situation is going to get really difficult. Dex is completely miserable. I was going to ask him to watch Sadie for me this afternoon, but with Olivia downstairs I can't even do that."

Stopping, I turn toward her. "If you need someone to watch Sadie, I could do it."

"You wouldn't mind?"

"Of course not, but if you're not comfortable with that, I totally understand. I know it's kind of a big step and—"

"I'm totally comfortable with that," she cuts in, smiling. "I trust you, Nate. Completely, absolutely, one-hundred percent."

"Good," I grin, unable to resist pulling her toward me for a brief hug. It's a huge deal for her to entrust me to watch Sadie. Even though I've done it before with Dex, it means a lot more for me to do it on my own.

"Hey Sadie," Amy calls to her. "Nate's going to watch you for a little bit today, is that cool with you?"

"Yes!" Sadie declares, bouncing happily on the sand. "Cool!"

chapter twenty

Amy

We leave the beach in the early afternoon so I have time to get to a mandatory meeting at the school. Now that August is underway, it's time to start preparing for the upcoming school year, and no one, not even kindergarten teachers, are exempt.

The meeting is relatively quick and painless, and mostly consists of familiarizing myself with the new group of students I'll have in the fall. As much as I'm dreading the end of the summer, I look forward to seeing the eager, adorable little faces in my classroom. They're always so excited to finally be starting school with all the big kids, but deep down there's a part of them that's terrified. I love being able to show them how much fun they're going to have and watching as they slowly come out of their tiny shells and start gaining some independence.

When I arrive back at the house and walk into my apartment, I stop short when the living room comes into view. I think I can actually *feel* my heart expand three sizes in my chest.

Nate's lengthy body is sprawled across the couch, fast asleep. There's a book lying open on his stomach, and curled up next to him, sleeping peacefully with her head on his shoulder, is Sadie.

Tears pool in my eyes as I take in the scene in front of me. Seeing them both so content and relaxed with one another is more amazing than I ever could've imagined. The way that Nate has his armed wrapped protectively around Sadie, and the way her little hand rests on top of his chest… it makes me realize what's truly been missing from our lives before now. I haven't made a habit of lamenting over my life as a single mother, and I have no regrets about the past, but seeing this perfectly wonderful image of the two of them… it fills a space and makes me feel whole for the first time.

I'm absolutely certain that Nate Miller is the one for me, the one who completes us and makes us whole. He's not simply taking someone else's place, or filling a vacancy, because it's always been his. This empty space in our lives was meant for him, and only him. No one else will ever fit.

I have an unbelievable urge to call Dex right this second to tell him about us. Not only because I'm sure that what Nate and I have is the real deal, but also because I'm *dying* to take things to the next level. I want him so badly that it physically hurts, and every time we're together it gets harder and harder to keep from giving in.

I haven't been with anyone since Duncan. It's been more than four *long* years since the last time that I had sex. After getting pregnant, I vowed to myself that I wouldn't make the same mistake again. I was never in love with Duncan, and when I slept with him for the first time, it was more of an obligation than something I truly wanted to do. I didn't understand the significance, and the magnitude, of what it really means to give yourself to someone. It should mean love, and trust, and desire. The only regret I have regarding Sadie, is that she wasn't born out of love. She isn't the product of two people's complete devotion to one another, which is how it should be. Realizing that made it important for me to promise myself that I wouldn't give myself to anyone again until I was in a serious relationship with someone I truly love. A *good* guy who I trust and desire.

Nate is that guy.

But as anxious as I am to be with him, I'm also unbelievably nervous. We've been wanting this for so long, and been so patient, that I'm terrified to fall short of expectations. It's been *four years*, and I can't help but worry that I'll be terrible in bed, or he'll be disappointed.

These fears—valid or not—are the only thing keeping me from running over to Dex's right now to tell him. However, I know that nothing, even my own nerves, will be able to keep me away from Nate for much longer. There's so much heat between us, so much fire, that all my worries and doubts go up in flames when I'm with him. It's only a matter of time before we both combust.

■　　■　　■

I go to our weekly family dinner at my parents' house with the intention of telling Dex before the night is over. However, my plan veers off track when, halfway through dinner, my mom asks why Olivia didn't come along as usual.

As Dex keenly awaits my answer, I seriously consider *not* telling them what I know about Olivia's plans for the night, but I realize he'll find out sooner or later, whether it comes from me or not. I chew my food slowly and swallow, before finally answering. "Olivia had a date tonight."

"Liv's on a date?" Dex stares at me, his face tight. "With who?"

I gaze down at my plate, avoiding his gaze.

"Don't even tell me she's out with that jackass from the other day..."

I let out a long breath. "Sorry, Dex."

"FUCK!" He yells, pounding his fist against the table and making the dishes clatter. Pushing away from the table, he knocks his chair over as he stands up and promptly storms off.

I move to go after him, but my mom stops me. "Let him go, honey. He needs some time to cool off."

"I shouldn't have told him," I say, slumping back in my chair. "I knew he would get upset. I'm sorry."

My dad squeezes my shoulder. "It's not your fault, Ames. He still has a lot to work through, and all these emotions involving Olivia are new to him. This may actually be a good thing. Maybe it will give him the push he needs to finally confront his feelings and do something about it."

"What's wrong with Dee?" Sadie asks, her voice full of concern. "Is he sad because Oleeva isn't here?"

"Yeah, baby girl. Uncle Dee misses her, but he'll be okay. I promise."

Sadie tilts her head to the side. "Do you miss Nate?"

I choke on the water I'm sipping, my cheeks instantly flaring bright red. "Why would you think that?"

"Because he's not here," Sadie shrugs. "And he usually comes over for dinner with us."

My parents exchange a puzzled look, and when my mom turns toward me there's a smile building on her lips. "Amy?"

My face is on fire. I can't believe my own daughter ratted me out. Clearing my throat, I stand up from the table. "I'm, uh, going to go find Dex."

Spinning away from their knowing grins, I head off in search of my brother. It's not much of a search, since I already know exactly where he is. A few minutes later, I find him sitting on the small sandy shore of the swimming hole.

"Want to finally tell me what's going on between you and Olivia?" I say as I take a seat next to him.

Dex explains to me that after they hooked up following our night out in Charleston, Olivia freaked out and said that it was huge mistake. In an attempt to make her jealous and encourage her to admit her feelings, Dex then went to the bar while she was working and made out with another woman right in front of her. Olivia was furious, and hurt, and basically told him she didn't want anything to do with him anymore.

"I really fucked up," Dex sighs, scrubbing a hand over his face.

"No shit, you fucked up!" I gape at him in disbelief. "What kind of an idiotic plan was that? It wouldn't work on anyone, but especially not Olivia."

"I know, I was upset and I…" He pauses, furrowing his brows. "What do you mean *'especially not Olivia'*?"

Apparently Dex has no knowledge of the fact that Olivia and her fiancé broke up because she walked in on him screwing someone else. When I fill him in on the details, he groans loudly, dropping his head into his hands. He looks completely torn apart, and if I ever had any doubts about his feelings for Olivia, they're gone now. Sure, what he did was awful—and incredibly stupid—but this is brand new territory for him. Deep down, I know that he truly cares for her.

"How do I fix this?" he asks, pain and desperation clearly written on his face. "Please tell me I can fix it."

"Have you tried talking to her? Groveling at her feet for a second chance?"

He shakes his head. "She told me to leave her alone. I didn't want to make it any worse."

"Wow, you really don't know anything about women, do you, bro?" I say with a slight smile. I never imagined that he was so clueless about this, and it makes me realize how different his life has been from most guys his age. I doubt there's much time for relationship drama when you're in combat. "Of course she told you to leave her alone. She was angry and hurt. That doesn't mean you give up. You have to fight for her and show her that you're serious. Are you serious?"

"I'm dead serious when it comes to Liv," he tells me. "I may have zero experience with this shit, but I would do anything for her."

"Then you need to quit playing games and be honest about how you feel. You got so angry because she wouldn't admit her feelings, and yet, have you ever once told her how *you* feel?" His silence confirms that he hasn't. Sighing, I say, "So far all you've done is show her that you're incapable of an actual relationship, and are no better than her dumbass ex. You need to prove to her that you can be different. Can you handle that? Are you sure it's what you really want? Because there's no going back after that."

"Liv is what I want," he says firmly. "I don't want to go back. She's all I want."

Lecturing Dex about being honest and owning up to his feelings makes me realize how much of a hypocrite I am. I should've owned up to my own feelings for Nate a long time ago. I keep telling myself how serious and real our relationship is, but how can that be true when we're merely existing inside our own bubble? How can it be real if no one else knows?

Nate

Until now, I'd never been in a serious relationship. I've never celebrated an anniversary, or met the parents. I've definitely never had to actually buy a gift for a woman—except for my mom—and now that Amy's birthday is coming up, I have to figure it out.

Obviously, I can't go to Dex for advice. Not only does he still not know about Amy and me, but he's just as clueless about this kind of thing as I am. Besides, ever since he finally worked things out with Olivia and made their relationship "official", they've been too wrapped up in each other to notice much else.

Not that it's a bad thing.

I can't remember a time when Dex was as happy as he is now. He walks around with a goofy smile on his face all day long, and the only time I've seen him the slightest bit upset is when Olivia had to spend three days in a row working and wasn't able to see him.

Now that Dex is in a good place, there's no excuse to continue keeping my relationship with Amy a secret any longer. Thankfully, she and I are in total agreement about that. I told her that I would do it myself, but she insists that it's something we should do together. So, we decided that this weekend we'll invite him over for dinner, sit him down, and tell him.

That leaves me with the dilemma of what to do for Amy's birthday. Since I have no idea what I'm doing, I decide that my best option is get help from the most romantic person I know.

My dad.

After all, he and my mom have been married for over thirty years, and he never misses a birthday or anniversary, ever. Hell, he makes sweet romantic gestures all the time for no reason at all. *"When you meet the right woman, you should treat every day like your anniversary,"* he always tells me.

When he comes into the shop on a morning that Dex isn't around, I decide to just go for it. "So, Dad, I was um, kind of hoping you might be able to give me some advice," I mumble, keeping my eyes fixed on the engine in front of me.

"I'll certainly try." He turns to me with a shrewd grin. "But only if you tell me who she is."

Of course he already has me figured out.

"Well, it's Amy. Amy Porter." I study his face as he puts it together.

"As in Dex's twin sister?" I nod, and he throws his head back laughing. "Oh boy, you must have it real bad to be stickin' your hand in the basket of forbidden fruit! Does Dex know?"

Groaning loudly, I shake my head. "We're going to tell him soon, we just..." I sigh, "We wanted to figure things out first."

"I get it," he says, giving me a soft pat on the back. "I know how much Dex means to you, son. I know you wouldn't be goin' after his sister unless you had real serious feelings for her. She must be somethin' special."

"She is," I tell him. "She's it for me. But I don't know how Dex is going to take it."

"Not gonna lie, he'll probably be pissed off," he says bluntly. "At first, anyway. No one likes to be kept in the dark." I let out another loud groan, and my dad grins. "He'll get over it, though. He loves ya, kiddo, and when he sees how important she is to you, he'll come around."

"I sure hope so."

"Now what is it you need my advice on?" he asks. "It couldn't have been about that, 'cause I didn't tell you anything you don't already know."

"Amy's birthday is coming up," I start.

"Aha! So you need help comin' up with something to give her?"

"Exactly," I nod. "I want find something that she'll love, but that's meaningful, too… and I have no clue what that would be."

I know that Amy couldn't care less about material shit, but I want to spoil her. I made really good money when I was doing those high-end restorations, and since I live fairly simply, it's just been sitting in a bank account untouched, gathering interest.

My dad wanders into the small office and comes back with a business card. "There's a jewelry store on King Street downtown." He hands me the card. "Ask for this guy, and he'll give you a good deal on whatever you find. I've bought your mama so much jewelry over the years that he's practically family."

"Jewelry?" I guess it's an obvious answer, but I'm worried that it won't be special enough. I want something that will really tell her how I feel, and I'm not sure that jewelry will do that.

"Trust me. All women love jewelry, so that part's a no-brainer. You can't buy just anything, though. You gotta go in there and search for something that has significance. Something that couldn't possibly belong anywhere else but on *her*. You'll know it when you see it."

■   ■   ■

I walk into that jewelry store thinking that my dad has officially lost his mind, and there's no way I'll ever find anything like he described.

However, when I'm browsing a glass case and my eyes land on three brightly sparkling stones, I immediately realize that I'm wrong.

My dad is a friggin' genius.

chapter twenty-one

Amy

On the day that Nate and I plan to finally tell my brother about our relationship, Dex calls to let me know that he's not sure if he'll be able to make it to dinner with us. Apparently he and Olivia have some kind of situation to take care of, and he doesn't know if they'll be back in time.

I do my best to hide my growing frustration, and I'm tempted to blurt it out over the phone just to get it over with. There was a time that the secrecy made it easier for Nate and me to be together, but now it's a huge weight that we're dragging along, preventing us from moving forward until we can detach ourselves from it.

I hadn't intended for Sadie to be around for the big conversation, since we don't know how Dex will react, so I've already arranged for her to spend the night at my parents' house. She loves her sleepovers with Grammy and Papa, so even when it becomes clear that Dex won't be able to make it, I don't bother to cancel the plans.

Instead, Nate and I enjoy a laid-back dinner, just the two of us.

We don't have many opportunities to be completely alone, so we soak up every minute of it, drinking wine outside on the deck while the sun sets and curling up on the couch to watch movies.

We almost make it to the end credits before our lips find each other. It starts off as a harmless peck, but soon our mouths are crushed together, tongues tangling and twisting. Nate presses my back into the couch, arranging his body over mine. I part my legs to make room for his hips to fall between them, moaning into his mouth when I feel the exquisite pressure of his hardness against me. He drags his lips along my throat, tasting my skin as he rolls his hips forward.

Reaching for his tee shirt, I grasp it in both hands and tug it over his head, tossing it to the floor. His bare skin is hot against my palms as I slide them up his back, memorizing the slope and contour of each muscle. Drawing back slightly, he lifts the hem of my shirt and begins kissing a slow path up my stomach, between the valley of my breasts and along my collarbone before pulling my shirt off completely. My hands are at his belt when I hear the front door burst open.

"What the fuck is going on here?" Dex's voice explodes through the apartment.

Nate instantly leaps off the couch, his eyes wide and the color draining from his face as he gapes at my brother. He looks terrified, and I don't blame him. I'm not sure I've ever seen Dex look so angry. With his fists clenched tightly at his sides, nostrils flaring, he looks as though he's ready for a fight. Olivia is standing behind him with a mortified expression on her face that quickly turns sympathetic when she realizes what's going on.

"Dex! What the hell do you think you're doing?" I grab my shirt from where it's strewn on the floor and quickly pull it over my head. "You can't just barge in here like that. Get out!"

"I saw Nate's car parked outside. I thought something was

wrong!" He looks almost embarrassed when his eyes meet mine, but any trace of remorse is gone when he turns to Nate. "And clearly I was right. What the *fuck* are you doing with my sister?"

"This is none of your business, Dex," I say. Nate's still frozen in place, completely dumbfounded, and I move to stand in front of him, positioning myself between them. "I'm a grown woman, not a teenager. You're not responsible for what I do."

I've been putting up with Dex's overprotective and controlling nature ever since I was a kid. I know that I should probably be feeling guilty, but right now I'm too furious and humiliated to find room for any other emotions.

"Where's Sadie?" Dex asks with narrowed eyes. "It's not very mature of you to do this while your daughter is in the next room."

I roll my eyes. "She's at Mom and Dad's house, you idiot." His comment should have me seething, but even through my anger I know that he would never consciously imply that I'm an irresponsible mother.

Dex glares at Nate, eyeing him as he pulls his shirt over his head. "Seriously, dude? Of all the girls for you to screw around with, you had to choose my sister?"

"I'm not screwing around with her," Nate says, speaking up for the first time. He steps up beside me and wraps his arm protectively around my waist. "I love her."

A gasp flies out of my mouth as I spin toward him. He squeezes me gently, as if to confirm the words, but keeps his eyes locked on Dex. A fluttery feeling fills my belly, and when I turn back to face Dex, I have to fight to keep the smile off my face.

It's obvious that Dex wasn't expecting to hear that. "You better not be fucking around with me," he cautions, aiming a suspicious look in Nate's direction. "The last asshole who told me that he loved her got her pregnant and then took off. How the hell do I know that you aren't going to do the same thing?"

"Oh, come on, don't compare me to that jackass," Nate groans, taking a step forward. "I'm your best friend, Dex. You fucking know me, and I'm telling you that this is for real. I've had feelings for Amy for a long time now, and I'm sick of pretending that I don't."

"And what about Sadie, are you really ready for all that?" Dex asks. "Because in case you haven't noticed, they're kind of a package deal."

"Of course I know that, and you know I love Sadie, too." Nate shifts his gaze to mine, addressing both of us at the same time. "I'll be in her life however Amy will let me, whether it's as a dad or just as a friend. I will never hurt either of them, you know that."

Dex studies me for a moment. "This is what you want?"

Tears prick at my eyes as look up at Nate, no longer trying to conceal the huge smile on my face. "Yes, absolutely," I say, nodding. "I've wanted this for a really long time, and I'm sorry for keeping it from you, but he makes me happy. I haven't been this happy in a really long time." I turn to Dex and glare at him with narrowed eyes. "You're my brother and I love you, but if you try and mess this up, I will hurt you. You don't scare me, Dex Porter!"

"Well, fuck," Dex chuckles gently. "I guess that's that then."

Olivia grabs his hand and begins pulling him out of the room. "Let's leave these kids alone. I'm freezing my ass off over here. I say we hit the shower."

As I take in the two of them, I notice for the first time that they have wet hair and damp clothes. "Yeah, what the hell happened to you two, anyway?"

Nate

As soon as Dex and Olivia are gone, I wrap my arms around Amy and pull her close. "I'm sorry that I told your brother before you, but I love you, Amy. I love you so much."

"I love you, too," she breathes, standing on her tiptoes to brush her lips against mine. "That didn't go quite as we planned."

"Not exactly," I say with a laugh. "But at least it's all out in the open now. The important thing is that he's okay with it… or will be."

"I guess the mood has officially been ruined, huh?"

Nothing kills the libido like having your best friend walk in on you half naked with his sister.

"Yeah, I think so." I cradle her cheek in my hand as I lean forward to kiss her again. "But we've got all the time in the world for that now."

I spend a while longer with Amy before we say our goodbyes and I head home. Despite the utter humiliation of having Dex catch us together, the fact that he finally knows and is somewhat okay with it makes everything worthwhile.

After weeks of planning and agonizing over this moment, and how it would play out, I should feel as though a huge weight has been lifted. Yet, as I pull up to my house, I'm still filled with the same restless anxiety as before.

Throwing the car into reverse, I turn around and go back the way I came. I'm at Amy's house in less than five minutes. When I see the dim light pouring through her bedroom window, I run up the outside steps, taking them two at a time, until I'm standing at her front door. I knock loudly, and a moment later another light flips on, and I see her walking toward the door in her tiny pajama shorts and a tank top.

"Nate?" She opens the door with a puzzled expression. "Is everything okay?"

"It's more than okay," I respond, urging her into the apartment as I close the door behind me. "I just decided that, even though we have all the time in the world, I don't want to wait another minute."

I pull her into my arms, bringing my mouth down to hers. "God, I'm so glad you came back," she sighs against my lips, weaving her fingers into my hair and pulling me toward her.

As our mouths work furiously against each other, I run my hands down her back and over the gentle slope of her ass, grasping it tightly and lifting her up. She lets out a squeal before wrapping her legs around my waist as I carry her into her bedroom.

I kick off my shoes before lowering her onto the bed and aligning myself on top of her. She quickly reaches for the hem of my shirt, tugging it over my head and throwing it aside. I can feel her taut nipples through the thin material of her tank, grazing against my bare chest and making me harder with each tantalizing stroke.

After making quick work of removing her shirt, I lower my mouth to her breasts. "I love these gorgeous tits," I tell her, skimming my tongue over one perky nipple and sucking it eagerly. She cries out, digging her nails into my back and sending me into a frenzy of lust.

Rising onto my knees, I hook my fingers into the waistband of her shorts and panties, sliding them down her long slender legs and taking them off. When she's bared completely, I gaze down at her hungrily, unable to decide where I want to begin.

"You're so goddamn beautiful," I murmur, grabbing both of her ankles and tracing my palms upward, pulling them apart as I go. She bites her lip nervously, her breasts rising and falling with each heavy breath she takes. "I've been waiting to taste you since I was eighteen."

I bring my head between her legs and drag my tongue over her wet slit, tasting her sweet arousal on my tongue before working my mouth over her.

"Oh God, don't stop…" she begs, clutching my hair in her fingers as I lick and suck her pussy until she comes loudly, muffling her screams in her pillow.

Standing from the bed, I keep my eyes locked on hers, watching her pant breathlessly as I unbutton my jeans and let them drop to the floor. My boxers soon follow, and as I tear open the condom, she raises herself onto her elbows and watches greedily as I slide it over my length.

"It's been a really long time," she blurts out, suddenly appearing nervous. "I might not be very… good."

I cock my head to the side and look at her. "You're crazy to even think that," I say, crawling on top of her and settling between her legs. Propping myself up on my forearms, I gaze down at her. "I've never wanted anyone the way that I want you, Amy. I love everything about you, and I can't wait to bury myself inside you. It only makes it better to know that this is mine, and only mine." I nudge the head of my cock against her slick opening, teasing her. "It's going to be so far beyond good, I promise you that."

She nods, and I gently push inside her tight heat, pausing only briefly to search her eyes for any sign of hesitation.

"I want you, Nate," she assures me, wrapping her legs around my waist. "All of you."

I thrust all the way in, groaning as her body squeezes me from the inside. "Christ, Amy." I grate out the words, drawing back slightly and then pressing back in. "You feel incredible. So fucking tight. So perfect. I'm not going to be able to last."

My pace starts off relatively slow, giving her body a chance to get used to me. I don't want to hurt her, so I restrain myself as much as I can, fighting against the urge to plunge hard and deep inside her.

She glides her palms down my spine and clutches my backside, her fingers digging into my flesh as she pulls me toward her. "Give it to me," she moans in my ear. "I promise I won't break. You don't need to be gentle, just give it to me."

Her words are my undoing. I pull nearly all the way out, and then drive my hips forward, slamming hard and deep inside her. She cries out, clawing at my back, and it feels so damn good I have to grit my teeth to keep from exploding.

"Holy shit, just like that." Her breath hitches as she tilts her hips up to meet mine. "God, that feels so fucking good."

"You like the way my cock feels in your tight pussy?" I growl, losing all control when I hear her beginning to let go. "I want to feel you come all over it, baby."

I pound into her with long, deep strokes until I feel her start to tighten around me. "Oh my God," she gasps, her voice needy and breathless as she trembles beneath me.

"I love you so fucking much." My balls are tight with the need for release, but I know she's close. I bring my lips to her breasts and suck on her pert nipple while I continue pumping inside her. She comes hard, crying out loudly as her pussy constricts around my length and sends me over the edge, bursting inside her with a strangled groan.

I collapse on top of her, both of us panting softly as we struggle to catch our breath. When I can finally breathe again, I sweep my mouth over hers and gently ease out of her before standing to quickly dispose of the condom.

She's still lying in the same position when I come back, gazing at me with a sated smile. I instantly crawl back into the bed, pulling her body on top of mine and holding her close. "There are no words for how amazing that was," I say, brushing my lips across her forehead. "Most definitely worth the wait."

"Definitely." She presses a kiss to my chest, and then looks up at me with a coy grin, her eyes greedy with lust. "But I'm glad we won't have to do any more waiting from now on."

"Oh, really?" I drag her onto my lap to straddle me, letting her feel my already firm cock between her legs. "You're in for it now, baby."

chapter twenty-two

Amy

In an effort to make up for barging in on us, Dex and Olivia offer to babysit Sadie so that Nate and I can go out for the night. Technically, it's our first real date, and I'm surprisingly nervous considering that we've been seeing each other for weeks now.

I change my outfit at least four times before finally settling on a short, stretchy skirt and a tank top with a cute pair of sandals. Olivia picks out a chunky necklace to go with it and helps me add a few wavy curls to my long hair.

"Wow, you look seriously fantastic," she tells me, stepping back to give me a quick once over before I head out. "You are, like, the hottest mom ever!"

I laugh, but the praise helps. It's rare that I get dressed up, and having Olivia around for the added reassurance makes me feel a lot better about it.

There's a knock on the door, and my stomach flutters knowing that it's Nate. "I better get out there before Dex pulls the brotherly intimidation routine on him," I say, rolling my eyes as I open my bedroom door.

"Don't worry, Dex is under strict instructions to be on his best behavior," Olivia says, following me out. "Besides, I think he's warming up to the whole idea."

When we get into the living room, Nate is standing by the front door in a pair of khakis and a navy blue V-neck sweater. His hair is combed back, and he looks ridiculously handsome. I can hardly believe that he's here for *me*.

"You look... wow." He exhales a long breath, raking his eyes over me, and grins. "Ready to go?"

"You look... too," I blush, hiding behind my loose hair.

"Okay, get out of here, you two." Olivia says, practically pushing us out the door. "Have fun!"

As we get outside, I pause when I see Nate's old Ford Mustang in the driveway. "I can't believe you brought the Mustang!" I say, rushing toward it. "I thought you got rid of it."

Nate opens the passenger door and helps me in. "No way. This is the first car I ever restored. I could never get rid of it. Besides, it holds a lot of fond memories... like the night I made out with a gorgeous, hazel-eyed brunette in the front seat and she stole my heart." He stares down at me with a wide grin. "It seemed only right for me to drive it on my first date with her."

A smile curves at my lips, and if possible, I think I fall deeper in love with him. When he climbs into the driver's seat and starts the engine, I turn to him. "So where are you taking me?"

"You'll see." He winks, reaching for my hand and twining his fingers through mine.

When we pull up in front of the bowling alley where I had my devastating first date in high school, I turn to Nate with questions in my eyes. "What are we doing here?"

"When I watched you leave on that date, all I could think about was what it would be like if it were me with you instead of him," Nate says, an adorable smile dangling on the corner of his lips. "Now I finally have a chance."

■ ■ ■

"Ugh!" I exclaim, watching my ball drift into the gutter. "This is so much harder than I remember."

We're on our last frame, and despite my horrific bowling skills, I'm having a great time. We ate greasy pizza and drank beer, all while enjoying endless laughs as we watch each other's bowling attempts.

"Let me give you a hand," Nate offers, stepping up behind me and pressing his chest against my back. He wraps his arms around my stomach, positioning them alongside mine as I grip the heavy ball. "Now, you need to spread your legs a little more," he breathes into my ear, using his thigh to nudge my legs further apart.

I can feel the firm outline of his erection, and I press my backside against it, smiling to myself. "Like this?"

He groans softly, and I shudder when I feel his warm breath against my skin. "Don't you dare tease me, Ames."

"Wouldn't dream of it," I reply, twisting around to wink at him. Stepping forward, I swing my hand back and use all my strength to heave the ball down the lane. It rolls down the wooden surface, weaving slightly, and then crashes through the pins, dead center.

"Strike!" I shout, throwing my hands up in the air. I spin around and run toward Nate, careful not to slip and fall as I jump into his arms.

"Way to go, babe!" He swings me around once before setting me back down on the floor. "I say we end this game on a high-note and get out of here, what do you think?"

Once we've turned in our bowling shoes, we leave the alley and climb back into the Mustang. Nate drives in the direction of our old high school, continuing past it until we get to Brittlebank Park. It's a quiet area overlooking the Ashley River, notorious for being the go-to spot for teenagers to park and make out. It's understandable, considering how beautiful and romantic it is, not to mention that it's deserted after dark.

"I've always wanted to come here," I admit, glancing at Nate with a small smile.

Reaching over, he grazes his thumb along my jaw. "I've always wanted to come here with you."

He brushes his lips against mine, so softly that they barely touch but leaves me breathless. When he leans down again, his kiss is firm and steady. I grab the back of his neck and pull him closer, parting my lips with a moan when his tongue finds mine. He drags me along the smooth leather of the bench seat, bringing me as close to him as possible.

It's not close enough for me. I throw my leg over him, straddling his lap with my back pressed against the steering wheel. I vividly recall being in this same position with him once before, back when I was desperate for him to be mine. That time I was left disappointed, but now everything's different, and I intend to make the most of it.

Nate runs his hands up my thighs, lifting my skirt until it's bunched around my waist. He hauls my hips into him, grinding me against his arousal and filling me with pure, anxious need.

Sitting back, I reach between us and unbuckle his belt, eagerly undoing his pants as quickly as possible. Lowering them down far enough to free him, I stroke his smooth length with my fingers as he fumbles to grab a condom from his wallet. I take the foil packet from his hands and tear it open with my teeth before slowly rolling it over him.

"God, Amy," he groans. "You're going to make me explode before I even have a chance to get inside you."

As soon as he's covered, he lifts me up and positions me above him, shoving my panties aside and teasing me with his fingers. I lower myself down on him in one swift motion, filling myself with every inch of him until he's deep inside me.

"Fuck," he exclaims, digging his hands into my hips.

I start moving on top of him, and he's so deep, and so big, that within seconds I can already feel my release building. "Oh my God, I'm gonna come," I chant, sliding up and down his length, getting closer to the edge with each delicious stroke.

"I want to feel you come all over me," he commands, thrusting upward and driving himself even deeper. "Keep riding me, just like that."

I grind my hips, bracing my hands against the ceiling as he pumps inside me, hot and thick, propelling me higher and higher. I dimly hear myself cry out his name as an intense orgasm tears through me, sending wave after wave of pleasure pulsing through me.

Nate stills, and I feel him jerk inside me as he follows me into oblivion. I rest my forehead against his as we both catch our breath while he holds me gently in his arms.

"If I'd had you in high school, I never would have let you go," he murmurs gently.

"You have me now." I nuzzle against him. "And I'm not going anywhere."

Nate

"So, exactly how long have you had a thing for my sister?" Dex asks over beers at the garage. It's the end of a long, busy afternoon at work, and when we finally finished for the day, we decided to celebrate with a couple of beers.

"I don't know, man, a long time," I answer with a laugh, thinking back to when I first started looking at Amy as more than my buddy's sister. "I had a thing for her in high school, but she was your sister, so she was off-limits."

He shakes his head. "How the hell did I not know about this?"

"I didn't want to risk a beating from you, so I hid it well." I take a long pull from my beer and swallow. "Then you left for basic training so I didn't see her that much, and that scumbag Duncan swooped in, got her pregnant and fucking left her." I clench my fist at my side to keep from punching something. Just thinking about Duncan sends fire through my veins. "God, I fucking hate that kid."

"You and me both," Dex grumbles. "At least he got a little bit of what was coming to him when he broke his arm and lost that football scholarship."

"You totally broke his arm, didn't you?" I ask, grinning. "I fucking knew it was you!"

The thought had crossed my mind when I first heard about Duncan, a few months after we found out that Amy was pregnant, but I didn't think that Dex would risk his military career over it. Clearly, I was wrong, and I'm glad.

He holds his hands up defensively. "I'm not admitting to anything."

The satisfied gleam in his eyes tells me everything that I need to know.

"Hey, I'm not judging." I turn to him with a pleased smile. "Do you remember his BMW that he loved so much?"

"Uh oh, what'd you do to it?"

"Rice in the radiator. Clogged the whole damn engine and destroyed it. I'd do it again in a second, too. After what he did to her, he got off easy."

A proud, grateful smile appears on his face, but it quickly turns into a scowl. "I never should have let that asshole anywhere near her. I should have known that he was no good."

"Oh, come on. There's no way you could have known that Duncan would turn out to be such a prick. He had everyone fooled with his bullshit golden boy act."

"Yeah, but I'm her brother," he mutters, staring down at the ground. "It's my job to watch out for her."

"And you do. You always have." I wish he could see that. Dex assumes responsibility for all the bad around him, even when there's nothing he can do to prevent it. "You carry around the weight of the world on your shoulders, and if you keep holding yourself responsible for the bad things that happen to the people around you... one of these days it's going to break you. Sometimes bad things happen. It's a part of life and it's not always anyone's fault. You can't change it. All you can do is move on."

■ ■ ■

The sharp ring from my cell phone cuts into my dreams, waking me from a deep sleep. Amy's curled up against my chest, sleeping soundly, and I quickly grab the phone from my bedside table to silence it before it wakes her.

I squint to read the small screen, and when I see Dex's name flashing across the front I answer immediately, knowing that he wouldn't call in the middle of the night unless it was important.

"Dex?" My voice is heavy with sleep. "Everything okay?"

"Hey, man," he says from the other end. "Sorry to wake you, but there was an incident tonight at the girls' house. Is Amy with you?"

"Yeah, she's here at my place, and Sadie is with your parents." I sit up in bed, stirring Amy awake in the process. "What happened?"

"Turns out Olivia's ex is a psycho stalker," Dex responds in a tight voice. "He broke into her place tonight and attacked her with a knife."

"Fuck, is she okay?"

"She's fine, thank fucking god. I showed up just in time. He got me once before I beat the shit out of him, but I only needed a few stitches. We're heading back to my place now. Sorry to wake you up, I just wanted to fill you in before you went back there and freaked out. There may still be police at the house."

"No, I'm glad you called," I tell him. "And I'm glad you're both okay. We'll talk to you in the morning."

"Thanks, man. I'm relieved that Amy was with you tonight. This whole thing could've been a whole lot fucking worse, and I feel better knowing that you're around to keep her safe."

I don't even want to consider what might have happened if Amy and Sadie had been at home when all of this went down. The thought of anything bad happening to them makes me sick to my stomach. They could've easily gotten hurt tonight, and it's pure luck that we decided to stay at my place for the night.

Luck isn't going to cut it for me.

There's no way in hell I'm going to let anything happen to Amy or Sadie. Ever. I intend to have a very long future with them, and I will do whatever it takes to keep them safe and happy.

chapter twenty-three

Amy

"You want to move in together?" I repeat, staring at him in disbelief.

"Yup, I do," Nate says with a grin. "What do you think?"

I bite my lip, trying to make sense of the warring emotions going on inside me. "Is this because of what happened with Olivia?"

I'll admit that it's terrifying what happened to her—and what *could* have happened—but I don't want fear to be the motivating factor behind the decision for Nate and I to move in together. I need the idea to come from him, and him alone, because it's what he *wants*, and not merely because he feels obligated.

"That's part of it," he says, causing my lips to curl into a frown. "But only a small part of it," he clarifies, reaching for my hand. "This is something I want no matter what, regardless of anything else. What happened last night with Olivia only made realize that I don't want to postpone it. The thought of anything happening to you..." He exhales a long breath, staring down at his hands. "God, it would break me. I never want to lose you, Ames."

"I don't want to lose you either," I respond softly. I so badly want to have confidence in what he's telling me. I don't doubt that he's being genuine, or that he loves me, but the nagging uncertainty in the back of my mind needs to be sure that this is what he *truly* wants.

He watches me for a moment, studying me in the way that makes me question whether he has the ability to see right into my head. "I know it may seem like I'm doing this for the wrong reasons," he says, "But when it comes down to it, I only have one reason, and it's the only reason that matters." He tilts my chin up, locking his eyes with mine. "And that is that I love you, Amy Porter. I want to take this step with you so that we can start building a future together. You, me, and Sadie. That's all that matters here."

My heart feels like it's going to float up out of my chest, his words erasing any lingering uncertainty. I know that I want this, but still I ask, "You don't think it's too soon?"

Nate chuckles. "Well, I've basically been in love with you since I was eighteen, and I waited six years to finally make you mine. Are you really going to make me wait even longer?"

"No, I'm sick of waiting," I tell him, a huge smile spreading across my face. "Let's do it."

"Really?" His eyes fill with hope and excitement.

I nod, choking back tears as he pulls me into his arms and slams his mouth against mine. Pulling back, slightly breathless, I say, "Of course, there's still one more person we have to convince."

■　　■　　■

Later that day, I sit down with Sadie to talk to her about Nate moving in with us. Nate and I had discussed the possibility of finding a new place altogether, but we both agreed that it makes the most sense to stay where Sadie is comfortable. Besides, as it turns out, Dex convinced Olivia to move into his place, so Nate and I will be able to merge the two apartments into one space for us to live in.

"Am I in trouble?" Sadie asks, concern filling her eyes.

I smile. "Of course not, baby girl. I just wanted to talk to you about Nate."

"Is he not comin' over for dinner tonight?" Her face falls.

I have to hold back a smile when I see how upset she is over the idea of Nate skipping dinner with us. I love that she's already so attached to him.

"No, he's still coming," I reassure her. "I wanted to see how you would feel about Nate being with us all the time, living here in the house."

"That sounds fun!" Sadie exclaims, clapping her hands together. "But why? Is it because he's your best friend?"

"Yes, he is my best friend." I hesitate, struggling to find the right words even though I've practiced this speech a hundred times. "But we also love each other. Do you know what that means?"

"Like Grammy and Papa?"

"Exactly." I smile. "And people who love each other want to spend as much time together as they can. But we'll only do this if it makes you happy, too. Would you like Nate to live with us?"

She bobs her head up and down. "Yes, Mommy."

"Okay, good. I'd like that, too." This was easier than I expected, though we're not finished yet, despite the fact that Sadie is quickly becoming bored with this conversation. "You know, baby girl, Nate doesn't just love me. He loves you, too."

"He does?"

"Of course he does! He loves hanging out with you, and taking you to the beach, and playing games with you. In fact, he told me that he can't wait to move in here so that he can read books with you *every* night before bed."

"Yes!" she cheers, bouncing up and down in her seat. "Can he move in now?"

"Not right now," I laugh. "But soon."

"Are you and Nate gonna get married?" she asks expectantly.

"Um, well…" I fumble to find the right words for a careful, sensible response. Then, I opt to listen to my gut and go with honesty. "I hope that we'll get married someday, and I think we will. Not quite yet, but eventually." This topic of conversation wasn't exactly on my agenda, but I decide to go with it. We might as well put it all on the table now.

She scrunches her little eyebrows together, looking down. "Does that mean Nate will be my daddy?"

My heart stalls in my chest. I'm not prepared to answer this. I'm terrified that I'll say the wrong thing or choose the wrong words. Then I remember what Nate said to Dex.

"That's totally up to you, Sade. Nate can be your friend, or your daddy, or whatever you want him to be. He's happy just to be in your life. You get to choose what he is to you, okay?"

"I think I might like Nate to be my daddy someday," she says in a small, timid voice. "Do you think he wants to?"

I gather her in my arms and hug her tight, kissing her forehead. "I *know* he wants to, baby girl."

Nate

I pull into Amy's driveway just as Dex and Olivia are loading the last of her things into the back of his truck. Olivia examines the huge stack of boxes that are currently occupying my back seat and looks at me curiously. "What's going on?"

"Didn't Amy tell you?" I respond, grinning. "I'm moving in."

She glances at Dex with a terrified expression, as though she's afraid he might take a swing at me. When he shows no visible reaction, she raises her eyebrows. "You knew about this?"

"Of course I did," Dex says with a smirk. "It was my idea. I wanted to make sure that Amy and Sadie were safe here."

"Actually, I believe your genius idea was to install an alarm system," I clarify, rolling my eyes. "I'm the one who suggested that I move in with them."

I'd gone to Dex first, before I brought it up with Amy. Not because I needed his permission, or even his approval, but because I felt I owed it to him. Considering the way he found out about Amy and me, I figured this time he deserved to be given him a heads up. Fortunately, their safety is his main concern, so he didn't even put up a fight about it.

"But I'm the one who came up with the plan to re-connect the two apartments and make more space for you guys," Dex retorts smugly.

"Enough!" Olivia laughs, shaking her head at us. "I'm just glad it all worked out."

"Me too," I say. Everything about this feels right, like the pieces in my life are falling into place. Amy, Sadie and me moving in together, Olivia moving in with Dex... this is how it's meant to be. It's unfortunate that it took an attack from a psychotic ex to put the wheels in motion, but at least it turned out okay in the end.

Sadie comes running toward me, a huge smile on her face. "Nate!"

"What's up, Sade?" I swoop down and pick her up. "Are you going to help me move in?"

Nodding she says, "Mommy told me to bring this to you."

She holds up a brass house key, and warmth radiates through me. "Should we go test it out?" I ask, carrying her up the stairs to the front door.

Together we insert the key into the lock and twist the knob, pushing the door open. Amy's standing just inside, waiting for us.

"Welcome home," she smiles.

■　■　■

It's a few days before Amy's birthday, and I've successfully managed to not only keep her present hidden, but also keep my mouth shut. That is, until I'm lying in bed, clad in only my boxers, and she comes out of the bathroom holding my cell phone with a puzzled expression on her face.

"Why did you just get a text message from Olivia about meeting her tomorrow while I'm at school?"

"Uhhh..." I stammer, searching my brain for a reasonable explanation and coming up empty. "I don't know. That's really weird."

"What's going on here?" she demands, shimmying over to the bed in her teeny tiny sleep shorts and a tank top that I can see her nipples through.

Living together is awesome.

"Nothing's going on," I reply as casually as possible. "What would be going on?"

She plants her hand on her hip, jutting it outward. "You're a terrible liar."

She's irritated, but not angry, which surprises me. Most women in this situation would immediately jump to conclusions and be furious, which she isn't. It dawns on me that Amy trusts me. Completely.

I grin widely. "I'm not lying."

Amy crawls across the mattress and sits astride me, one leg on either side of my hips. "I'm going to find out what you're up to," she says, a devilish gleam in her eyes.

These moments right before bed are my favorite part of the day. She's so insanely beautiful; her hair in a messy bun, her face scrubbed free of makeup, and the adorable pajamas that she insists on putting on, even though she knows I'm going to strip them off her as soon as she climbs into bed next to me.

Lounging back against the pillows, I gaze up at her, thoroughly enjoying the view of her above me. "I'm not up to anything, babe."

Shifting slightly on top of me, she quirks an eyebrow and glances down at the obvious bulge in my boxers, smirking. "Well, something's definitely up."

"What do you expect?" I say, running my hands up her smooth thighs, playing my fingers along the ruffled edge of her shorts. "It's been a long day, and I've been looking forward to this moment since I left the house this morning."

"Don't try and change the subject," she warns, trailing her finger along my elastic waistband. "What aren't you telling me?"

"I love you?"

She laughs. "Nice try, but *that* I already know." Leaning forward, she sweeps her lips briefly over mine.

"You're beautiful?"

"Try again..." Her tongue glides along my bottom lip, and she nips it gently between her teeth.

Groaning, I pull her toward me. "This is sexual blackmail."

"You know what they say, all's fair in love and war." Molding her mouth over mine, she skates her palms up my chest, leaving a path of fire beneath her touch. She rocks her hips against my arousal, letting me feel the heat from her pussy along every inch of my length as she rubs against it.

"Damnit, Amy..." I reach up to cup her breasts, palming them in my hand and teasing her nipples through the fabric of her shirt. "I need to bury my cock inside you."

"Just tell me what I want to know, babe." She yanks her tank top over her head, giving me a perfect view of her luscious tits, and then climbs off me to remove her shorts. Before returning to her position on top of me, she tugs my boxers down my thighs, letting my erection spring free.

"You're trying to kill me, aren't you?" I say through gritted teeth.

Shaking her head, she sinks against me, and it takes every ounce of control I have left to resist plunging inside her. I can feel her wetness as she slides over my cock, teasing me with every shift of her hips.

"Fuck it," I growl, flinging my arm to the side and fumbling in the bedside table for a condom. Once I find one, I tear it open and slide it over my length. "We're throwing you and Dex a surprise party."

The instant the confession leaves my lips, I lift her up and position myself at her entrance, slamming her down over me in one smooth motion.

■ ■ ■

"Are you really throwing us a surprise party?" Amy asks a short while later as we lay naked in bed.

"It's not much of a surprise anymore, but yes."

"If that hadn't been so amazing, I might feel bad for making you tell me," she says with a satisfied smirk.

"Baby, you're welcome to exchange sex for secrets any time you want," I tell her. "In fact, I think there are a few other things I haven't told you…"

She bats my arm playfully, making me laugh. "But seriously, I want you to have a great birthday, and since I already let it slip about the party, I may as well give you this now, too." I grab the small jewelry box from its hiding place at the back of my bedside table drawer and hand it to her. She stares at it for a moment until I say, "Open it."

Carefully she tears open the paper, and when she lifts the lid from the flat box, she gasps. "It's beautiful, Nate. I can't believe you did all this."

"I wanted to give you something special to mark the beginning of our life together," I say softly. "When I saw this in the store, I knew it was meant for you. I thought the three stones kind of, you know… represent the three of us. Me, you, and Sadie."

She runs her finger over the three diamonds that make up the pendant. "I absolutely love it. It's perfect. This is the most amazing gift I've ever gotten." She brings her lips to mine, lingering on them for a moment.

"You're the most amazing gift I've ever gotten," I say, not caring how cheesy it sounds. "And I can't wait to give you another diamond sometime in the near future."

She blushes slightly, dipping her chin to her chest. "Do you really mean that?"

"Of course I do." I caress my hand over her silky skin, dragging my mouth along the slope of her delicate neck. "I can't wait to marry you, and make babies with you, and grow old with you. This is only the beginning, Amy Porter."

"Only the beginning," she repeats with a smile, and then we lose ourselves in each other once again.

epilogue

Amy

"Okay, kiddos, snack time!" I address my students from the front of the classroom. "Grab your snacks from your cubbies, and then take your seats at the tables. This week's classroom helpers—Tina, Sadie, Mike and Beth—will hand out the juice boxes."

I can't resist winking at Sadie as she scampers over to the juice cart and starts wheeling it around the classroom, carefully placing a juice box in front of everyone. She started kindergarten in the fall, and I was lucky enough to get her in my class. I was worried at first that it might not be the best thing for Sadie to have her own mother as her teacher, but it's been wonderful. She doesn't try to use it to her advantage, and she's very good about keeping the roles separate. When we're at home, I'm her mom, but when we're in the classroom, I'm her teacher. I want her to have a normal learning experience, and as much as I love having her in my class, I don't treat her differently or favor her over the other students. At least, not *too* much.

There's a knock on the classroom door, and before I can glance up to see who it is, I hear Sadie squeal happily. "Daddy!"

She runs right over to Nate, who doesn't hesitate to lift her into his arms, smiling widely at her. "Hey, baby girl. Are you having a good day at school?"

She nods proudly. "I'm classroom helper this week."

"Wow! I bet you're doing a great job, too. I'm sure Mrs. Miller really appreciates it," he says, winking at me from across the room.

He lowers Sadie to the ground so she can rejoin her classmates for snack, and then walks over to me. "How's my other favorite girl doing?" he asks, dropping a kiss on my forehead as he hands me a small, brown paper bag. "I brought a snack for the teacher. Olives and a brownie."

"Have I told you lately how much I love you?" I say, gazing up at him gratefully as I open up the bag. "My day has been pretty good so far, but it just got a whole lot better."

"And how's my boy doing?" Nate gently rests his hand on my swollen, pregnant belly.

"Kicking up a storm," I respond as I struggle to twist the lid off the jar of olives. "Apparently at the six month mark, he's learned to use his legs. We may be growing a future soccer star in there."

He lifts the jar out of my hand, opening it easily before handing it back to me. "I don't care if he turns out to be a synchronized swimmer, just as long as he's happy and healthy."

My cheeks glow as I beam up at him, no longer surprised by the fact that he still gives me butterflies. I didn't think it was possible for me to love him any more than I do, but somehow I fall more in love with him each day. He's the most amazing husband, father, friend, partner and lover that I could ask for. He takes such good care of both me and Sadie, always making sweet gestures—like dropping off my latest pregnancy cravings and bringing me flowers for no reason—just to let us know how much we're loved.

"Can I sit with you and Daddy while I have my snack?" Sadie comes up to us, her eyes pleading. "Just this once?"

Nate's expression softens when he looks at her, and there's a gleam in his eye that is reserved exclusively for her. I remember the first time she called him "Daddy." It was right after we got married, and I seriously thought that Nate was going to collapse from pure joy. They have such a special connection, and it goes far beyond DNA or a name on a birth certificate. Sadie is his, and Nate is hers.

And they're both mine.

"Of course you can sit here," I tell Sadie, unable to deny her anything when she looks at us with that adorable face. "But only because Daddy's here for a visit."

Nate pulls up a chair next to mine, and Sadie climbs on his lap. I bite into the fudge brownie that Nate brought, and a faint moan escapes my lips when I taste the chocolaty goodness.

"Oh my God, this is good," I murmur in between bites. "At this rate, I'm going to be a total cow at Dex and Liv's wedding."

"You're perfect," Nate says, giving my thigh a gentle squeeze. "Even with chocolate all over your face, you're the most beautiful thing I've ever seen."

"Hey!" I laugh, feigning offense. "It's your fault for feeding my brownie cravings."

"I'm more than happy to feed *all* of your cravings." He grins devilishly, his eyes twinkling as he leans over to whisper in my ear.

"Especially your late night cravings. I happen to enjoy those the most."

I blush slightly, thinking of how... *insatiable*... I've been in the bedroom lately. Fortunately, Nate is more than happy to give in to my needs.

"Those cravings have nothing to do with pregnancy, Mr. Miller," I say with a wink. "See you later tonight?"

"Looking forward to it, Mrs. Miller."

three months later

■　■　■

Nate

"Are you ready to meet your little brother?" I ask Sadie, standing with her at the door to the hospital room.

She nods, taking my hand as I lead her over to the bed where my exhausted, yet beautiful, wife is waiting for us with the newest member of our family.

"Hey there, big sister," Amy says with a weary smile, her voice hoarse from hours of screaming. "He's been waiting to meet you."

Amy watches us as we approach, our son cradled safely in her arms. Her face is glowing with happiness, despite the fact that she's barely able to keep her eyes open. She's been up all night and desperately needs to rest, but we've been waiting for this moment ever since we found out she was pregnant, and it's an important one.

I lift Sadie up and carefully sit her down on the edge of the bed, leaving my arm wrapped around her and resting protectively across Amy's thighs. "Sadie, this is your baby brother. Ryan James Miller."

Amy tilts him toward her, tucking back the blue blanket that's wrapped around him so that Sadie can get a better look. She stares at him in awe, examining every feature on his tiny, wrinkly face.

"Hi, Ryan," Sadie says, laying a gentle hand on top of his head. "I'm Sadie. I'm your big sister. I love you so much."

Joy swirls inside my chest, filling me with such warmth I can barely breathe. When Ryan's mouth opens in a wide yawn, Sadie jerks around to look at me, a broad smile stretching across her cheeks. "Did you see that?" she squeals softly. "He is so cute!"

"I think he's excited to see you," I tell her, reaching for Amy's hand and squeezing it lightly in mine. We share a proud smile, her eyelids drifting shut as she falls asleep.

"He is?" Sadie says, unable to take her eyes off him.

"Absolutely," I say quietly, not wanting to wake Amy. "You're his big sister. He's going to look up to you and love you so much." I drop a quick kiss to the top of her head. "You're going to teach him things, and watch out for him, and protect him... you'll help him when he needs it and always be there for him. And he'll do the same for you, because that's what siblings do."

Sadie bends forward and kisses his forehead, whispering sweet, quiet words that only he can hear. There's no doubt in my mind that she'll be an incredible big sister, best friend, teacher, and protector. I'm amazed by her every day. She accepted me into her life with ease and showed me a different kind of love that I never knew existed.

As I watch the three of them—my beautiful wife sleeping peacefully, our perfect newborn son cradled in her arms, and my remarkable daughter with her hand resting protectively over him—I know with absolute certainty that this is where I'm meant to be. The only place I *want* to be. The love I feel for them, for my family, is stronger than anything else in the world. They own me.

Now and forever.

the end
. . .

Turn the page to read the first chapter of Dex and Olivia's story,
***Break Away,* available now...**

break away

Ellie Grace

When Olivia Mason catches her fiancé cheating, her life gets turned upside down. With no family and no real place to call home, she heads south for a fresh start in Charleston, South Carolina. Determined to gain her own independence and protect her heart, the last thing she needs is a sexy, tattoo-covered guy to cross her path and test her resolve. Just as she's beginning to put her life back together, she uncovers a piece of her past that shakes up everything.

Dex Porter has his own demons. A former Marine, he's haunted by the past and uses whiskey, women and fighting to drown the pain and guilt that consume him. When Olivia arrives in town, he finds himself drawn to her immediately and is surprised by his desire to get to know her. She's unlike anyone he's ever met but he knows he can't get close to her without exposing the part of himself that he keeps hidden.

As Dex and Olivia strike up a friendship and fight their attraction to one another, they begin to chip away each other's walls and help each other heal. However, the past is never far behind and they soon learn that no matter how fast they run, it will always catch up with them.

prologue

Olivia

For the first time since I'd arrived at the office, I glanced up from the piles of reports and spreadsheets that littered my desk and checked the time. It was already almost noon, and despite the fact that my morning coffee and muffin were practically untouched, it was also time for my lunch break.

It never ceased to amaze me how quickly time went by while performing the menial office tasks that went along with working at an investment firm in New York City. My official job title was "Assistant Analyst," which was really just a fancy term for someone who pushes paper all day and takes care of all the tedious duties that all the higher-ups were too busy and important to do themselves. I'm not sure what I had originally planned to do with my business degree, but being a glorified secretary wasn't exactly what I'd had in mind.

I'd been working at Chambers International for almost a year, since graduating from New York University. Investment banking wasn't something I was particularly interested in, but my fiancé,

Steven, was a senior analyst at the company, and his father also happened to be the CEO. Oh, and his grandfather was the company's founder. Needless to say, Steven had planned his whole life around working there and eventually taking it over, so when he suggested how great it would be for us to work together, I eventually agreed. He ended up proposing to me a few days later, leaving me to wonder if he was motivated by love or by the fact that I had finally added myself to the grand equation of his life.

Of course, Steven's office was upstairs with the other big-wigs and executives, so we didn't actually work together or see each other aside from the occasional lunch when his schedule permitted. Not that I minded. I wasn't working at his family's company because I wanted any handouts or special treatment. The truth was, I had taken the job because it was convenient, and I hadn't known what else to do.

I normally ate lunch by myself in the employee cafeteria, but today I decided to call up to Steven's office and find out if he wanted to join me. The phone rang only once before his secretary answered in her usual cheerful tone.

"Good afternoon, Steven Chambers' office. How may I help you?"

"Hi, Lynn, it's Olivia," I said. "Is Steven available by any chance?"

"No, hon, I'm afraid he's not. He went home for the day… said he wasn't feeling very well and thought he might be coming down with the flu."

"Oh, no problem. Thank you, Lynn." I hung up. That was strange; he hadn't mentioned that he was sick, and normally nothing could keep him out of the office. I hoped it wasn't anything too serious.

I made my way down to the first floor, but instead of going to the cafeteria, I decided to go to our apartment to check on Steven, stopping at a bistro along the way to pick up a bowl of his favorite chicken noodle soup. He was always making comments about how "cold" and "distant" I was, and even though he claimed to be joking around, I had the urge to do something nice and prove him wrong.

After greeting the doorman of our building, I stepped into the elevator and made my way up to our apartment on the fifth floor. Steven moved into this exclusive apartment complex when he was first hired full-time at the company. At the time, I was still a junior at NYU and hadn't wanted to move from the cozy, on-campus apartment that I shared with my roommate, Nora. However, after graduation when Nora moved back home to South Carolina and Steven and I got engaged, moving in with him made the most sense.

I still hadn't adjusted to living in such an elegant place and being a part of the glitzy lifestyle that Steven had always known. It was an entirely new world for me, and I would probably never get used to it. The only way of life I'd ever known was penny-pinching to make ends meet, shoebox apartments, and always earning my own keep. I didn't like Steven to pay my way, but he insisted on it. I did my best to reciprocate by always taking care of him—cooking his meals, cleaning the apartment, doing his laundry, ironing his shirts and basically catering to his every need. He seemed to like it that way.

I would have preferred paying rent.

Still, I was grateful to Steven. He'd come into my life and taken care of me when I had no one else. So no matter how much I hated cooking and cleaning, I would always do it for him.

The summer after I graduated high school, and only a month before I was to begin my first year at NYU, my mother died in a car accident. I'd never known my so-called father; he left when I was three, and we never heard from him again. My mom was an only child and lost both of her parents when she was young, so she was all the family I had. We moved around a lot while I was growing up. My mom would relocate to wherever there was work available, and since we were never in one place for an extended period of time, I'd never had any true, lifelong friends who stayed in touch. When I lost my mom, I was all alone.

As devastated as I was when my mom died, I began college in the fall as planned, mainly due to the simple fact that I hadn't had anywhere else to go. I went through the motions of school and classes, but it was all a haze. I'd become completely numb to everything around me. My roommate, Nora, was a big help, but she had her own problems. Within the first couple weeks of school I'd met Steven at the college library. He was a junior at the time and, unlike me, seemed to have his whole life together. He was determined, and always seemed to know the right thing to say. All of a sudden, I wasn't so alone anymore. He took care of me and was there for me when no one else was.

So, I became the person that he needed me to be.

I stepped off the elevator and into the hall that we shared with one other apartment. Letting myself in quietly, I slipped my heels off and set them down next to the door before making my way across the apartment. It was quiet, and I assumed that Steven was either resting in the bedroom or working in his home office. Before I had a chance to check, the bedroom door opened, and he walked out with a towel wrapped around his waist, his normally perfect hair all mussed up.

"Olivia, what are you doing here?" he said, closing the door tightly behind him. "Aren't you supposed to be at work?" A look of panic flashed across his features as he positioned himself between the door and me. His surprise was odd considering that our apartment was only a fifteen-minute walk from the office. It wasn't like I worked across the state and a quick trip home was out of the question.

"I'm on my lunch break," I explained. "Lynn told me that you went home sick and I wanted to check on you. I brought you some soup from that place downtown that you—"

I stopped mid-sentence when I heard the sound of the shower turning on. Before I had a chance to comprehend what was happening, a woman's voice called out from behind the closed bedroom door.

"Stevie! What's taking so long? Get your sexy ass in here so I can lather you up, you dirty, dirty boy…"

The door flung open and out waltzed an attractive brunette holding a towel that did little to hide her nakedness. She stopped in her tracks when she saw me, her cheerful expression morphing into fear. Steven was still standing there like a statue, all the color draining from his face as his eyeballs moved back and forth between me and the whore as though he was desperately searching his brain for some kind of explanation that didn't involve him being an asshole.

"Well, *Stevie*…apparently you have been a dirty boy," I spat out, anger boiling inside me. Was this seriously happening? He could have at least found a more original way to reveal himself as a cheating scumbag. I mean, come on. The whole situation was just so…cliché. I honestly wasn't sure whether I wanted to yell, cry, or laugh out loud. Maybe I really was a frigid bitch after all.

"Fuck, it's not what it looks like," Steven said, fumbling for words. He inched slowly toward me as though I were waving a loaded gun around and threatening to blow them both away.

I scoffed, rolling my eyes in disgust. "Don't be an idiot, Steven. It's exactly what it looks like." Finally moving from the spot where I was standing, I stormed into the bedroom and grabbed a small duffel bag from my closet, haphazardly packing the few things I had that meant enough to take with me. My closet was full of fancy clothes and expensive shoes, but I had no intention of taking any of that stuff with me. Steven had bought it all for me for the various parties and events that we'd attended over the years, and I didn't want anything from him anymore.

"Olivia, I'm so sorry," Steven said, slowly coming up behind me. "I was stupid and I let her seduce me, but I swear to you, it was a one-time mistake, and it meant nothing. You've been so distant lately, and after more than four years together, you still won't let me in. I was frustrated and upset. But it will never, ever happen again. I promise to make it up to you. Please, don't go. I made a mistake. We'll fix it and move on."

"You're seriously going to try and blame me for the fact that you couldn't keep it in your pants?" I asked, clenching my fists at my side. "That's the worst excuse I've ever heard! You are a pitiful excuse for a man, and I can't believe I wasted four years of my life with you. Go to hell!"

There was a flash of anger in his eyes, and I knew I'd struck a nerve. I'd never raised my voice to him like this, and Steven was someone who was used to always getting what he wanted. From everyone.

"Where are you going to go, Olivia?" he sneered. "In case you've forgotten, I'm all you've got!"

I zipped up the duffel bag and stood inches away from his face, glaring at him with narrowed eyes. "As far away from you as possible. I'd rather have no one than be with you."

Throwing my pitiful little bag over my shoulder, I turned and walked out of the room, muttering a sarcastic "good luck" to the woman still cowering in the hallway on my way out. I grabbed my purse, left my engagement ring and cell phone (that Steven paid for) on the counter and walked out the door without looking back.

Maybe I *had* always been a little bit closed off, but it was for good reason. Men were scum! Just look at my so-called father. He had claimed to love my mom and me, but at the first chance he got, he abandoned us. I never wanted to suffer through that kind of pain and heartbreak, which was why I'd chosen someone exactly the opposite of my dad. Steven was supposed to be the safe choice. After growing up in a state of constant change and instability, I had vowed to live my life differently. The reason I'd been so attracted to Steven in the first place was because he was predictable, uncomplicated and risk-free. I thought I would always know what was coming with him. Turned out I didn't know him at all.

I kept waiting for the crushing pain to hit me, but it never came. I felt angry, hurt, confused and slightly terrified about what I would do next, but somehow I also felt strangely relieved, like a weight had been lifted.

Unfortunately, I had no idea where the hell I was going or what I was going to do. Steven was right about one thing; I really didn't have anyone else.

chapter one

Olivia

I'd been in the car for almost fifteen hours now. When I first got on the road, I hadn't known where I was going. But after driving southbound for a while, I realized that there was only one place I wanted to go. The last place that had ever felt like home.

Charleston, South Carolina.

I'd never actually lived in South Carolina, but my mom was from Charleston and I'd spent time there with Nora when we were on break from school. There was something about the area that immediately drew me in. I couldn't explain it. Maybe it was because I felt a connection to my mom there, or maybe it was simply because the city was so beautiful, but as soon as I'd arrived there for the first time, I just had this feeling—like it was where I was meant to be. It was comforting and peaceful, and somehow being there put me at ease. Since my mom and I had moved around so much over the years, I'd lived in my fair share of places—Pennsylvania, Ohio, Maryland, Virginia, New York—but none had ever felt like home.

After leaving Steven's apartment, I'd wandered around the city for a while trying to decide what I was going to do. All I had was my purse, a few toiletries and a change of clothes. I didn't even have a cell phone anymore. Eventually, I'd hailed a cab to take me upstate to Scarsdale, where my mom and I had lived before she died.

All our stuff, including the old Honda she owned, was sitting in a storage unit there. I could never bring myself to go through it or throw any of it away, so I'd been paying for the storage until I decided what to do with it. Everything from my old life was in that unit. I hadn't wanted to bring any of it to Steven's—it never seemed right to have it there. I kept those two parts of my life separate. But now that I'd left my "new life" behind, it was all I had.

My old clothes were still there, and even though they were from when I was a teenager, I would have to make do until I could buy new stuff. I had started to sort through one of my mom's boxes, but it was too much. As soon as I opened it, the smell of her perfume hit me, opening a floodgate of memories that crashed into me like a freight train. It was amazing how a scent could transport me back in time and make me recall certain moments with absolute clarity. It brought me back to when I was a little girl, watching my mom as she sat at her vanity and got ready for work, dabbing a small amount of perfume on my wrist and my neck, just the way she did it. It made me feel so grown up.

I'd closed the box after I found what I was looking for. I left most of her stuff behind until I actually had a safe place for it, other than the trunk of the car. The only thing I'd wanted to bring with me was a pair of her earrings. They were beautiful, antique diamond drop earrings that had belonged to my grandmother. No matter how tight money was, my mom would never sell them. They had been special to her, and for some reason, I wanted to have them with me.

After loading up the car and saying a silent prayer that the old hunk of junk would still start, I hit the road, ready for a fresh start.

Once I'd decided on a destination, I drove straight through, making only a few stops along the way for food, bathroom breaks and a quick nap at one of the rest areas. I'd also grabbed a paper and thumbed through the classifieds in search of an apartment near Charleston. I knew that Nora was there and I could probably stay with her, but I wanted to do this without anyone's help or handouts. I never wanted to be dependent on anyone ever again. I needed to know that I could survive on my own.

The only apartment that I could afford was in Folly Beach, just outside Charleston. I called the number and arranged to see it the following morning.

After driving more than four hundred miles on I-95, I was desperate to see anything other than the same two-lane highway lined with trees, advertisements for fireworks and stands offering the area's famous handmade woven baskets. When I finally turned onto the exit for Charleston, I was full of nervous, excited energy. It wasn't long before I arrived in the city and saw the familiar cobblestone streets, live oak trees, and historic antebellum houses. It was still fairly early in the morning and the streets were quiet, not yet bustling with cars and crowds. It was like arriving in another time period, one that was enchanting and perfectly simplistic, a seamless blend of past and present.

I crossed the small bridge into Folly Beach and found the address that the woman had given me on the phone. It was a two-story house that sat on the edge of one of the river inlets. There was a small dock on the water and a hammock under the shade of tree. It was paradise.

As I climbed out of the car and stretched my tired limbs, a woman about my age came down the outside stairs from the top floor apartment. Her brown hair was pulled into a messy ponytail, and she carried a little blonde girl in her arms.

"Hi! You must be Olivia!" she greeted me happily. "I'm Amy, and this is my daughter, Sadie."

"It's so nice to meet you," I said, smiling and shaking her free hand. "Thank you so much for seeing me on such short notice."

"It's no problem at all! We live in the upstairs apartment, so we're here anyway. You're also the first person to inquire who isn't a creepy, middle-aged man," she laughed. "It's just the two of us, so I really wanted it to be a woman downstairs. Ready to take a look around?"

The apartment was perfect. It had a bedroom, a small kitchen and dining area, and a living room with glass doors leading to the backyard and a small patio. The lawn sloped down to the shore of the inlet and had a gorgeous view across the fields of marsh. It seemed too good to be true, and I couldn't believe how lucky I was to have found this place. I could easily see myself there.

I liked Amy and Sadie immediately. Amy was incredibly friendly, laid-back and easy to talk to. She was a single mother raising a four-year old daughter, so I already had an enormous amount of respect for her. I knew firsthand just how hard it was to be a single parent, but it was obvious that she was a great mom. Sadie was sweet and absolutely adorable. It seemed impossible not to smile around her. Although the two apartments in the house were separate, it would be nice to be around Amy and Sadie, and I hoped that I would get to know them better.

The downstairs apartment was empty, so thankfully I could move in right away. I signed the lease and wrote Amy a check, eager to get settled in. She helped me unload the few bags that I had with me, and after telling me to stop by for a glass of wine sometime, she left me to unpack my things and adjust to my new home.

Dex

I stared down my opponent, taking time to study him carefully and form a plan of attack. We stood across from each other inside a circle drawn in chalk on the cold cement of the basement floor, surrounded by dozens of people shouting last minute bets before the fight started. The air was musty, tinged with sweat, and buzzing with adrenaline, but I blocked everything out and zeroed in on the man who would try to beat the shit out of me as soon as the bell rang. He had a deadly expression on his face, but he couldn't intimidate me. I had already won the fight; he just didn't know it yet.

My lips curled up into a smile. He would find out soon.

"What are you smiling at, you fucking pussy?" he goaded. "You're not even a Marine anymore. You ain't shit, Porter. I almost feel bad that they put me up against your sorry, has-been, disabled, ex-Marine ass."

My smile only got wider. I couldn't wait to teach this prick a lesson. There was no such thing as an "ex-Marine." Once a Marine, always a Marine. The fact that I was no longer considered "fit" for active duty didn't change that. It pissed me off that pieces of shit like him didn't understand that. If it weren't for the partial hearing loss in my left ear, or "acoustic trauma" as the doctors referred to it, I would still be overseas with the rest of my unit. Everything in me wanted to be out there fighting for my country alongside them. But I was stuck here, honorably discharged and forced to retire before the age of thirty.

My body still hummed with the energy and lethal power of a

Marine. My brain still functioned and strategized like a Marine. The only way to take the edge off was by beating the shit out of other guys, which is why I participated in "underground" fighting. It was strictly other guys in the military – some who had been discharged for whatever reason, and others who weren't on active duty – but never any outsiders. Outsiders couldn't be trusted, and keeping it secret was crucial because any active military would be kicked out immediately if they were caught fighting. Sure, there was a lot of shit talking and rivalries between the different branches of the armed forces, but there was also a bond of trust. We were all warriors. Fighters.

We got together every couple of weeks and some people fought while others would just watch and place bets. In the end, we were all looking for the same thing: a way to take the edge off so we could function in our "normal" lives. No one ever got seriously injured. There was always someone assigned to monitor the fight and ensure that it didn't get out of hand. There was an element of structure to the whole thing that set it apart from the average bar fight and kicked the intensity up a notch or two.

Reece—the guy who was in charge and organized all the fights— would send out a mass text message when there was an upcoming fight to let us know where and when to show up. With both the Parris Island Military Base and the Citadel nearby, there was never a shortage of fighters or spectators. The locations rotated between different basements, garages and warehouses in the area, usually every couple of weeks or so. Reece took bets on the winners, and it was crazy how much money people were willing to throw down for one fight. I wasn't in it for the cash, but it sure as hell didn't hurt that I made a nice chunk of change every time I won. Which was often.

As barbaric as the whole thing sounded, it provided an outlet for those who needed it and was done in a controlled environment that made it safer for everyone. Before I found this group, the rage was practically eating me alive, and I was picking fights with random strangers in order to get my frustration out. It was better for everyone if my opponents were willing volunteers. Not to mention, it made for a much better fight when I was going up against someone who had the same kind of training that I did.

It was also one hell of a rush.

Some people had counseling or medication, but I had this. This was my fucking therapy. My momentary dose of freedom. The relief was fleeting, and I wasn't stupid enough to believe it was a cure, but it was all I had.

The bell rang, signaling the start of the fight. I watched as my opponent lunged forward, wasting no time before coming at me full force.

That was his first mistake.

I never struck first. Instead, I watched and analyzed my opponent. I examined their technique and looked for their weaknesses. Then, I waited for them to tire, and I used those weaknesses against them. I fought smart and efficiently because that's what I'd been trained to do. I let them think that they had the advantage, and then I took them down.

My opponent landed a few decent punches. A pair of body shots to my ribs and a hard right hook to my face that split the skin and started bleeding. He was strong, there was no doubt about that, but he was already running out of energy.

His breathing got heavier, and I went in for the kill. As he came at me with another hit to the side of my head, I ducked, throwing him off balance and making him stumble slightly. Before he could completely regain his balance, I had already landed a solid blow to his side and an uppercut to his jaw that sent him tumbling backwards. He flung a sluggish punch that I dodged easily and countered with a powerful shot to his ribs.

The fight was as good as over.

I threw a vicious right hook that landed on his cheek and propelled him into the crowd before he dropped to the floor, not moving. The ref slammed the ground three times, declaring a knockout, and half the crowd began to cheer while the other half groaned.

"That's the match, folks!" Reece yelled over the megaphone. "Your winner, and still undefeated champ, is Dex Porter!" He raised my arm above my head and slapped a pile of cash in my other hand.

Piece of cake.

acknowledgements

■ ■ ■

To the readers: I cannot thank you enough for taking the time to read this. With so many amazing books out there to choose from, I truly appreciate you giving mine a chance. I started writing because it's something I love to do, but I had zero expectations. I never imagined that so many people would actually read what I'd written, and I am forever grateful.

A huge thank you to Autumn Hull and Andrea Thompson of Wordsmith Publicity, for their continued advice and support. I was on the fence about writing Amy and Nate's story, but their enthusiasm gave me the push I needed, and I'm so glad that I did!

Tawdra Kandle, for all her hard work with the editing, and once again fitting me into her hectic schedule. I've learned so much from her, and she's truly helped me become a better writer.

Becca Liberty from Prisoners of Print: What can I even say? Thanks for not only dropping everything to beta read this book for me, but also for being such a good friend to me along the way. I'm so happy I met you!

Angela McLaurin of Fictional Formats, for her wonderful interior design and formatting, and Sarah Hansen of Okay Creations for yet another beautiful cover.

To all the bloggers out there who signed on to my blog tours, taking the time to read and spread the word about my books, thank you!

Last but certainly not least, my family, who have always supported me and been there for me no matter what. Especially Will, my biggest cheerleader, who puts up with me on a daily basis and can always put a smile on my face. I'm one lucky gal!

about the author

■ ■ ■

Ellie is a reader, writer and overall book lover. When a story popped into her head that she couldn't seem to shake, she decided to pursue her childhood dream of becoming a writer, and released her debut novel *This Time Around*. Now, she spends much of her time dreaming up new characters and stories to write, or curled up with her Kindle reading books by her many, many favorite authors.

To connect with Ellie:

Facebook: Ellie Grace Books
www.facebook.com/elliegracebooks

Twitter: @elliegracebooks

Website/Blog: www.elliegracebooks.com

Also by Ellie Grace:
This Time Around
Break Away

Made in the USA
Lexington, KY
15 July 2016